THE PROMISE OF RAIN

Also by Shana Abé:

A ROSE IN WINTER

THE PROMISE OF RAIN

Shana Abé

BANTAM BOOKS

New York Toronto London Sydney Auckland

ISBN 0-7394-0078-9

Bantam Books are published by Bantam Books, a division of Bantam Doubleday
Dell Publishing Group, Inc. Its trademark, consisting of the words "Bantam
Books" and the portrayal of a rooster, is Registered in U.S. Patent and Trade-
mark Office and in other countries. Marca Registrada. Bantam Books, 1540
Broadway, New York, New York 10036.

PRINTED IN THE UNITED STATES OF AMERICA

For my father, Ted—a strong Texas man
with the kindest heart in the world.
I love you, Daddy.

I also offer my deepest thanks to Darren for
his patience and all the late dinners, and to

my mother Gwen and the rest of my family
for their continuous support. And of course,
none of this would have been possible
without the invaluable and highly appreciated
help of Ruth Kagle and Stephanie Kip.
You all are the best.

Author's Note

This book is a work of fiction.

All events, locations, and characters herein are purely the result of my imagination.

The island earldom of Lorlreau; the estate of Rosemead; the village of Glencarson, Scotland; and all the people and things that dwell in these places exist only between the pages of this book and in our shared minds—I who wrote about them, and you who read about them.

I invite you to journey through the looking glass and enter my world with an open mind and a joyful heart. May the story of Kyla and Roland touch you, and may you leave here a happier person.

—S.A.

THE PROMISE OF RAIN

Prologue

*T*HE THIEF IN BLACK melted into the shadows of the room so completely it was easy to believe he had done this a thousand times.

Yes, Roland thought, as he lay still. *Be cautious. Your enemy is close by.*

He watched the figure through slitted eyes, feigning sleep determinedly. It had been excruciating waiting these last few nights, and he had begun to suffer from the exhaustion. But now he was full awake. His mission was almost finished.

The feeble light from the embers in the fireplace was so dim the moonlight shamed it. He saw the intruder's legs, first the right, then the left, block the sullen red glow as he passed the grate; slow, so slow Roland could not be sure it wasn't simply the passing of time that turned the red to black.

But no, it was the thief, coming closer to his goal. Roland shifted slightly and sighed, as if in his sleep: a test, and the thief halted and disappeared once more into the shadows.

Very good, Roland thought. *How patient are you, my friend? How careful will you be?*

After a long while, Roland saw the shadows shift again, coming closer to where he lay prone on his pallet. Coming closer to the box.

He could hear the softest of sounds, the whisper pad of the intruder's footsteps on the rushes littering the floor. Roland hated rushes, hated the crumbling mess they became over time, but tonight he was glad for the dry reeds, and he silently thanked the faceless servant who had scattered them days ago.

No doubt his guest was cursing the same event.

The rushes gave the intruder a significant pause in every step. Roland imagined himself prowling through the room, between the reeds, imagined how he would roll his feet around the sound they made, imagined how the sharp anticipation would taste as he neared his goal. He wondered if the intruder felt the same things.

He had left the wooden box out in the most obvious of places, lid not quite shut, the folded paper peeking out coyly. If he were the thief, Roland would have retreated as soon as he saw the box on the table by the door, an open invitation, ready for the taking.

It was all much too easy.

Luckily, his prey didn't think so. Or did he?

The intruder had halted halfway to the table, as if uncertain of the surety of his situation after all.

Go on, Roland urged silently. *Go.* He was running out of time, and the intruder was still too far away.

But now the thief had turned and faced Roland's pallet. From where he lay, Roland could see his head tilt, just so slightly, could almost hear the unspoken questions forming in the intruder's mind.

Before Roland could think to move, the thief had crossed to him instead of the box with the swiftness of a greyhound, had pulled out a respectably wicked dagger and was holding it quite nonchalantly—and very professionally—at Roland's throat.

"Give me one reason not to kill you," the intruder hissed, breaking the silence at last.

Roland opened his eyes fully, glanced down at the polished blade, and then up into the masked face of the outlaw he had been tracking for this past half year.

"Because without me you'll be dead soon," he replied.

"But you will be dead much sooner than I, my lord." The thief's voice was surprisingly light, even though he was obviously trying to mask it, but Roland passed that off as a quirk of his youth, when voices were unpredictable things.

The dagger blade turned delicately against his skin. Youth or no, he obviously knew just what to do with the knife to create the most excruciating pain. Roland felt the warm trickle of blood slipping down his neck.

"What matter is it to me if I die?" the boy asked. "You will go first. I can ensure that you will go most painfully first."

"You don't want to die, Alister." Roland could see the use of the boy's proper name had startled him. The tip of the dagger shifted against his throat; a short dart of deeper pain jabbed through him. Roland ignored it. He kept his tone calm and reasonable. "You can't afford to die. Not yet. I still have something you want."

But now the boy was in greater control of his emotions and did not spare even a flicker of a glance for the table with the box on it. Roland focused on the eyes staring at him through the black, meshed mask, and caught a chill of emotion there, a frigid thing so deep it seemed to burn him to the core.

My God, he thought suddenly, *he's serious. He wants to kill me.*

And that, of course, made him smile, because there was his damnable sense of humor again, always coming to the fore when he least needed it to. After everything he had managed to live through, to be killed by this slip of a boy with a grudge, it was too ironic. He turned the smile into a placating tone.

"Don't you want it, Alister? Don't you want the letter that would save your father?"

Again came that chill as the boy looked down at him, held the dagger rock-steady against the artery in his neck.

"I've learned many things," said Alister lightly. "Many creative things, my lord, involving all sorts of unpleasantries with knives and anatomy. I could, for instance,"—here the blade shifted again, higher now—"cut out your tongue through the bottom of your jaw. A most effective means of silencing undesired chatter. Or"—he trailed the blade lower, leaving a stinging path down to the base of Roland's throat— "I could simply sever your windpipe. It's a little less messy that way. But just as painful, I assure you."

"The letter," Roland said. "Your sister."

"Yes," said Alister. "You would like to trade the letter for Kyla, isn't that right? I believe that is how the message went. Tell me this, Lord Strathmore, what makes you think I would trade my sister to you for a tattered bit of vellum?"

Roland managed another smile. "She likes me."

"Really?" said the boy mockingly. "She never mentioned that to me."

"Perhaps she didn't wish for you to rush out and kill her intended out of spite."

"Spite, my lord? What is spite to me?" Alister's voice grew sharper. "What is mere spite to one who has lost everything, *everything,* damn you! I come for revenge, Strathmore, nothing so petty as spite. Revenge is much more delicious than that."

The moment had come. Roland knocked the blade away with a hand-numbing blow, heard the dagger go clattering across the floor. In an instant he was up off the pallet, stifling the dismayed cry of the boy by clapping one hand over his mouth and using the other to pin his arm to his side, easily lifting the boy's feet off the floor.

A part of him registered that Alister was surprisingly slender in his arms, though he wouldn't stop struggling long enough for Roland to handle him gently. Instead he crushed the boy into him with sheer force of muscle, turning the boy's head until Alister's ear was by his lips.

"Listen to me," he whispered urgently. "Stop fighting! There are guards everywhere, you know that! Don't be a fool!"

It seemed that his words had some impact after all, for suddenly Alister grew still, his breathing ragged and muffled beneath Roland's palm. The boy's heartbeat thudded heavily against the arm Roland had pinned to his chest; he could feel the faint trembling shaking the slight body. One less cautious would assume it was fear making him shake so. But Roland was quite certain this young man knew no fear of him.

It was fury shaking Alister, plain and clear. Pure fury.

Interesting, that the weight of the form in his arms was not so heavy as he had expected. Curious, the softness of the shape he held pressed to him. Not like a boy at all, not even a young one. . . .

"Ah," said Roland.

The puzzle fell into place with sudden clarity. He took his hand from the thief's mouth and pulled off the black hood.

He released her as her hair tumbled free past her shoulders, a glorious sight even in the murky light. It was red, he noted distantly, not the reddish orange of just about every Scotsman he had met, nothing ordinary like that, but a deep, rich red. More like the color of a fox, Roland thought. A gorgeous, furious fox.

There was a penalty to be paid for his bemused distraction. He saw her arm pull back just before she punched him in the jaw, snapping his head to the right. He took a step backward, cradling his chin.

"Ah," Roland Strathmore, Earl of Lorlreau, said again. "Lady Kyla, I take it. How delightful to meet you at last."

Chapter One

 RAINBOW DANCED ACROSS the smooth expanse of thick paper, turning the flat vellum into a moving spectrum of colors, sharpening the inky black of the letters written upon it.

"Alister, do stop," said Kyla Warwick absently, trying to make sense of the lines scrawled there.

"I can tell you what it says," said her younger brother, turning the crystal prism he held up to the sunlight. "I heard Uncle Malcolm speaking about it. He was quite loud."

The rainbow paused and trembled on the paper, transforming the particular word Kyla was studying to bright violet. Even without the color, this word stood out from all the rest.

"Strathmore," she said under her breath. "Lord Roland Strathmore. Earl of Lorlreau. How interesting."

Kyla cupped her chin in her palm and stared past the errant sunbeam that stole through the gloomy parlor. The view from the window in front of her showed only a moderately clear day, a handful of thatched huts with shuttered doors, half the slope of a hillside covered in green, and misty purple-and-white peaks in the distance.

The idyllic scene was more striking for what it did not show than what it did. She could see nothing of the trouble haunting the edges of her window view. There were no English soldiers surrounding the manor. None of the serfs of her uncle's estate walked about on their daily business. The hillside was deceptively peaceful, only an idle wisp of smoke curling up from a hut betraying the presence of people at all.

Kyla knew, however, that the soldiers were out there, making their plans, and the serfs were inside, sharpening their harvest tools, of all things, to meet them.

"You haven't thanked me yet for pinching the letter." Alister held the prism closer to the desk, turning it until the rainbow flitted like a fantasy butterfly across the profile of his sister. Without looking at him she reached out a hand and pushed his to the side, so the brilliant light slid over her and back onto the paper.

"Thank you."

"You're welcome."

She read the name again, then sighed, tracing the uneven corners of the note with her fingers, as if to feel for some hidden meaning she might have missed. Alister put the crystal down on the desk and touched her arm tentatively.

"Don't worry, Kyla. We won't let him get you."

She looked at the freckled face of her only living family member. He was so young still, only twelve, much too young for the sharp anxiety that hovered behind his blue eyes.

"I am not worried, Alister. I am merely thinking."

"I won't let him get you," he repeated.

"Nay, I know," she said. "I am far more likely to go after him."

Alister dropped his hand from her arm, caught halfway between the manly desire to comfort and the childish urge to hide in her arms. She watched him struggle to maintain the man, but it was so hard to see that she smiled over her fears and grabbed his hand. "I know you would protect me. You have done such an excellent job of it so far. It cannot be easy looking out for me, I'm always in some sort of trouble or another."

"No," Alister replied seriously. "You're actually quite good. You've only just been in trouble recently."

Now she really smiled and took him into her arms,

hugging him tight, willing him to be a little boy for just a bit longer. "And you have kept me sane throughout. What would I do without you?"

Immediately she regretted the words, knowing what they would remind him of, feeling him stiffen in her embrace. She held him tighter, searching for the right thing to say to hide her blunder.

"You won't be without me," Alister said, very still. "You'll always be here, won't you?"

"Aye, my love, I always will. Never fear."

She wanted to add more to comfort him, she wanted to erase the memories she had inadvertently brought forth, but she couldn't think of what more to say. The pain rose in her throat, blocking any further words.

Their gentle mother, murdered. Their beloved father, dead a few weeks after, despite how hard Kyla had tried to keep him alive. It was now her responsibility to protect her brother. She was the elder by six years. She was the one who had led them to Scotland during the harrowing winter without being caught, but this disastrous chase had stretched them both so thin she could barely think straight any longer.

She was going to end it, no matter the cost. And the letter from Roland Strathmore had given her the means to do it.

"You won't die," Alister said, fierce. He wrapped his arms around her neck and squeezed. "Not you, Kyla. I'll save you."

She nodded into his neck.

On the desk the prism was suddenly lit with a blinding spark that fell just in her eye. That was the only reason she was crying.

"OUT OF THE QUESTION."

Malcolm MacAlister, the dour result of generations of Scottish pride, brushed past his niece without a second glance. He was on his way to a meeting with his steward and the leader of the village men to address the matter of the note from Strathmore that had been delivered early this morning. Kyla kept his pace.

"Uncle, hear me out."

"Enough. I am busy, Kyla."

The narrow corridors of the manor house prevented her from walking beside her uncle, but did not stop her from dogging his steps. They were almost to the end of the hall-way, and then he would disappear behind the doors of his study and she would be powerless. She had to make him listen before that.

"Please," she said, holding her skirts in both hands to keep up. "Please. Let me see him. Let me hear what Strathmore has to say—"

Malcolm rounded on her suddenly, both of them stopping short. "And how did you happen to learn of the missive, dear Kyla?" His hazel eyes gleamed down at her. "It was not meant for you. This is men's work."

"I beg to differ, Uncle. It was *addressed* to me. I believe that makes it my work."

Malcolm shook his head. "You think you know what you say, but you're only a woman. You know nothing of war and death. You could not possibly understand what is at stake here. I will handle this."

This bald proclamation startled her, then fueled the anger blooming inside her. "I *am* a woman, as you say, and I know naught of war, but plenty of death. I have seen enough to last me forever. I do not want to see more, not when I could prevent it."

"You! You can't prevent it! What, think you that you hold some magical key to unlock the hearts of the English? Think you that you can see into the minds of these men who have sought for centuries to conquer our family? Foolish chit, you have seen the message he sent. Can you not recognize a ruse when it's in front of your nose?"

"What if it isn't a ruse? What if Lord Strathmore would actually leave us be if I went to him? Can you take that risk?"

The message came back to her vividly. The words were surely etched in her mind for all time:

Lady Kyla,
    I would seek an audience with your ladyship. I wish to end
this chase as surely as you must.
    I have a certain note that mentions your father most
plainly. Methinks it would be of interest to you to see it your-
self. Conner Warwick is an innocent man. My note will prove
this.
    Meet with me at once, and the note is yours. If you are
agreeable to this, I promise you that no harm will befall you or
your kin from me or my men.
    I await your ladyship most anxiously.
    Yrs.
    Strathmore

She had not needed the rest of his title to discern his iden-
tity. Roland Strathmore, King Henry's own Hound of Hell,
so he was named, had bothered to write her personally to end
the nightmare she was now living. The fact that he was her
ex-betrothed might or might not have influenced the personal effort he had made to contact her. She didn't really care.
All she knew was that she couldn't allow this opportunity to
slip through her fingers.

"Of course it is a ruse. The mere fact that you would
question that makes clear the weakness of your thoughts."
Malcolm paused, giving her his full attention. "I do not
doubt you mean well, Kyla. I do not doubt your heart is set
on goodness. But you cannot trust a beast. These English are
no better than beasts, believe me."

"Nay." She faced him calmly, trying to force reason into
her tone. "I have heard Strathmore has honor. If he sent the
note, then he must have the means and the mind to meet his
condition."

"Fool," said her uncle flatly. "It is Strathmore who gave the
command to attack us not yet an hour past. The soldiers are
coming even now. Will you still trust him?"

Without giving her time to answer he walked off, slamming the door to the study behind him.

Kyla stared at it open-mouthed, absorbing what she had just heard. Could it be true? Was the letter nothing more than a lie from the servant of Henry, after all?

Were the soldiers coming?

No. She refused to believe it. It would be too ugly to end her hopes like this, not after she had determined that the sacrifice of herself was such a small price to pay for the security of Alister, and her father's good name.

Conner Warwick, Baron Rosemead, had once assured his daughter that the man she had never before met but would spend the rest of her life with—the Earl of Lorlreau—was an honorable one. And Kyla knew her father would not lie to appease her. Conner had valued honesty too much for that. He would have asked the king to break off the betrothal if he thought for a moment Kyla would be harmed by it. And she knew Henry had liked her father enough to do it, had he asked.

Aye, Conner had been popular with all who knew him, a big bear of a man who bestowed smiles and astute advice with equal friendliness. Even the sober king was not immune to his constant good humor and keen observations.

It must have been so, Kyla often thought, for her father spent more time at Henry's court than at their own manor house not three days' ride away. The king needed him, Conner would explain sadly to her mother, the patient Helaine, who would comfort him with gentle pats and kisses, then send him back to Henry in London.

Perhaps that had been her weakness, Kyla thought now, heading blindly back to the living quarters; perhaps her mother had been too kind in letting her husband always go bowing to the whims of the sovereign. Perhaps if she had only shown a little irritation with Henry's repeated demands upon Conner's time. Surely he would have attempted to stay at home with her more.

Because everyone knew of the unabashed love Conner had for Helaine. Everyone knew that.

Which was why, perhaps, everyone could be so easily

persuaded that he had killed her in a fit of jealous passion. It could hardly have been anything else, considering the circumstances.

Kyla shook her head, trying to rid herself of the same circle of thoughts that had been haunting her for the past half year.

No matter what the evidence, no matter what anyone said, she knew her father would never have killed her mother. Never. He had been so broken without her.

But King Henry was quite convinced Conner had killed her; that much was plain. He would send an army after the Warwicks to appease his pride, to make sure everyone understood that a man who murdered his wife and one of the king's noble courtiers could not simply run, could not save himself and his family from just punishment.

And now Kyla's only chance to set things right was about to vanish unless she did something to prevent it. She had to find Alister. If the English were coming, she had to get to him. She had to. . . .

For now she knew that Malcolm was not going to listen to her. What a shock he had turned out to be, such a baleful old man, a man who had hated the English side of them that was their father's even as he had embraced them for his sister Helaine's sake. And she and Alister had thought to find safety with their Scottish kin.

Yet it was an uneasy situation from the start. Malcolm had the red hair of the MacAlisters—just like Helaine—and the tall figure, but burning eyes Kyla had not recognized in any of her family.

When she and Alister had arrived, weary, uncertain, he had allowed them to stay, having heard their story, and Kyla had swallowed her misgivings when she saw the relief of her little brother, his slender shoulders slumping with exhaustion. It had been hard on him, brave Alister; he had come along without complaint the entire journey, had wept enough for both of them over the loss of their parents, had helped in every way he could from the beginning.

She thought he would never be a boy again and regretted

that, for he had been such a cheerful, happy child, and she didn't like to see the tired wariness that marked him now. She had wondered if it would ever leave him, and when Malcolm himself had shown them to their rooms two weeks ago she had felt her soul lighten at last, just a little, at Alister's obvious joy.

It had been a horrible winter. But it was not over yet.

Malcolm had been scarred by the defection of his young sister to the side of an Englishman. Kyla hadn't realized it at first. Yes, she had known there was some tension between her mother's brother and father. After all, not once had Malcolm ever come to Rosemead, though he was invited every year.

One late evening not even a week ago, after most of the manor people had gone off to seek their slumber, Kyla had encountered her uncle in the sitting room, drinking whiskey, shards of broken glass all around him.

When she had exclaimed over the glass and gone to him, he had seen Helaine. It was Helaine he grabbed painfully by the arms, Helaine he had ranted against for leaving him, for going to the side of the enemy. It was Helaine who betrayed him for the English, a generations-old hatred, and it was Helaine he had never forgiven.

The broken glass had been an empty decanter. It reflected thousands of glints of firelight all around them as Malcolm held her, alternately shaking her then embracing her, reeking of whiskey, spilling what was left in his cup on them both.

He was tearful and mostly incoherent. Kyla had broken from his grasp and fled the room.

To the best of her knowledge, Malcolm did not remember that night. He certainly never mentioned it. And she almost had cause to forget about it entirely until Roland's messenger arrived this morning, an army behind him, offering his bargain for peace.

She was ready to take it—eager to take it. It was such a perfect solution, a thing to clear Conner's name of her mother's murder and restore her family honor. Nothing could be more important than that.

But Malcolm did not want peace, no, he wanted a battle. How awful to be held up as a new cause for hatred. He had seen his chance to rage against the injustice fate had dealt him when he lost his sister. This was a golden opportunity for revenge.

And now the soldiers were coming.

Where was Alister?

She found him standing over the pallet that he slept on each night in the chamber next to hers, his back to her, looking down at something on the covers she could not see.

She slipped into the room quietly but he heard her anyway, throwing a quick glance over his shoulder to confirm her presence.

"They want us to surrender." His voice was subdued.

"What?"

"The English." He said the word as if it were foreign to him, as if he himself were not English at all but rather a reflection of something else.

Malcolm, she thought, and felt a chill.

She walked over to him and saw that he was looking at a broadsword, a ridiculously large one, she thought, lying flat amid the furs. The blade gleamed dully, spots of rust speckling its length.

Her mind refused to make the connection between the weapon and her brother. What was he doing with it? He shouldn't be allowed to handle such a thing, he might hurt himself. Without thought she reached out to pick it up.

Alister stopped her by taking it first. He used both hands to lift it. His face twisted with the effort.

"What are you doing?" Kyla tried to keep her voice mild, fighting the urge to snatch the sword from him.

"Didn't you hear?" he asked, concentrating on balancing the blade, turning it this way and that.

"Hear what?"

Outside the room she did hear something now—how could she have missed it before?—an ominous rush of sound, booted footsteps in the hallways, masculine voices, deep and filled with an emotion that brought goosebumps to her arms.

Without thought she crossed her arms over her chest, rubbing her sleeves to warm herself.

"Lord Strathmore has ordered Uncle to surrender us. 'Surrender the Warwicks.' He said if Uncle didn't, then Glencarson would suffer the consequences."

Alister rested the sword point on the pallet, his head bowed. Kyla noticed that he was dressed in a hauberk, chain mail, all of it much too large on him, a grown man's battle gear. The blood went rushing from her head.

"No," she said, but it was just a whisper.

"It's true." Alister looked up at her for the first time, eyes grave. "I saw the demand myself. It came this afternoon, after the first letter. Uncle showed it to me."

"No," she said again.

Outside the strange noise was rising, a sinister thing she had never heard before, yet she knew what it portended.

A cloud passed over the sun, plunging the room into shades of gray.

"He's relentless, Kyla. That's why they call him the Hound of Hell. He'll never stop, unless we stop him here. Otherwise it will never be over. He'll take you if he can." Alister's small hands clenched the hilt of the broadsword. "I won't let it happen. He won't kill you, too."

She stared at him speechlessly, the brother she knew hidden behind these words of a stranger. But they were the wrong words, they would get him killed.

"Listen to me," she began urgently.

"Alister," interrupted a voice by the doorway, and her chills came back. Malcolm was here.

"It will be all right, Kyla," said her brother. "I will protect you."

"I won't let you do this." Her voice was strange even to her, high and brittle.

Malcolm spoke again, a silhouette with the light of the hall behind him. "You are mistaken if you think you have a choice, Kyla. You will stay here with the rest of the women. This doesn't concern you."

"I won't let you!" she cried, running to him, trying to get past him, trying to get through the door.

Malcolm blocked her easily, much larger than she was, holding her at bay with both arms. "Alister," he said again, a low-pitched command that pierced her to the bone. Behind her moved her brother, edging around them both, leaving the room.

"No!" Kyla called, reaching for him. "Come back!"

Alister looked over his shoulder at her again, a still look that spoke volumes, then moved off down the hall. She turned on Malcolm furiously.

"It's only me they want," she said. "Let me go, I will bargain with Strathmore. It doesn't have to be like this."

"Never," Malcolm replied, and meant it.

"He is only twelve!" she cried. "God have mercy, he is but a child! Do not misuse him so!"

He brushed her protests aside with disgust. "He is a man, or he would be if you would not coddle him so. It is his God-given right to fight those who killed his father."

"He will die!"

"If he does, it will be as a man. That is the end of it."

"We will all die! Don't you understand? They outnumber us! You would set these villagers to fight with hoes and sticks against arrows and maces?"

"If God wills it, so be it."

The bloodlust in his eyes said much more than his words. With cool efficiency Malcolm pushed her away from him. She fell sharply to the floor, scraping her palms and tangling her skirts. Before she could arise he had closed the heavy wooden door and bolted it shut behind him.

"We will see you later tonight, Niece." His voice was muffled by the thickness of the wood.

"No!" she screamed now, scrambling to her feet, stumbling to the door.

Of course, it was too late. She was trapped.

A few hours later, when she smelled the smoke of the burning manor, she knew it was over.

---

*T*HE BATTLE AT GLENCARSON was as grim as any that had been seen so far in these bitter Highlands. To someone who, perhaps, had climbed up one of the many rocky hills surrounding the valley, there would at first appear to be nothing notably amiss. The sky was a boiling gray soup overhead, true, but that was typical weather in Scotland in this early spring. There was mud everywhere, also true, but what could one expect when the rains came almost every day? But walking farther up the hill it would not take long to notice the peculiar smell mingled with that of the wet earth; a sharp, metallic odor that raised the hair on the back of the necks of man and beast alike.

The good brown mud of Glencarson was pooled with red this evening. Red was everywhere, forming puddles, trickling with dirty scarlet streams around the bodies of the fallen. And there were so many bodies.

Kyla picked up each foot with measured determination, fighting the mud, which sucked at her boots and caked her skirts. She stepped around severed limbs and dead horses without much thought about it, keeping her mind on reaching the men lying near the center of the field. That was where she would find him, she was certain. He would be there.

A misstep on a slippery sword blade caused her to fall onto her hip in the muck. She caught herself with her hands, and they sank wrist-deep into wreckage of the field. For a broken moment the sounds came back to her as she had heard them even locked inside the manor house, the screams of men, the screams of the horses, and now the screams of women left behind, women like her who were searching the valley for their kin.

The cries of the women bothered her the most.

She stood up again and wiped her hands absently on her skirts, smearing the bloody mud around her thighs. She didn't want to hear the women sobbing any longer. She didn't want to hear each fresh wail as the next body was turned over, the next face identified as a husband, a father, a sweetheart.

Kyla moved on resolutely. There was only one sound in her head now, one name, over and over.

Alister, Alister . . .

Of Malcolm she cared nothing. It was his fault this battle had taken place and she wished him to hell for it. But of Alister, sweet Alister, still so young the broadsword given to him had dipped and shivered in his hands, oh, God, Alister. . . .

And he was there, limp, quiet, in the mud, his hands and face pale beneath the streaks of sweat and blood and dirt. So very pale. So peaceful.

She didn't know how long she knelt beside him, cradling his head in her hands. She didn't see the clouds grow thicker, hear the rumbling in the skies. She didn't feel the rain drenching the valley.

The water washed away the filth on him and smoothed his hair back to dark red, like her own. He was all she had had left in this world, all that had mattered to her.

Kyla Warwick did not cry. Her hands did not tremble as she wiped the water from his brow. And her knees buckled only a little when she bent over and picked up the body of her little brother and carried him out of the valley of Glencarson.

Chapter Two

"A BLACK DAY," said the old woman, stirring the pot over the smoky fire.

There was nothing to say to this. It was such an obvious remark that Kyla couldn't even summon a proper response. She stared down at her hands, at the dirt beneath her fingernails that repeated washings could not remove.

"Ye'll be leaving soon," the woman continued. Outside the mouth of the cave a goat bleated in the darkness once, then again.

"Yes," Kyla said.

"They'll be looking fer ye." The woman, Lorna, banged the wooden spoon against the rim of the pot.

"I know."

But Kyla couldn't seem to do much right now. Her hands lay open and lax in her lap, fingers curled upward. Her skin seemed very white to her; they could have been a ghost's hands. She remembered how her mother used to pamper her own hands, rubbing them with special creams each night, keeping her own white skin so smooth and perfect.

Kyla's hands were cut and blistered right now, unused to labor still.

"I'll go before they come," she said.

"Aye." Lorna had been her uncle's chatelaine for many years. But the modest manor was gone now. Tonight Lorna was just another of the homeless, the ragged remnants of a clan that would be living inside these rocky hills for a good while to come, Kyla supposed. The entire village had been burned to the ground.

The cave was damp and cold, but then again, so the manor house had been as well. Lorna banged the spoon again for emphasis. "Yer father's people will take ye."

"I'll go," Kyla repeated.

"It's fer the best."

Again, another statement for which she could think of no reply. Was it for the best? She had no idea. Would the English chase her still? Did she matter to them now that Alister and Malcolm were dead? Would they persecute this clan further to flush her out?

Such heavy questions. She wished she had some answers for once.

The fire threw a dull light that gleamed against the gold hilt of the dagger Kyla had tucked into the sash at her waist. She had buried Alister without it. It had been their mother's, a jeweled thing with a dangerously sharp blade. Kyla didn't think either of them would mind if she kept it.

The goat bleated again, and a new shape stooped to enter the cave. It was Colin, ancient Colin, come to tell her to go. Kyla stood.

"We'll give ye yer uncle's horse, lass," he said, not unkindly. "He's a right brute, but ye've got a way with him."

"Thank you." Kyla picked up the leather saddlebags she had been sitting on and carried them out of the cave.

The night air was clear and sharp; it felt painfully good to take a deep breath. Malcolm's stallion was remarkably uninjured from the battle, surely the only thing left so. He lowered his great, sleek head to her as she approached. Kyla ran her hand down his nose, then stroked his neck. An all-black horse, she thought with some amusement. How fitting the outlaw's daughter would ride a black horse.

Someone helped her up, she didn't notice who. There was no saddle, but sitting bareback was nothing new to her. Her skirts fell carelessly around her shins.

The circle of people around her were specters in the moonless night; distant, proud people who had reluctantly taken her in with her brother, and now were thankfully seeing them both gone.

It wasn't a personal dislike, Kyla knew. It was simply that they could not afford to house someone with such a price on her head. The wrath of the king was already great against these people. She was lucky they hated the English enough that they had not turned her over to them for the gold.

Colin handed her a weighted sack. "Food for four days, mayhap," he said in his old man's voice. "Head south, lass. Head for Glen More."

"Thank you," Kyla said. "Thank you all. I'm sorry."

The stallion turned and the people parted for her to pass. There were no good-byes to follow her. The only sound to be heard was the steady *clip-clop* of the horse's hooves in the dirt as she guided him south toward the English border.

For a while it was soothing just listening to the rhythm of the stallion's steps. She drifted in and out of awareness, letting the animal set the pace and the direction. He knew the land better than she did, anyway. She was fortunate to have him. They didn't have to give her anything. They owed her nothing, while she owed them more than she could ever repay.

The stallion took her to a loosely knotted forest of pine and birch. There were boulders and streams, but no real place to hide. Kyla patted the horse down as best she could and then lay down on the cold ground, using the saddlebags as pillows.

She didn't care if Lord Strathmore and his soldiers found her. She didn't care if they came and killed her in her sleep. There was even a part of her that wanted that, wanted an ending to this brutal life she had inherited.

She had deliberately left the stallion untied, free to roam if he wished. If the soldiers came, he could run away. He would survive.

That thought gave her some comfort as she sank into slumber.

But the soldiers did not come, no one came, and when she awoke the next morning the stallion was standing patiently nearby, grazing on a patch of wild grass.

Her cloak was still damp with dew from the ground, but at least it wasn't raining.

"What ho, my friend," she called to the horse softly, sitting up and stretching her sore neck. "Have you not the wits to abandon a lost cause?"

The stallion rolled his eyes in her direction but did not stop chewing. The crunching sound from his teeth seemed unnaturally loud in the forest. It made her realize abruptly that she had not eaten in over a day—years, it seemed—and so she opened the cloth sack Colin had given her and ate an oatcake in somber contemplation of the fallen log across from her.

Slowly, horribly, the feeling of numbness that had taken her over since the field of Glencarson was beginning to fade against the bright light of this new day. Reality was coming back, no matter what she did to let it know it was not welcome.

She was a gentlewoman, born of nobility, now utterly alone in the world, and utterly without recourse. Despite Lorna's words, Kyla knew that her father's people could not take her in, because her father had no people left. Malcolm had been their last slender thread of hope, and he had proven to be a false one.

The oatcake was gone too quickly but she was loath to eat another despite the rumbling in her stomach. She didn't know what else she was going to do for food. There was a stream nearby, she could hear the treble gurgling of it from here, and so that might mean fish. She knew how to fish. Her father had shown her that much.

It had been at her own insistence. When it had become clear to her that Conner was not going to be shaken from the coils of grief that held him, it was she who had acted to save them. With the money she had taken with them she bought the necessary supplies for their journey. When the money ran out, she gamely tried to teach herself the survival skills needed. She nearly caught consumption from the dousing in the Highland waters she received while trying to catch fish with the blunt spear she had fashioned.

That had roused Conner—if only briefly. He had taken the spear and broken it over his knee in the first spark of anger she had seen in him since their mother's death. He had caught the fish that night. But she had watched, and learned.

It didn't seem odd to Kyla that she had understood the import of what was happening those first ghastly days after the murder and her father had not. From the instant they had heard the news, he became as dead to the world as they had learned her mother was.

In truth, Kyla couldn't recall how she had managed to behave so normally. She just knew if she didn't, no one would, and then they would all be lost.

It was she who had held the household together for as long as she could in the face of the scandal. For days after the discovery of her mother's body she had seen the speculation growing in the eyes of the servants, had noticed the subtle shifts in attitude that had affected the entire estate. It had been a creeping chill in the air, a lassitude of service, and that ever-present whispering hum of gossip she could not help overhearing but never quite make out.

When the nobles had begun to trickle over to Rosemead, they didn't come to express their condolences, though the pitying looks they threw her seemed real enough. They came to stare at her father. They came to see the killer, to talk and gape with appalled fascination while he sat there, oblivious to all. It had terrified her to the depths of her soul.

The stallion finished with the grass and now strolled over to where she sat idle on the ground, staring into space. He bowed his head down next to hers and blew through his nose.

"Get enough to eat, friend?" she asked him, dusting her hands free of the crumbs from the cake. "I hope so. Let's go see if we can find the water."

The stream was farther than she thought, and by the time she led the big horse there the sparkling water was a welcome sight. The stallion waded in to drink and she followed, taking care to remain upstream.

Sunlight danced and winked over the liquid passage,

disrupted by her hands dipping into the stream and splashing handfuls of water over her face.

It was shockingly cold. Kyla sucked in her breath, then repeated the process. Belatedly she realized she had nothing with which to dry herself, and so she sat back against the bank of the stream and lifted her face to the sky, letting the water trickle away to nothingness.

She became aware of the evenness of her own breathing, of the steadiness in her arms as she rested her weight against them, and the soothing warmth of the sun on her skin.

Conner had not killed Helaine. But someone had, and in doing so they had managed to destroy her entire family. And now Kyla thought she knew what she would do next, after all.

She was young, she was strong, and she was clever. And she had nothing to lose. What was left of her old life was already dead. She would gladly risk this one to exact vengeance.

There was one man who held both the key to her questions and the burden of responsibility for the tatters of her existence. Her former fiancé had made a point to write to her, bragging about the note he held, the note that would save them. Then he had betrayed them all.

Aye, she would find the Earl of Lorlreau and he would give her some answers. He would, or she would kill him. Perhaps she would kill him anyway.

The hunted was about to become the hunter.

"REALLY, STRATHMORE," drawled Sir John Hindrige. "It was merely some miserable little Highland village, barely worth mentioning. I fail to see the cause for your rather excessive concern."

Roland kept his back to the man, examining the courtyard scene below him through the thick, wavy glass of the window in the inn's sole private parlor. Only the slight tightening of his hand on the windowsill betrayed the anger he felt.

"That miserable village," he said quietly, "was the only

home to more than one hundred and fifty people, all of whom were innocent in this game."

"Oh, come," scoffed Hindrige. "Hardly innocent! They were harboring the fugitives! Malcolm MacAlister was sheltering them even as he taunted us! Those people got exactly what they deserved. They disobeyed the law. They disobeyed the king. They had to be punished."

"Perhaps you are right." Roland turned around and faced Henry's minister of war. "But it was my job to punish them, not Reynard's."

"Well, as to that, I cannot help but agree with you. He overstepped his boundaries there. As I told you, the king has reprimanded him."

"Yes."

Roland turned back to the window. Below him bustled the population of this busy border town, securely on the English side of Hadrian's Wall. His eyes picked out a woman down there, watched her bargain with a baker as she hung on to five children at the same time. He wondered how many children there in the Highlands were now homeless, orphans because of Reynard's enthusiasm. How many of them would last the year without proper shelter?

A reprimand from the king. *Yes, indeed,* Roland thought sarcastically, *that was certainly a fitting punishment for the slaughter of a village.*

Hindrige spoke again around the joint of lamb he was eating. "Well, Strathmore. What now? You still have no proof of Rosemead's death. If his children did survive, they are hardly likely to come forward at this point. You return to Henry empty-handed."

Roland said nothing, watching the woman now head for the smithy, children scattered in a string behind her.

"She is most likely dead, you know," said the minister in a different voice, somewhat gentler. "She would not have survived the winter in the wild. I heard she was a delicate thing, like her mother."

"Perhaps."

"You have no obligation to the family now. You know that."

"So I keep hearing."

Behind him Roland heard the minister sigh into his goblet of port. "A tragic thing," he murmured, for surely the hundredth time since Roland had entered the little room at the inn for this meeting. "Such a lovely woman, the baroness. Such a tragedy. Who could have known. . . ."

"Who indeed," said Roland, cutting him off. "Forgive me if I do not stay, Hindrige. I find myself rather fatigued after the journey."

"Yes, yes. Miserable Highland weather. Miserable place. Can't understand why anyone would want to live there."

"Indeed. Good eve to you, Minister." Roland strode to the door.

"Strathmore," called Hindrige, just before he could make it.

He looked back, his hand on the door handle, the impatience to escape burning in him.

"She is no longer your betrothed, even if she has survived the winter," Hindrige said. "You will do well to remember that."

"Aye," said Roland, and left the room.

---

*U*NLIKE MOST PEOPLE, Roland thought Conner Warwick dead and his children alive. He had been on their trail almost from the beginning, almost from the very night they had fled into the anonymity of the countryside.

He alone had believed the reports he had gotten back from his scouts of the two younger Warwicks traveling north. As incognito as they might have wished to be, Lady Kyla was said to be a great beauty, and accounts of a young woman matching her looks had been steadily leaking back to him through his own private network of spies.

There was never mention of anyone but the two of them. Roland could not believe that Conner had abandoned his children to the merciless winter by choice. No, they were trying to survive alone because they thought they had to.

Not that he didn't trust the reports from the king's men,

which had placed the trio of Warwicks anywhere from Kent to Ireland to Wales. Actually, it was more a matter of not trusting their zeal for their work.

The king had promised a great reward for the capture of the man who had ruthlessly murdered his cousin, Lord Gloushire. And since Lord Gloushire had been discovered in bed with Baroness Rosemead, both of them quite dead, there had really seemed to be no reason not to think the lady's husband had done them both in.

Roland frankly did not know, nor did he care, who killed Gloushire. He had never liked the man anyway, had always found him to be an annoying peacock who used his connection to the king shamelessly to curry favor in court and abroad. Roland didn't think even Henry had liked his cousin, but of course now that he was dead, the king could not allow the slight to go unattended.

So Henry had sent Roland to apprehend Baron Rosemead, because that was what Henry depended upon him to do—to clean up loose ends. He was not known as the Hound of Hell for naught, as those who crossed the king soon discovered.

The fact that the daughter of the murdered woman and fugitive man was to be his wife was something the king had dismissed out of hand.

"Find them," Henry had ordered him. "Bring them to me. I shall decide what to do about the children then. Bring them back to me alive, Strathmore."

And that was what Roland intended to do.

The betrothal had been the king's invention, anyway, something arranged without his—nor the young woman's, he assumed—consent. It wasn't unusual for Henry to match up his nobles, especially those who had avoided matrimony for what the king considered far too long a time.

In fact, Roland had been rather surprised it had taken Henry this long to try to wed him off. He supposed it was sort of a compliment, that the king had chosen the daughter of one of his favorite advisers, and a reportedly beautiful one as well.

Roland could only remember seeing the Lady Kyla Warwick of Rosemead once before, and she had been a child then, a lanky ten-year-old with large eyes and very white skin. She had been at court with her parents, and was busy tending to her little brother, as he recalled. Someone had pointed the mother out to him, and he did remember being struck by *her* unusual beauty. If Kyla did indeed resemble Helaine, he thought he could have done worse for a bride.

It had taken a good month for that memory to surface after he had been informed of the betrothal, and then he had immediately dismissed both the girl and the wedding from his thoughts.

Henry had picked his bride for him; no doubt Henry would arrange the ceremony, as well. He enjoyed things like that. Roland had decided he would wait for the king to tell him when the wedding was, then he would show up, endure the ceremony, and take his new wife back to Lorlreau.

She could fend for herself from there.

But fate had taken the good king's plans and tossed them recklessly into the air to fall where they would, leaving Roland with the rather bizarre task of tracking not only the father of his ex-betrothed but also the lady herself, and her younger brother, across the kingdom.

It hadn't bothered him. Not really. At least, not until now.

For although the evidence against the baron had seemed insurmountable, Roland had been left with nagging doubts about the neatness of the crime, the way all guilt pointed to a man who had seemed genuinely frozen in grief over the death of his wife.

It had taken days for him to gather up his children and leave. Days, when it seemed to Roland that a guilty man would have run away immediately, and most likely alone.

Roland had arrived in London just after the murders took place, and thus he had a chance to witness for himself the dazed bewilderment of the great hulk of Baron Rosemead, there to claim the body of his wife and transport it back to his estate.

He had seen only the shadow of a man, not the personable, outgoing adviser he had met many times before. But this was not the calculated demeanor of a murderer, nor even the panic of a man who had killed in the heat of passion.

Yet still, he had taken the body to Rosemead and then fled. It didn't sit well with Roland. For the first time ever he felt a vague distaste for his job, pursuing this man who had fallen steep and hard from such a lofty place.

And there was the matter of Lady Kyla. There was another mystery for him, the fact that the father would take the two children, especially when one was said to so closely favor her mother. Very strange, indeed.

Either way, it was an unpleasant task. He was stalking either an innocent man and what was left of his family, or else a ruthless killer who nevertheless had not abandoned his children.

And both ways, he was in the awkward position of hunting down his would-have-been bride.

A curious sort of guilt folded and doubled inside of Roland, enveloped his sharper senses with the soft notion of saving the Warwicks somehow, of proving Conner's innocence, mad as the notion was.

At least he might save the children. He could save Kyla. Surely he owed her that much, that ten-year-old waif who had grown up into a woman he could not envision.

Roland walked out of the inn, blended in with the crowd in the square. The peasant woman with the children was gone, but in her place were a hundred more such women, all of them nameless, faceless, struggling to survive another day.

A ragged herd of sheep clattered across the cobblestones in front of him, driven on by a brown dog and a shepherd boy in a tartan.

He wondered what Kyla and Alister were doing right now.

As it turned out, he wouldn't have to wait that long to find out.

Chapter Three

*S*HE HAD THOUGHT the whole thing was rather too easy.

First there was the serendipitous coincidence that the very lord Kyla sought had not bothered to leave the rustic English border town since the massacre at Glencarson five weeks ago.

But she had explained that away as a commonsense move on his part, to keep his base entrenched on his own English soil while hunting for her up north. She would have done the same thing.

And how quickly she had been able to pinpoint the inn where the soldiers were staying. Of course, the town only had two inns. It had to be one or the other. The soldiers constantly milling about The Hound's Taile had resolved that issue.

But perhaps she should have taken a longer look at the arrangements before leaping forward with her plan. She had given herself only a day to scout the area. It had seemed simple enough. A small inn, a courtyard with easy access to the stables and the main road. . . .

Oh, it had been so sweetly arranged. That tiny twinge of warning had been all but vanquished once she had seen the man she sought, strolling so casually across the courtyard.

And it had to be him. It had to be.

No other man in this remote little town could have walked with such confidence, seeming to part the very air in front of him with a wealth of power and grace.

The day had been cloudy, so when she first spied him what she had noticed was the presence of him more than anything, an overall impression of complete and absolute command.

Then the woolly clouds blocking the sun had passed. With breathtaking abruptness clear sunlight spilled all around him, and she almost gasped out loud.

What twisted fate had left the man who had the soul of the devil with a person so blessed? It was bitterly unfair, watching such perfection move across the yard without any apparent awareness of his own beauty.

Honeyed hair fell in waves around a firm jaw, to wide shoulders, and she could swear a crooked smile curved those sculpted lips, a smile given to no one but the birds in the trees, it seemed. She could even make out the color of his eyes, a vivid greenish blue, bright against the tan of his face.

They were the exact match to the color of a small stone she had seen once at court, set in the ring of a Moorish prince. *Turkeis,* the prince had called it, with a knowing smile at her, and then translated the strange word: "turquoise."

She hated Strathmore with sudden force, hated that he lived and Alister had died. Hated that the man who would have had her in marriage would now have her in chains, yet still walked like a man who had not a care to trouble him.

But mostly she hated him for who he was: the man who had hunted what was left of her family to death.

Kyla, crouching in an alley behind some empty ale barrels, had closed her eyes then, willing him to go away.

When she opened them again, he was gone.

She had faded back into the shadows of the building to wait until nightfall. After that, she had merely chosen the most auspicious room—the largest one, of course, the only one with its own balcony—and had no trouble at all scaling the stripped branches of a summer vine that had buried its roots into the walls of the inn. It had taken less than a minute.

Yes, it had been so easy.

And that was what she got for using her heart and not her head, for now he had caught her, and she would die without the revenge she had been nursing since Glencarson. He had trapped her here in this little room with him, and in an instant he would hand her over to Henry's men. Hound of Hell, indeed.

Her hand ached from the punch she had delivered to his jaw. She sincerely wished she could do it again.

He was standing there, almost grinning at her after having made that ridiculous, formal introduction, as if they were at a ball, and not toe-to-toe in the darkness of the inn where she had come with half a mind to kill him.

"Give me the letter," she said in a low voice, rubbing her knuckles.

Roland took a careful step away from her before replying. "Sorry," he said. "Don't have it."

He watched with interest the despair that flickered across her face and was gone. Her eyes narrowed in the half-light. What color were they? Something light. Green, he would guess, or robin's-egg blue, perhaps, to go with that cherry hair . . .

"You lie," she hissed.

"I'm afraid not, my lady. The letter is not here."

She hesitated; he watched her fight the urge to look at the wooden box on the table, the revealing corner of paper sticking out.

"It's blank," he said gently.

She shifted on her feet, allowing a thick fall of hair to cover half her face. With abrupt intensity Roland found himself wanting to touch it, wanting to feel for himself the fire of its color. It almost made him miss the forward leap she made for the window.

He caught her, but not without a struggle, and he was desperately afraid they were making too much noise. For lack of a better idea he forced her over to the thin pallet and made her sit still while he lowered himself beside her, holding her against him.

Again he felt her tremble, but he couldn't be distracted by that now. He was going to save her even if she didn't want him to.

Roland placed his lips close to her ear.

"Take me to your brother. I promise you both safe passage to London. I will speak to the king for you."

She said nothing in response to this, but he thought he felt the trembling increase.

"I can help you, Kyla. You know that. I can help you both."

He felt the moment stretch out, growing longer and thinner with an undefined emotion that hummed and sang between them.

"Spawn of the devil!" she burst out loudly. "Leave me be! I'll kill you!"

Instantly he was on top of her, smothering her with his body as he clapped a hand over her mouth. Her eyes widened, she twisted her body beneath his with surprising strength, but he was able to hold on to her as the door opened.

"My lord?" came the gruff call. "All is well?"

"Aye, Gilchrist," Roland said with a lazy humor. "This wench and I are having a bit of sport. She's a saucy thing." He kept his arm in front of her face, blocking the view of the soldier in the doorway.

"Ah," said the man with dawning understanding, and a chuckle. "Good sporting, my lord."

"There is no doubt of that," Roland said pleasantly.

"Good eve to you, my lord." The soldier shut the door.

Kyla bit the inside of his palm.

"You are not endearing yourself to me, my lady," said Roland in the same pleasant tone he had used with the soldier.

She didn't care for that, it was clear. If possible, her eyes got wider, then narrowed again. She tried a mighty heave to throw him off of her.

As interesting as the position was, he was going to have to do something to calm the lady. He didn't want her to hurt herself, not to mention him. He would try reason one more time.

"Kyla," he said quietly. "I can help you. Let me. I can take you and your brother to London under my protection. No harm will come to you, I swear it."

He lifted his hand from her mouth.

In the gloom she stared up at him, eyes wild and her mouth a little bruised from the struggle. It came to him then that she was not merely beautiful, as he had first thought, but she was amazingly beautiful, quite the most incredible thing he had ever seen.

If her face was a little too thin, her mouth a little too sensual, her brows too straight, her neck too long, none of it mattered when the sum of the parts made up the whole. He found himself caught up in the spell, mesmerized, and she allowed him this, seemingly diverted in her own perusal of him.

Roland came back to himself with a slight shake of his head. It was unlike him to play the part of a smitten boy, no matter how bewitching the woman. He was her protector, not her lover.

Not even her betrothed—anymore.

But embers in the fireplace let him see the movement of the tip of her tongue as she moistened her lips, and he felt himself respond with an immediate rush of passion.

He sat up, scowling. This was not supposed to happen.

"Where is the real letter?" Her voice was husky. She didn't move from the pallet, a sweet temptation with her hair spilling around her face, and her body not nearly concealed enough in her black tunic and hose.

He heard the question. Yes, he heard it, it floated out into the room, and certainly she deserved a response. But what he wanted to do was hold her, tenderly, and break the news to her as gently as possible.

"There is no letter at all," he said instead. "I made it up."

Her lips parted slightly in shock. She shook her head mutely.

"It was a trick, to trap you," he said ruthlessly, trying to slay this soft, unfamiliar thing inside of him she had found. "It was successful."

Her eyes closed, squinted shut, as if to fight off the words. The weakness inside of him rolled over, horrified at his own callousness. She looked so helpless. How could he do this to her?

"Kyla. It's over. Take me to your brother."

She opened her eyes, looked past his shoulder to the ceiling of the room. "All those lives lost," she whispered. "And it was only a lie, all along."

The weakness exploded into life again. He fought it, he didn't have time for it; weakness would not help anyone. Weakness would leave him vulnerable, and Roland had spent the last few hard years of his life making sure that vulnerability would never be a factor for him again. He stood.

"We need to get back to London. I know your father is dead. Take me to Alister, and we may go."

She came back from someplace far away, and he saw her focus sharpen on him again. Saw the loathing she had for him. It was such a contrast to the immediate memory of the lushness of her body beneath his. . . .

"You knew I would come if you lied," she said.

"Well," he conceded. "I thought it might be your brother, instead. I thought he might be the more impulsive of the two of you."

There had been no news of either Kyla or Alister after the massacre of Glencarson. An entire village of people had vanished, seemingly without a trace, save those left in the field. By the time Roland arrived, those that had been left behind had been too long dead to identify. He had a feeling that the Warwicks weren't there, anyway. Searching the hills would have been an exercise in futility; the villagers were far more knowledgeable than his own people about surviving in the Highlands. He had pulled back to this place to rethink his options.

Roland wasn't about to let anyone know, least of all this angry young woman, how lucky for him it was she had been spotted that very day by his squire, who had seen her once in London. The man had alerted him immediately, and he had known one or the other of them would show up tonight. He had known it in his bones, and these feelings were never wrong.

"Where is Alister? Is he ill?" he asked now, already making plans to surprise the boy before he got wind of his sister's capture.

Kyla ignored his questions. "You made up the story of the letter. You made up the proof of my father's innocence."

Roland said nothing. He just watched her, waiting for her to accept it.

"You sent word to me that you had a letter to prove he didn't murder my mother." Her voice cracked slightly. "You told me you would give it to me—"

"If you met me at Glencarson," Roland concluded. "And you did not."

She was silent, contemplating him. Then:

"I don't know why I should be surprised that you would lie. You are naught but a slave to the king, everyone knows that. You have no soul. You have no remorse. Of course you would lie."

"Of course. Take me to Alister, Kyla."

She gave a muffled laugh, then turned her head to the side. Roland felt something in him freeze up, go numb.

Damn, he thought, *damn, damn. . . .*

"How did he die?" he asked.

"How do you think," she spat, sitting up quickly and scrambling to the other side of the pallet.

"The cold," he said, following her form with his eyes, wanting to believe what he said. "The Highland snows—"

"It was not the cold, my lord Strathmore. It was not the snow. It was you. It was your command to attack at Glencarson that killed my brother."

There was a surfeit of pain in her voice, calm as it was. It spoke measures beyond a scream or a cry. It sliced him to the core, hearing that pain come from her.

But perhaps the torment came from within himself. He wanted to deny that he was responsible for the attack. He wanted to deny the indecency that had taken place in his name. He wanted to, but he couldn't.

He had not been at Glencarson. But he should have been.

"I'm sorry," Roland said. "I'm very sorry. What happened at Glencarson should never have occurred. It was a mistake, and I will always regret it."

Kyla took a heavy breath and let it out slowly, staring at him all the while. She seemed to make up her mind about something.

"I'll be going now." She walked over to the dagger, which had landed on the floor amid the rushes.

Roland crossed the short distance and took the knife from her hand before she could close her fingers around the hilt. "We're all leaving soon. Have you any other supplies to take?"

He saw her shoulders stiffen beneath the tunic she wore.

"I would sooner travel with the devil himself than with you," she said flatly. "Leave me alone."

"If this is all you have, I suppose it will have to do. I'll see what I can do about getting you some proper clothing. Perhaps the barmaid has something you could wear."

He tucked the dagger in the heavy leather belt he wore. Kyla shook her head at him. Her eyes were shadowed.

"Again, my lord, you manage to astonish me with your audacity. Perhaps I have not made myself clear to one as thick-skulled as you. I came here to kill you. By the grace of the Lord I have decided not to do that. But now I am leaving."

He blocked her by stepping in front of her without touching her, maneuvering her until she was backed up almost all the way against the wooden wall.

"Forgive me, my lady. I think I have been the one who was not clear. You are accompanying me to London." Roland kept the threat in his voice to a velvet purr. He had found this usually had the maximum effect. She was so much smaller than he was. He wanted to smile at the fierceness of the look she threw up at him.

"I will die first!"

"No," he said softly.

"I will kill you, then!"

"No," he said again, then waited.

He listened to the raggedness of her breath, felt the tension radiate from her to him with almost physical force, then felt it begin to wane. *Good,* he thought, *almost there.*

"Give me back my dagger," she said tonelessly.

"I think not, my lady. Not just yet. Perhaps later."

She moved one hand a fraction.

"It's mine."

"I'll keep it safe for you."

Again that tense silence from her, that blaze of emotion he could almost feel, the anger, the uncertainty.

"When we are in London," he said, placing one of his hands on the hilt of her dagger, "we will look for that proof of your father's innocence."

"Oh yes," she said scornfully. "*Now* I believe you. There's certainly no reason for you to lie to me *now.* Everyone knows the Hound of Hell would offer his word to keep a village safe, even as he burned it down."

He turned the anguish her words caused him into a careless shrug, backing away slightly.

"If you wish to leave, Lady Kyla, you are free to do so. The soldiers outside will retain you, of course. I will see to that. And my men would never harm a lady." He gave a fearsome smile from the shadows and had the satisfaction of seeing her take a step back. "Some of the soldiers here, however, are Henry's men. And they have been promised a fortune to bring you back, living or dead. Although I think they might prefer you living, at least for the next few nights. There are more than forty of them, after all."

He turned away from her indignant gasp and walked back to the table by the door. "It matters not to me which path you choose. As you say, the Hound of Hell has no soul, and certainly no reason to regret the foolish choice of someone who does not recognize her redemption when it is offered to her."

He let her see him take hold of the door handle. "I offer you my protection. Whatever else you think of me, I *will* keep you safe. It is my mission to do so. What say you, my lady? Where will you cast your fate?"

An ember in the fireplace popped then with a brief flowering of golden sparks, illuminating her for a fraction of a moment. It was enough for him to catch the look of resignation shrouding her, and although he should have been happy with the turn of her thoughts, he was slightly ashamed of himself, of his blatant manipulation of her fears.

Another irksome quality she had unearthed in him. How inconvenient. He would have to see what he could do about banishing this new sensation as soon as possible.

"I cannot trust you," she said in a frustrated tone. "You would as soon have me dead, no doubt."

"Oh no, my lady," he said quietly, so quietly she had to strain to hear him. "Not I. I would have you live a long and fruitful life."

She made a sound of disbelief. Roland turned the door handle, opened the door a crack.

"And in the final outcome, what does trust matter, Lady Kyla? It seems to me your choices are quite clear. Either come with me peaceably, or come with me forcibly."

She watched him toy with the handle, then glanced longingly at the balcony window. Her hands were balled into fists.

"You have tricked me, made it impossible to leave. I cannot win."

"That's what I do," Roland said, and opened the door wide.

———————— ⟨⟩ ————————

*H*ER EYES WERE gray.

Not green, not blue, but a peculiar silver-gray with smudges of black streaking through. He had never seen anything like it.

She rode solemnly beside him on her stallion, silent and watchful of him, of the armed men surrounding them both, letting those striking eyes form her judgments without audible comment.

The dress he had procured for her from the innkeeper's wife was ill-fitting, much too loose on her slender frame, yet she had taken it from him without saying a word and donned it obediently in the room he had rented for her. A very, very well-guarded room.

And that had marked the beginning of her silence. She had not broken it once since emerging from that room in the plain bliaut of brown and green. Without a word, she had even accepted the sidesaddle he had managed to purchase for her; there was merely a slight lifting of her brows, as if such a thing surprised her.

No doubt riding bareback she was as lovely as a sylph, and she must have been doing it for Lord knew how long. But he couldn't see bringing her to London like that. Henry would not approve.

Even now she could have been a druid, emerging from the woods for the first time, as alien to this world of soldiers and sweat and pain as anything could be. Hair of molten flame, skin so pure in cast she looked almost like a statue of alabaster, and those eyes—strange, enchanting eyes, like sunlight through thunderclouds. He had no idea how she had survived the wild. It was surely a miracle, except that she seemed such a natural part of the wilderness, anyway. Silent, wary sprite, out of her element now.

Every so often Roland saw her reach a hand out and stroke the neck of the great beast she rode, but that seemed to be the extent of her animation. You'd think she was being led to her execution.

Of course, she probably thought she was.

Roland couldn't blame her for not trusting him. There was no reason on earth for her to do so. Indeed, he might even have thought less of her if she had. It would have implied a gullibility that defied reason in the face of all that had occurred between them.

But no, she was not gullible. She must have plenty of good solid reason in her, to survive on her own for the past weeks as she made her way out of Scotland to him. Plenty of reason, and plenty of reasons to despise him.

It was a shame, he thought, and then didn't know why. It was not logical of him to care one way or the other what she thought of him. She didn't have to like him in order for him to save her. He had a duty to discharge, a duty of honor, and if she couldn't understand that, so be it. It would not change his course.

Roland Strathmore had never let things like emotions get in the way of whatever he truly wanted. Emotions, all in all, were rather tedious things that tended to befuddle his life whenever they were allowed to. He had no use for them.

The only emotion he had never been able to fully control was his sense of humor. As always, he could see the irony of this, and it brought forth the crooked smile that so many men had learned to fear. He had to concede that his humors were odd, but constant. A small corner of him held on to this notion, unwilling to abandon the last traces of feeling that he could still muster.

But it was easier to feel nothing. He liked feeling nothing.

Feeling nothing had allowed him to conquer his past and climb triumphantly into his present position. He had always thought the term Hound of Hell wasn't really suited to him, for surely a demon hound would feel some anger, some devilish fury. But such things hardly ever affected Roland. Hardly ever.

Those few black times in his adulthood when the fury had come he preferred not to think about. There were not many things that could set it off. And fortunately, the few things that could were now dead and gone.

Concepts like honor, justice, revenge, these were things he understood intimately. These qualities had none of the disturbing, blurred undercurrents that emotions carried. The precepts he lived by were sharply defined. He liked that, liked their easy clarity.

It suited him well. It allowed him to do the things he needed to do to serve his sovereign, and to protect his own self-rule at Lorlreau. He would finish this business with Kyla

Warwick, and then Henry would allow him to retire to his family castle. That was the agreement. Roland was willing to do just about anything to see it fulfilled.

The fact that Lady Kyla had eyes that could pierce him with a glance should mean nothing to him. That her hair was even more lustrous than he would have believed last night, shining with autumn richness under the sun, was merely a mildly interesting side note. If she was anything to him, she represented a certain phantom voice in his head, a slight qualm in his heart, that last bit of living emotion, begging him to right a wrong.

So, he supposed he would. He would speak to Henry for her. He would send some people to do a more in-depth investigation of the murders of Gloushire and Baroness Rosemead—discreetly, of course. That was all he could do. It was more than anyone expected of him. It was enough.

As for Kyla herself, why, she would not be required to pay for the sins of her father. Although she had steadfastly refused to answer any of his questions regarding the murders or the subsequent escape of her father, her brother, and herself, she would answer to Henry. And then she would be the king's problem.

Not his. No longer. Lorlreau called.

Lady Kyla would fare well enough, Roland was certain. A young woman as fair and wealthy as she was would have no shortage of suitors at court. Even though her family stood in disgrace. Even though she might spend the next few months in a room in the Tower, awaiting Henry's pleasure. . . .

But that was not his problem.

At lunch she sat alone, chewing pensively at the mincemeat pie he had handed her. She had stayed near her stallion, who hovered over her and every now and then blew in her hair. Roland watched her reach up and feed the horse an apple she had on her lap. The horse grunted approvingly.

Kyla watched the stallion crunch the apple to pieces. She supposed she should think of a name for him. Malcolm had not called him anything that she had ever heard, so it was at her discretion now.

"A fine name for you, my friend," she whispered to him, tilting her head back. "What would you like?"

The men had not quit staring at her since this morning, when she had walked out of the inn and guided them to her carefully concealed horse. The morning was long past and now she was more than a little weary of the looks. Never before in her life had she been subjected to such open appraisal from the opposite sex, and certainly not from such a rude lot. If anything, she had been treated with a sort of familiar respect by the men in her father's circle, and had never noted anything more out of the ordinary than a few of the nobles in court staring at her from behind their fans and ornate handkerchiefs. That had been rather amusing.

But this boldness from these soldiers was startling; it made her want to wrap her cape up around her body and duck her head in embarrassment.

Instead she let the cape flow free around her and kept her head high constantly, concentrating on staring icily ahead, or else meeting those insolent stares with an unflinching gaze of her own. She would show them she was immune to their brutish ways, that she thought no more of them than she would an insignificant fly buzzing around her.

Kyla stood up, brushing her skirts into place, still ignoring the others. She turned to the stallion and began to stroke his fine nose.

"Adonis, mayhap? What think you of that?" The stallion nuzzled her hand. "No? Well, then, how about Apollo? Priam? Zeus?"

"Auster," said a deep voice over her shoulder. "Call him Auster."

The stallion nodded.

Kyla didn't bother to look at the man who had walked up next to her. "It is commonly considered impolite, Lord Strathmore, to eavesdrop on a lady's conversation."

"Even a lady's conversation with a horse?" he inquired innocently.

She threw him a frigid look. "Any conversation. But of

course, I could not expect that you would understand anything about courtesy."

"He likes Auster," said Roland, running his hand down the thick black neck. "It's a good name for him."

Kyla frowned. "Auster," she said experimentally, and the stallion turned his head to look at her. "Oh, very well," she grumbled.

Roland couldn't help but think it was a pleasure to hear her speak at last, even when she was obviously so displeased. Her voice had a particular husky resonance that drew him, conveying in smoky tones things she could not possibly know anything about.

Not yet.

"Auster, because he'll run like the wind," he said to distract himself, trying not to think of the unspoken promises in the sound of her voice.

"Yes. He does." Kyla had plenty of proof of that.

The one glorious memory of the past weeks was when they had encountered a smooth valley between the mountains, a valley that was invitingly dry and free of stones, with fringes of wild heather decorating the edges in a moving sea of green and pink and purple. She had let the stallion have his head then and he had burst forth in full glory, floating above the ground with her clinging to his back, tears in her eyes, laughing, watching the world streak by.

"Are you so fond of pagan mythology, my lady?"

Kyla turned and found Roland studying her. She ducked around under the horse's head and pretended to check his bit. "I am fond of knowledge in general, Lord Strathmore. But history has many lessons for us."

"Indeed."

He didn't appear to have anything more to say, just kept looking at her in that fixed manner, much like his men. Since there had been nothing wrong with the bit in the first place, Kyla sighed and faced him boldly. A tickling breeze blew a few strands of hair in her eyes, and she pushed them back impatiently.

"Are we ready to leave, my lord? I find myself bored of this journey and would wish it to end as soon as may be."

His mouth tightened. "Aye, my lady." He bowed low and walked away. She heard him give the order to the soldiers to prepare to mount up.

---

*I*T WAS TOO FINE a day to be thinking about death, but Kyla was. They were traveling at a leisurely pace; apparently now that she was captured there was no good reason to push the horses to rush back to London. For now, she couldn't help but be glad for that.

As they traveled farther south the small patches of woods grew more and more frequent, turning into great lengths of ash and pine and birch, beautiful old trees that were budding with spring leaves. Birds sang from high above in the green boughs. Speckles of sunlight littered the ground like last year's leaves as they came and went through the clouds and branches.

Kyla found herself lulled by the steady rhythm of the ride, to the point where her thoughts flowed freely from one to the next, random but smooth. Her eyes half closed. Her chin sank just a little.

She didn't think Henry would kill her. She was not the one, after all, accused of the crime. All she had done was run away with her father, and if it came down to it, she could always say she had been persuaded against her better judgment.

Of course, she would never say that. She would not lie, not to the king, not to anyone, not even to save herself. Her loyalty was unequivocally to her family, no matter what the repercussions might be. The true story was just the opposite of what Henry believed. She would throw that in his face, let him consider that.

No, she didn't think Henry would kill her, and the reason was as simple as that he had liked her. But he had liked her father as well, she reminded herself bitterly.

She had met the monarch on more than a few occasions, and every time he had gone out of his way to converse with her, to hold her hand—even, of late, to compliment her. It had to have been one of the reasons she had been getting those long looks from the courtiers, she was sure of it. Henry didn't treat her the way he did most of the young women at court, she had seen that with her own eyes. At the time she had supposed it was because of her father, or perhaps her mother, who had once been a favorite lady-in-waiting for Queen Matilda.

Whatever the reason, she didn't think the king would be so harsh as to kill a woman he had often referred to as "Our most-prized ruby" merely for fleeing.

So what would her punishment be? She would not admit her father's guilt. She would not apologize for running away. She could not forgive Henry for pursuing her family to the point of destruction, and she was not sure, in all honesty, if she would be able to keep her contempt for him from showing.

Henry was an intelligent man, a just man, she had heard, but like all kings, a very proud one. He could not afford to lose face in front of everyone when she appeared. But he might grant her a private audience. That might help. He might be more forgiving then.

A bleakness swept her, a terrible sense of isolation and foreboding. Whatever else her future would be, it would always include the shadow of her disgrace and the disgrace of her father, unless she could manage to clear his name. And there was hardly any chance of that now. Lord Strathmore had seen to that.

The announcement of her betrothal last year to the man riding beside her had been unexpected, but not entirely unwelcome. She had been sharing the household duties with her mother for some time, at first a reluctant apprentice and then, eventually, taking over certain aspects that interested her most. Her mother had been patient and kind with her, as always, and although they were careful never to mention it, the happy flow of months into years made it quite apparent to both of them that it was almost past the time for Kyla to wed.

Conner had complained half-seriously that they couldn't bear to lose their daughter, for who would soothe Cook's tremendous tantrums when supper was delayed? Who would play chess with him each night? Who would prepare the special wine he favored? No one but their Kyla knew the intricacies of the countless little trifles her father came up with, a list so ridiculous that even her mother had sighed and shaken her head. But truly, both of them had been pleased for her, despite the bittersweet moment of it.

Kyla herself had been taken aback by the betrothal, but thought it rather exciting, as well. Marriage meant her own manor or perhaps even a castle. It meant a new name, a new family, a husband beside her always. For surely all men were like her father, she had rationalized. How wonderful to create a family like her own.

That was before she had heard of the Hound of Hell's reputation. Conner's assertions that Strathmore was indeed a gentleman, a good man, had been her sustaining hope. The point had been moot, of course—ultimately she had no choice and she knew it, but to have her father's approval was reassuring.

It had been her father's voice that had spoken in her head that instant in the inn, when she had to choose between allowing Strathmore his life or taking it.

Kyla had been certain she could do it. She was skilled with the dagger, and she was filled with enough hatred. How effortless it would have been. How much he deserved it.

But then came her father's face in front of her, his voice resounding in her ears, speaking again the words he had said when she had run to him in a panic over a servant's gossip: "Don't believe what you hear of him, my dove. Don't believe the envy that paints him so black. He is a fine man, he will be a worthy husband for you. . . ."

Conner had liked him. Conner had thought highly enough of him to give him his only daughter. And so it had been Conner who had saved Strathmore, whether he knew it or not, whether he deserved it or not.

Now Strathmore lived, as she lived, but what would become of her?

She would not marry well now. She doubted very much she would marry at all, for who but the most base of men would take her? The thought of being wed to some grasping, desperate man, eager only to ingratiate himself with the king, was worst of all.

She would not suffer that. She truly would die before that.

Yet it seemed her choices were as narrow as Strathmore had earlier claimed. She would be taken to London, paraded before the court, kept locked in the Tower for days or weeks or even years, and eventually be expected to grovel before Henry while he made up his royal mind about whether or not to forgive her. In turn, if she was lucky, she would be wed off at some point to a minor noble with all expectations of her heartfelt gratitude, and would then spend the rest of her life being reminded how fortunate she was to have a man take her at all.

She would grow old and dry and withered, unwanted, reviled, laughed at, wondered at. Forever.

Or, she could escape.

Her life, whatever else it became then, would at least be her own again.

Kyla let her eyes drift shut, turning the bright colors of the outdoors to a muted red behind her lids. Auster kept the pace as she relaxed her legs and then her back after what she hoped was a suitably long enough period. She began to allow her body to bend in the saddle, just a little at first. Her head dipped down to her chest. She swayed rather dangerously to the left.

Sure enough, a command to halt came and she found herself swept up into solidly muscular arms. She pretended to come awake with a start.

"Oh, dear," she said, hoping she sounded chagrined.

"My lady." Lord Strathmore was looking down at her with concern. "Are you well?"

She lay across him in his saddle, her upper body and head propped up by his shoulder. He was close enough now for her to really see him—and it was the first time that she truly looked at him, for she had been ignoring him all day.

Again came that pang to her heart, for he was so very handsome, and he did look worried. She could even swear she saw a measure of warmth in his blue-green eyes, lit like the bottom of some enchanted sea pool.

Stupid, Kyla silently chided herself. Now was no time to fall for the charms of a rogue. She fluttered one hand up to brush her throat, as if in alarm. His look followed the movement with unexpected intensity, a glare of that exotic color that discomfited her in the midst of her charade.

"My lord . . . I am so tired. Please, could we not stop for a rest?"

His arm shifted beneath her, moving her more securely against him. The fine corners and links of his chain mail dug into her skin. "I have not slept in so long," she added softly, which was true. She tried to go completely limp without sliding down from his horse.

Roland tightened his grip. He smelled of something she could not name, sweat and pine and earth. Distracted, she turned her head to his chest, trying to pin down the disturbing emotion that was sweeping her. She suddenly wanted to stay in his arms, feeling safe and secure, surrounded by that masculine thing she could not define.

He dismounted, managing to get them both out of the saddle without much effort, swinging her up into his arms again. "We'll camp here for the night," he said. "It's as good a spot as any, and we had only an hour or so of daylight left, anyway." He took her over to a mossy bed beneath a tree. "Rest here, my lady. I will have your tent set up immediately."

She almost felt guilty then at the gentle quality of his concern, but pushed that aside. She could not afford to lose her nerve now, no matter how pleasant it was to be held by him. He was no friend of hers, and she must not forget it.

Kyla concentrated on the meeting with the king that

awaited her, on the tiny, cramped rooms in the Tower of London assigned to prisoners.

She had been to one once, on a clandestine visit to a man who had later been beheaded.

When she was younger she had thought her father's work was all glamour and excitement, which was why everyone loved him and admired him. She had wanted to be like him. She had wanted that exciting life for herself.

No one had told her she could not be an ambassador for the court because she was a female. Neither her father nor her mother had used that excuse. Instead, they had tried to explain that what Conner did was business, just business, and usually not very pleasant business at that. It was nice, yes, Helaine had admitted, to have the king like you. Yes, said her father under pressure, sometimes he got to meet wonderful new people from distant lands.

Kyla had refused to heed her parents' warnings. She didn't want to believe the king's business was anything other than what she had imagined it to be. She wanted to go to the Tower, where most of her father's work was done.

They absolutely, positively forbade her to go.

So she had arranged everything herself, carefully hoarding her allowance until she had enough coins to bribe a minor courtier's son, who agreed to smuggle her in the next time his father went there on the strict condition that she never breathe a word of it to anyone as long as she lived.

She had gone dressed as a boy, of course, and was introduced to the father as a friend of his son's. The father had grunted and then told them both to listen only and not be heard as he conducted his interview with the traitor.

It was only then that Kyla realized they were going to see a prisoner.

The room had been cold and dark, even in the midst of the hot summer day. There had been a cot with no covers, a bare wooden table, a single candle melting in greasy puddles on the wood. The stealthy scuttling of rats shivered across the beams above. One lone, narrow window slit the wall, barely wide enough for a sliver of sky to press through.

But worse than any of that, the room had smelt to her of fear, of hopeless desperation. Of death. She had seen that death reflected in the sunken eyes of the prisoner, a French man accused of conspiracy against the crown. He had kept his focus on her the entire visit, beseeching her with terrible black eyes clouded with cataracts. His hands had quivered un-controllably, even when he had flattened them down on the table.

She had listened and not said a word, as instructed. She had tried not to cover her mouth with her hand to block out the stench of the man. She had tried to ignore the prisoner's choked pleas to the courtier to end his life, to end his torture in that room, as he stared at her.

She had finally pinned her own gaze to the floor, concen-trating on the blackened grime between the pitted stones, trying to think of anything but the trembling man who sat before her, weeping.

That day part of the flame of adventure in her died a little. She never bothered her father about his work again.

Now Kyla deliberately relaxed against the tree, took a deep breath of the forest scent surrounding her, the sweet spring breeze, and promised herself that soon her steps would match that free, windy path.

Chapter Four

*T*HAT NIGHT SHE SLEPT securely in the tent they had set up for her, wrapped for warmth in furs and blankets. It was luxurious by the standards she had become used to, and she meant to make the most of it while she could. Her night was peaceful, surrounded by six armed men, by her count, all standing ready outside the walls of the indigo-blue wool tent.

History held valuable lessons, indeed. Kyla had always shown a keen interest in her studies, so much so that her parents had hired extra tutors for her and Alister. She knew mathematics, Latin, French, geography, even astronomy.

And she knew history.

History had told her of the Roman conquest centuries ago, of the difficulty the emperor's soldiers had infiltrating this particular area of Britannia. The woods here in these odd pockets of low country often gave way to swamps and marshes without warning. She had read of the thick fogs that would billow up from the ground, covering everything in their path, obscuring even the boldest marker.

The Roman soldiers had not done well here, those regimented formations proving to be no defense against nature. Kyla had amused Alister on their way to Scotland with the stories she remembered, embellishing to keep his mind distracted from the reality of their situation. It had worked for a while, especially when they saw for themselves the odd white fog, blotting out the countryside every morning for a week.

Once they even had to halt and camp for a day and a night,

the fog grew so voracious. They made a game of it, pretending they were the Romans forced to camp.

"Do you think the ghosts of the soldiers are still here?" Alister had asked that night, all agape and wide-eyed as they huddled together.

"Nay," she had replied. "They would not dare haunt us. Our ancestors vanquished them centuries past. We have our own guardian spirits to guide us."

She had said it with all the fervency of a real desire that it be true. Alister had nodded, eager to banish the thought of ghosts in the mist.

So when the next morning dawned outside the indigo tent after her fine night's sleep, and all were fed and the supplies were packed away again, the Lady Kyla mounted her horse with complete poise, noting quite calmly the thickness of the mist on the ground, listening carefully to the uneasy remarks of the men around her.

" 'Tis naught, it will pass," she heard the man she thought might be the captain say in unconvincing accents. The mutters of the soldiers indicated they doubted as much.

Thank the heavens, the soldiers had the right of it.

Instead of the mist clearing under the burning warmth of the sun, the day turned gloomy and dour, encouraging a heavy fog to build and reach up in snaky tendrils to cover the horses' legs and then the riders' torsos, until the very path was obscured from view, and all that could be seen was the vague outline of men and horses, and all that could be heard was the eerily steady clinking of armor against shields.

Six men to guard her tent! Kyla smiled to herself, adjusting her leg over the annoying horn of the sidesaddle. She supposed she should be flattered. At least Lord Strathmore was attempting not to underestimate her. But, from the moment she had realized there would be no way to avoid this journey back to London, Kyla had devoted her time to thinking about ways she could lull her keepers into a false sense of security.

She had not thought it would be very difficult. Her experience with men was limited, true enough, confined mostly to servants, tutors, and merchants, and occasionally those perfumed gentlemen who favored the court life. But she had discovered long ago that if one pretended to be weak or incapable, a man simply accepted it as a fact of nature, an inevitable example that the female mind was inferior to the male. She had had so many tutors reveal identical expressions of astonishment when exposed to her prowess, or at least her interest, in their academic fields. This was something she had become used to.

She had learned that if she said that she did not understand something, it would provoke a pitying look, a murmur of comfort, an urging to move to some other—easier—topic.

The same remark from her brother prompted a deeper explanation of the theory involved.

It was an inequity she had learned to adjust to. She formulated her questions carefully, posing them in the most ridiculously complicated terms she could think of. But she never fully escaped the superior looks of the men who taught her. And after all, she always tried to learn from her mistakes.

Therefore it was not hard to fool these soldiers into thinking she was nothing more than a simple, weak woman, lost and confused. She picked at her food, she kept her expression sour, and she knew the natural pale ivory of her skin would aid her. It wasn't hard to look pallid.

She probably should have cried at some point, she thought, but then knew she could not have gone that far convincingly. She had never been one to cry easily. What she had accomplished would be enough, she told herself. It would have to be. She had demonstrated to them that she was frail and scared, fatigued easily and was most likely in ill health. Fine.

There was no doubt in her mind that she would not be able to escape without her horse. And there had been no way to take Auster from the group of steeds last night without alerting the guards assigned to keep watch over the horses, and, of course, those other six men. That simply meant she had to be mounted already when the time came. And it would be soon now.

She wasn't silly enough to think she would be able to suddenly discover a clear path that branched off from the one they were on. That would be too much to ask for. All she was looking for now was a hint of the proper circumstances to help her.

There was only her one, true enemy to watch out for. Something told her he would not be fooled as easily as the rest.

Lord Strathmore stayed close to her as they rode, keeping his horse within an arm's reach of hers. She had not expected anything less from him. Every now and then she moved her head casually to catch a look at him from the corner of her vision. He rode bareheaded, shunning the heavy chain mail headpiece, which might, she supposed, dampen his hearing further than it was already by the fog. Very prudent, she silently approved.

But the shifting layers of mist could not disguise the grim set of his mouth, nor the hawklike sharpness of his gaze. He maintained a constant vigilance, keeping his sword ready. Even through the murky whiteness she could easily identify the golden-brown hair, the rather massive build of him, and once, when he caught her looking at him, the vibrant turquoise of his eyes, a burst of warmth amid the coolness.

He had smiled at her then, as if to reassure her, and she had instinctively smiled back, because she had wanted to, because he had a smile that made her want to trace his lips with her fingers to feel that graceful joy for herself.

Kyla caught herself and turned away again. She had to keep her head about her. She could not make a mistake now. He was handsome and charming, and he was her nemesis. It would not do to forget that.

The warmth from his look lingered, a gentle ghost in the blankness around her.

"Ho," came a distant call, a disembodied voice from far ahead in the line.

"Ho," echoed someone else, the call repeated down the column of men to Kyla and Roland, each one growing louder and more distinct. The horses were slowing.

With an almost casual ease Kyla turned Auster to her left,

where the soldier guarding her had drawn ahead just enough to allow her to slip behind his horse's haunches and off the forest path. She didn't dare look behind her, she made no overt noise or movement, merely pulling lightly at the reins to indicate where she wanted to go. Auster willingly obeyed. She maintained the walk that had been keeping pace with the others and hoped the mist had swallowed them without a sign of their passage.

Her mouth was dry, her heartbeat thudded in her ears and she had to strain to listen to the sounds of the men behind her. Nothing yet. She bent as low as she could in the saddle and urged Auster on.

Now came the raised voices, a commotion of sound with no visible origin. She heard her name being shouted, repeated.

Quickly she slipped to the ground and led Auster on foot, not willing to run in the obscurity of the fog. She was betting they would not risk their mounts to run in pursuit. Tangles of black branches materialized suddenly out of the whiteness, grabbing and catching at her. She bent them back as best she could for Auster, still walking, fighting the urge to run.

The soldiers were coming. They were not bothering to be quiet about it. She could clearly make out Lord Strathmore's voice, calling her name. There was a resignation there that affected her more deeply than anger would have. Resignation suggested that he was sure she would only be caught again. She was merely delaying her fate, not escaping it.

"Lady Kyla! You don't want to make this more difficult!" The cool assurance that carried to her as he called out was far more frightening than his wrath would have been.

Her throat closed. *I am not afraid,* she told herself firmly.

She remembered his look, friendly, consoling, and felt a small jump within herself, a shock from the memory.

A pair of gnarled branches caught and held her hair, yanking her painfully backward and almost causing her to fall. Her hands shook as she broke off the ends, leaving them snarled in the mat of her hair. Precious seconds flew by.

She had to think. She didn't know where she was. She didn't know the direction she was headed. All she knew was that only a few dear feet separated her from Strathmore, and London, and the Tower. She had to preserve her advantage.

The fog was making her hair cling to her neck and face in damp, cold curls. The bliaut melted to her form, dragging at the leaves and twigs around her. And still they came behind her, edging closer, not slowed by preposterous things like long hair or skirts.

Every now and then a whirling sweep of air would clear the ground ahead of her, highlighting the brown earth, the clumping bushes, an ancient tree or two.

That was bad. If the fog was lifting, she might as well give up now. She heard the muttered cursings of the soldiers, the sounds traveling to her clearly now.

"Blasted woman," said someone, and others growled agreement.

"Blasted witch," another amended, and got a louder round of approval.

She needed to loop around them. She needed to be somewhere they would not think to look right away. She needed to turn back toward them.

Leading Auster abruptly left, Kyla prayed she had enough time to cross their path before the soldiers were upon her. She began moving at a half run on her toes, squinting, bending low, keeping one hand up in front of her to ward off the dangerous branches and limbs, letting her arm take the brunt of the blows.

Still they came closer. Hadn't she reached the end of their line yet? She and Strathmore had been almost at the end of the column when she turned off. She wouldn't have believed they could organize and fan out so quickly.

She was heading right for them. Their horses were snorting and stumbling through the haze. She could clearly hear the steady *clink, clink* of the men's chain mail against their shields and armor once more. It was a nightmare coming true, faceless monsters come to hunt her down, they were going to get her . . . .

She wasn't going to make it.

In a heartbeat she turned Auster around, away from the

soldiers, and let go of the reins. He didn't move, just stood placidly as the others approached. Kyla pushed at him, put both hands against his mighty shoulder and shoved. He still didn't move.

In desperation she slapped him lightly on the flank, then pushed again. The stallion turned his head and looked at her reproachfully.

Please, she thought, *oh, please, my friend, go now.* . . .

And the horse had looked away from her and ambled on, almost immediately invisible behind the curtain of the fog.

The moisture clinging to her face now was mingled with salty perspiration, but Kyla rubbed her eyes with the sleeve of the gown and began to stumble on, running on a straight path that crossed the line of men.

But she still wasn't going to make it.

To her left she thought she saw the shadow of a horse, but then it vanished again, lost in the mist. The soldiers were talking to one another in lower tones now. They had abandoned the notion that calling her name would bring her back, she guessed, and so they were keeping track of one another, cursing and noting markers when they saw one. She did not hear Lord Strathmore anymore.

And then the shadow beside her took shape and she saw that it really was a horse, with a real man atop him, and Kyla whirled around and darted ahead. There was no call to halt or to follow her. Maybe she had not been seen? That horseman would be between two others, and they were too close now for her to circle around them. It was only a matter of seconds before they spotted her.

Just ahead rose one of the many thick tree trunks, blessedly not an oak—a barren, long-trunked oak—but instead a heavy old pine, and without a second thought Kyla was on it, grabbing at her skirts and climbing faster than she would have thought possible.

The sap stuck to her skin, collecting pieces of bark and needles, which dug into her palms. It didn't matter. She was only a few feet off the ground when they passed her. She froze, flattening herself against the trunk.

"Waste of bloody time," one man was saying, slapping his thigh for emphasis. "Ought to leave her out here for the wolves."

"Go on, then," said his companion, riding to his right. "And I'll takes that fat reward for her m'self."

As they passed by she could make out their heads and torsos through the pine needles and the mist, both men dark-haired and large, mounted. They were exactly at eye level to her. If they turned their heads toward her even a fraction, she would be caught.

They moved so slowly. She was afraid to breathe, her body was screaming to move, to run in panic, and she had to close her eyes to erase the sight of them, pressing her cheek against the roughness of the bark. She heard one of the horses snort in alarm, and had to bite her lip to fight the whimper that wanted to come out.

"Here now," said the man on the horse, "what's gotten to you, boy?"

She opened her eyes and the soldier was close beside her. And he was turning to look around.

"Her horse!"

The cry came from far ahead, bless Auster, and immediately drew the attention of both of the men.

"What was that? Did he say he found her horse?"

"Aye, that's what it sounded like to me."

As if to confirm it, the call came again, and then more cries from the soldiers scattered about. The two men pushed ahead into the fog, leaving her alone again in the whiteness.

The whimper came out now, unbidden, this time signaling relief. She waited, listening carefully, but all the sounds were up ahead, where they should have been. She began to climb down the tree, one step, then another, searching carefully with her foot for the next hold.

"Where would you have gone, I wonder, if you had escaped?"

She couldn't stop the little scream that came out; her hand missed its grip on the branch she had been reaching for, plunging her off-balance. It was too late to stop herself from falling.

The branches bent or broke beneath her, scratching her, ripping her clothing, and then she landed hard on something that grunted and collapsed to the ground under her.

A shower of pine needles drifted down in her wake, a pin-sharp snowfall.

Her wind was gone, her head was spinning. She couldn't move as Lord Strathmore grunted again and shifted her off of him. He leaned over into her line of vision, examining her curiously. The memory of the turquoise look merged with the present, only now his eyes were brighter, and almost laughing. None of the anger she might have expected was reflected in that look. Instead a sort of mischief glittered there, the end result of that resignation she had heard before, an I-told-you-so boyishness. A lock of his golden hair curled down against her neck.

Kyla blinked to get the spots out of her vision.

"Well," Roland said, slowly breaking into a smile. "We seem fated to keep meeting under the most unusual of circumstances, my lady."

And then he lowered his lips to hers.

Chapter Five

ᏸᎷᎷᎧ

*H*ER LIPS WERE soft and succulent, even better than he had imagined them to be, and he had been imagining quite a bit since he met her.

She tasted warm and spicy, yet the mist had cooled her skin, a delightful contradiction that pleased him in some whimsical way. He reached up a hand and cradled her cheek, marveling at the smoothness, rubbing his thumb through the thin film of moisture left by the fog.

She seemed stunned, immobile, those gray eyes large and startled as she looked up at him. He drew back his hand slightly and passed it over her eyes, gently, just enough so she would close them. Then he closed his own, deepening the kiss this time.

Her mouth opened beneath his. Perhaps she was just jolted from the fall, but he took advantage of it and touched his tongue against hers, and now she did gasp—but he used his other hand to stroke her hair, running his fingers through the silkiness of it, encountering the leaves and twigs left from her run, smoothing around them to find the line of her neck, her jaw.

He knew this was a serious breach of conduct. He was shamelessly taking advantage of someone in his personal care, a woman who had no other refuge. He should stop. It was wrong.

But it felt so good.

The hunger inside of him that had been born that night at

the inn had not abated, no matter how he rationalized it, no matter how he sought to dismantle it through logic, reason, or honor. The hunger had grown all yesterday and today, watching her, wanting her, and now the hunger took over completely because she was beneath him again, and she was twining her arms around his neck. She was kissing him back.

Roland felt the melting of her caution and systematically slipped in where her defenses had been, moving her body closer to his, teasing her lips with small, ravenous kisses, tracing them down her cheeks to her jaw, behind her ear, until she made a small sound in her throat, all feminine, that fed the fire in him to fever pitch.

Kyla arched into him when he bit lightly at her earlobe, he felt the sudden heat as her chest pressed against his. He took her mouth again with ferocity now, forgetting the time and the place, forgetting all but this woman, a stranger two days ago whom he thought he had known forever.

Because he knew just what to do to evoke that small cry in her again, he knew how to kiss her, how to stroke her arms, to cup the gentle swell of her breast, oh God, so sweet.

And she knew him, yes, how to touch him back, to frame his face with her own hands, trembling, as if in wonderment, and the kisses she gave back to him were hot and melting, her breath was honey against his skin.

Her body was lithe and taut beneath him, he could feel her even through the chain mail, such torture between them, but he moved to cover her completely with his body and she took his weight willingly, not seeming to notice until he pressed the fullness of his arousal against her thigh.

Then she gasped again, and he heard the difference. Her eyes opened wide, the heat dissolving in the silver and black, leaving clear lucidity. And fear.

Roland paused, caught between an agony of want and reality. The reality won. He pulled back, then rolled off of her.

He took a deep, shuddering breath. "See what happens to young women who attempt to leave their protection?" There was self-mockery in his voice.

She sat up beside him, looking uncertain, then defiant. "You said you were my protection."

The crown of cherry hair was littered with leaves and pine needles, bringing back to mind his earlier comparison of her to a druid. She surely looked the part now. Without thought he reached up a hand to untangle a mossy twig from its silken bonds. "Yes," was all he replied, at a loss for more. She was right and he had been wrong. They both knew it.

She sat still for him, allowing him the tending of her hair. Her breath was coming unevenly, and the thought that he was the cause of it made the shame grow, but worse, made the hunger spring back as well.

"Let me go," she said suddenly, urgently, and he knew she wasn't talking about just this moment.

"I can't."

Unexpectedly she reached out a hand and held on to his arm, her grip firm. The mist followed her movement in a white echo. "Please."

He could guess how much that cost her, that simple word. He tried to keep the torment from his voice. "My lady, it is impossible."

"No. It isn't." She kept her hand there. He could feel the strength of her fingers pressing through the chain mail. "You never found me. No one found me. I disappeared into the countryside. I'm still in Scotland. I'm dead. It won't matter to anyone but me."

"Ah, there you are wrong, my lady." Roland took in her face, the fairy beauty. "You would be sore missed."

"You don't understand! It's nothing to you! The king will not be angry at you! You did your best, I disappeared, and that is all! I am not worth pursuing further. Henry has my home, my wealth, the bones of my family. There is nothing left for me there, don't you see? In the end, it won't matter at all."

"You matter, Lady Kyla."

"I do not. Not in any important sense. Nothing I say or do there will mean anything to anyone, I assure you. What harm is there, my lord, in letting me slip away?"

"I can't," he said again, helpless to let her change her fate.

"You can. You won't." She took her hand away from his arm; he felt the absence there keenly.

She turned her head away from him, looking askance through the fog, seeing something there he could not. It was hurting him, watching her struggle with the pain, and he was appalled for both of them. What was happening to him?

Her lashes were long and dark, spiked with wetness, and for one horrifying instant he thought she was crying, until she looked up at him and he saw the anger sparking there.

"You would condemn me to death, all for your pride? I suppose I could expect nothing more from you."

"Death!" He smiled in spite of himself, relieved if this was the direction of her thoughts. At least he could dispel this notion. "No one will put you to death, Kyla. Be reasonable. Henry wants to talk to you, that's all. He wants to know what you know."

"And when he has done with me, what then, do you think, Lord Strathmore? Do you think he will just allow me to go without a by-your-leave? Just stroll right out of the Tower and back to Rosemead?" She didn't wait for him to answer, cutting him off with a flick of her hand. "Nay. He will have to do something with me. I am an enormous embarrassment to the crown. I know that. He will sell me off to pay a debt, or to incur one, no doubt. I am too conspicuous to be left alone."

The clarity of her observation left him no room for comment. She was right. Of course she was right. He began to see what she was driving at, but it didn't change his position.

She pulled her knees up to her chest and wrapped her arms around them, then rested her chin on top pensively. The swath of hair shifted down her side, cascading dark red, covering half her face. "How did you know where I was?"

"In the tree, or at the inn?"

"In the tree."

"Luck."

"At the inn?"

"Luck."

A wry smile twisted her lips. "You must have a lucky star, indeed, Lord Strathmore."

Again he couldn't reply; she had made the contrast between them so open that he could not bridge it with words. It left him feeling rather annoyed, that she would so quickly trounce him, exposing him in such ruthless brightness, picking out flaws he had never before considered.

Had he a lucky star? He would see about that when they returned to London.

Roland stood up, then took her arm and pulled her up beside him. "Come," he said, and then gave a low whistle. His horse materialized out of the mist, looming large and sudden where before there was nothing.

He lifted her up into the saddle, then quickly vaulted into place behind her, wrapping one arm securely around her waist. The top of her head reached just to his chin.

"My men will have captured your horse by now. We will meet them back at the trail."

Kyla made no acknowledgment, but her hands clenched together in her lap.

⸻

*T*HE FOG WOULD NOT LIFT, no matter that they waited until it was almost time for the sun to set. Roland had already ordered the tents unpacked and set up, expecting this, so there was no worrying about where to place the Lady Kyla while the soldiers straggled back in pairs and threes from the woods.

She had led them all on a merry chase, as Gilchrist, one of Henry's captains, had complained sourly, and they had lost the entire day for it.

The fact that the fog prohibited travel anyway, which Duncan, Roland's captain, pointedly mentioned, did nothing to sweeten the tempers of the men.

Actually, it wasn't Roland's contingent who were grousing at all. They were seasoned enough to handle just about anything. But Henry's men were loud and obnoxious, no doubt disguising their unease at the foul weather with bitter humors. Roland wasn't concerned. The king's men would not dare openly rebel; technically they were all under his command until the completion of the assignment. No matter what was said, all would obey him, and that was enough.

Everyone was tired. Everyone was sick of the extended stay up north and anxious to get back to London. And beyond London, for Roland, lay Lorlreau, at last Lorlreau, and he thought no one could be more eager to get home than he was.

He heard Duncan reassuring the others in their huddled groups around the smoking fires and knew he should be there with him, helping to soothe the fractured nerves, the surly demeanors of a group of fighters who had no battles to fight. But he would let Duncan handle it. The men respected him, they would listen. If there truly was trouble brewing, Duncan would alert him and he would deal with it then.

In the meantime, Roland decided it was far past time for him to sup with the cause of all this discord. He told himself it was only to ensure her health and safety. He needed to see for himself how she had fared after her adventure. She had not been eating her food. She might have some lingering illness. It was up to him to deliver her safe and sound to Henry. It had nothing at all to do with the fact that the memory of their kiss filled his mind, so spicy, so sweetly given. . . .

Still, he walked around awhile amid the men before reaching her tent, and then he entered without warning, passing her guards with a reserved nod. His men nodded back.

She was sitting on the pallet of furs, staring glumly at the untouched platter of roasted pheasant before her. She didn't look at him.

He settled down in front of her on the other side of the tent. "Is it not to your liking?"

She didn't seem to want to answer him, but then she sighed and said, "I'm sure it is fine."

"You haven't eaten any."

"I am not hungry."

"Not very gracious of you."

That got her attention. "Gracious?" she repeated, astonished. "My finest hunter went to all the trouble of finding you a pheasant. Not just any pheasant, mind you, I told him that wouldn't do. I told him it must be the king pheasant, the grandest bird out there. And I assure you it was no little feat for him to find it. He had to pass up a great many lesser birds. But here it is, the King of Pheasants, just for my lady, and you too proud to take even a bite. Most ungracious," he finished mournfully.

She studied him, puzzled, as if what he had said might be true and not some silly nonsense that popped into his head. Roland reached over and plucked a sliver from her platter to taste. It was dry, bland, and burnt on one side. He smiled. "Definitely the king."

"You have a very odd sense of humor." She tucked her hands under the furs covering her legs, then eyed him cautiously, as if unsure of what he might try next.

Roland looked affronted. "King Pheasant didn't find it humorous, I think."

A tiny furrow creased her brow, such a serious silver look, and he found himself wanting to charm it away all the more. It pulled at something inside of him, that tiny wrinkle, a short stab at the softness in him reserved for her alone, apparently. Roland racked his mind to think of something to say to bring peace to her, but before he could speak she pushed the platter away and lay down on the furs on her side, facing him, and he was too wrapped up in the elegance of her movements to catch his thoughts.

"Why are you called the Hound of Hell, my lord?"

"You don't know?" he hedged, not wanting this conversation.

"Oh, well, I have heard different things, of course. Battles, victories, that sort of thing. Nothing in particular that could explain it."

Roland pushed the platter of pheasant back to her. "Eat, and mayhap I will tell you."

"Mayhap?"

"Eat," he ordered, and somewhat to his surprise she reached out a hand and took some. She brought the bite to her mouth, watching him as she did it, closed her lips around it, began to chew. After a while, she swallowed. "Well?" she prompted.

"I suppose," he said slowly, "it is because the hounds from hell are supposed to be . . ." She took another bite. Her lips distracted him, luscious ripe berries, or velvet rose petals, he didn't know which was more apt. . . .

"Wicked," she said flatly, finishing the sentence for him when he lost his thought again.

"Relentless," he said instead. That was it. Relentless in the pursuit of their goals, fiendish though they were, forever and ever. Relentless in the destruction of their enemies. Roland gathered himself. "Henry named me thus."

Whatever he had said had affected her. She jumped a little at his words, her eyes darkened. He caught a bitter spark there, the curl of her mouth was derisive.

"So"—she took another bite—"you are his dog."

He smiled sharply to show she hadn't offended him. "Some would say so."

"A lapdog?" Her eyes were bright now, the pheasant was disappearing faster.

"Nay," he replied, his voice low. "A hunter. What else?"

He saw her glance at the mark she had made on his throat with her dagger, that night at the inn. "You hunt down the innocent."

"I serve my sovereign."

"You have no will, only a master."

"You have a biting tongue and a quick wit, my lady, but I'm afraid you're wrong in this. I am my own master. I choose to serve, because it will get me something I want."

She paused in eating. "And what would that be?"

He hesitated, unwilling to spill his inner self to her so openly, not when she obviously had such a low opinion of him and could skewer him with a single, well-chosen word. "Nothing of interest to you, Lady Kyla."

She finished the meal, licking her fingers, watching him, and then stretched out fully amid the furs. "Well, hound, you dogged me into eating. You should be pleased with that, at least."

"Tomorrow perhaps you shall have the pheasant queen."

"Yes," she said, turning her head to study the tips of her toes, peeking past her coverings. "She would be better off on my plate than living the rest of her life alone. Don't you think?"

And of all the things she had said, that was the one that stabbed him. For he knew she meant herself, but he saw himself there as well.

Roland grabbed the plate and stood. "Sleep well, Lady Kyla. Tomorrow we ride hard."

He left without another look.

———————⟨∞⟩———————

𝒯HE JOURNEY BACK TO London went swiftly after the last of the fog wafted away and they passed through the low country. The small army of men drew gawkers whenever they passed a village, people pointing and talking, running in from the fields, crowding into the muddied lanes to stare.

And all noticed Kyla, the lone woman, head back, hair free, the cape a flowing mantle behind her. The slack of the rope that linked her tied hands to Roland's pommel swayed between their two mounts. He had done it as a safety precaution, hating to embarrass her but unwilling to let his prey slip away this close to the end. Something told him she would be swifter than all of them on that stallion, and he had no desire to put his theory to the test. The rope went around her wrists in the morning and came off again in the evenings, when they camped.

So naturally the people asked about her—Was she a criminal, a rogue princess? What manner of woman needed to be bound amid all these men?

Kyla ignored all of them. She really could have been that princess, so thoroughly did she scorn to answer the questions hurled at her and around her. Roland would have spared her this if he could have. The soldiers brushed off the peasants as they passed, only pausing to reassure them that they had nothing to fear.

Lady Kyla had taken to silence again; she had not spoken except in simple words since that night in the tent with him. She exhibited neither fear nor apprehension as they drew closer to the great city, merely kept to herself with a frosty demeanor that discouraged all but the most determined of men. He didn't know what to make of her.

The land they were passing through was becoming less and less wild, the villages closer and closer together. Signs of civilization cropped up more often: dots of white sheep decorating the hillsides; even, narrow strips of earth holding the new growth from the plowed fields. People everywhere, tilling the soil, scattering seed, herding the livestock, staring, staring.

He began to perceive her agitation rather than see it as they came close to a small village that he did not recognize. A flush lit her cheeks, making the paleness of her skin stand out all the more, and for the first time she dropped her royal pose to keep her head down, her hair cloaking her.

He could not fathom the change until the villagers spotted their group and came running over. Nothing unusual about that, but these people were saying her name, talking out loud in shocked voices as they pointed. The crowd swelled to impressive proportions, people coming closer from all over, erupting from the forests. And then Roland saw the stately manor house of warm rose-colored stone, the gabled contours of it set back peacefully amid a green, and saw Kyla look too, just once, before lowering her head again.

What had he been thinking, to bring her past Rosemead, to publicly shame her like this? He had not known they were so close. He had never been here before, he would never have done this on purpose. The lead captain would pay for this, Roland vowed to himself grimly, and was turning to the nearest man to pass a message along to quicken the pace when a young woman, no more than fifteen, broke from the crowd. She ran right up to the column of soldiers, fearlessly darting between the horses until she was at Kyla's side.

"Milady," the girl panted, half running beside them, tugging on Kyla's skirt. She pressed a ragged posy of field daisies into Kyla's fingers. "We're for you, milady," the girl cried boldly, rousing a chorus from the watching villagers.

Kyla didn't seem to know what to do. Her fingers closed around the flowers, she looked down at the girl in bewilderment.

"We're for you," the girl repeated, then dropped back, letting the procession go by.

---

*R*OLAND WAS TIRED. The nearer they came to London, it seemed, the more tired he became. His close observation of Lady Kyla revealed the same of her. She had been thin at the start of this journey, but now, despite his best efforts to get her to eat, she was growing thinner, her eyes more radiant, her hands more delicate. No doubt she was a fighter, but the worry was wearing her away, and it frustrated him that he could not stop this. Passing Rosemead had not improved her disposition. Indeed, to him it seemed far worse, for now, interspersed with the regal hauteur, he would see crumbling moments of her misery as she clutched the wilted daisies, fighting valiantly against the distress inside her.

To battle the weakness she had created in him Roland focused on Lorlreau, on what his people would be doing right now: sowing their own crops, airing out the castle from the winter chill, the fishing boats casting out every day now, almost, since the weather would be fairer at last. Madoc and Seena, taking charge of the spring, cantankerously directing the very air in the proper way in which to flow.

Harrick, gently persuading everyone to keep calm spirits, and Elysia . . . how tall would she be now? Would she even reach his hip yet?

But still, through all these musings would come the echo of that moment in the fog with Kyla, the hungry need of that kiss, her plea to him to release her, and his immediate, instinctive refusal. Doubts began to circle his thoughts, questioning not only his decision but also his motivation.

What would have been the harm in letting her go? She had shown him quite clearly what she had to look forward to for the rest of her life, the stigma that would scar her forever. She knew the rules of court as well as he did, probably better. Would it have been more merciful to let her fade away into the mist that day, to give her that final bit of freedom?

But then he would catch himself. Of course he had been right. Perhaps she was an enchantress, eclipsing his reason with her will. Of course he had to capture her. Of course he had to hand her over to Henry. It was not only his duty, it was the best thing to do. He would not consign even his enemy to die in the wild, unwanted, unprotected. And Kyla was not his enemy, no matter what she thought of him.

If he had released her, she would have died quickly this time. He was sure of that. The thought was so appalling to him that he couldn't bear to examine it.

This ethereal woman, this determined sprite, obviously needed to be protected. But who would do it?

Two days after Rosemead they rounded a grassy hillock and before them spread the outer edges of the city proper, gray stone and wood and dirt and people. The soldiers perked up noticeably, the banter back and forth became more hearty, full of glad tones.

Kyla said nothing, of course, but Roland fancied he could see her hands tighten on her reins. After a while she spoke, looking down at the midnight mane of her horse.

"I have heard the Tower is very dark."

Roland frowned, trying to interpret the hidden message in her words. "Some parts are," he said cautiously.

There was a long pause, and he began to cast about for something else to say to draw her out when she spoke again, very softly, almost so he could not hear her.

"I don't like the dark." Before he could respond she continued, her voice stronger. "I know you owe me nothing, Lord Strathmore, but I would ask one favor of you. I ask it in the name of my father, if need be. He was a good man, and he spoke well of you."

Roland waited.

"I would ask you to care for Auster while I am . . . away," she said, now finally meeting his eyes. "I do not trust the palace guard to watch him well, and you show a certain fondness for him. And he for you. Would you do this one thing?"

"It will not be necessary. You'll see."

"Will you do it?" she persisted.

"There will be no need."

"Will you?"

Roland sighed, the tiredness coming over him again, making him rub at the bridge of his nose. "Lady Kyla, I promise you right now, there will be no need for me to look after your horse. You will be able to entrust him to whomever you choose."

"Then I choose you."

"I don't—"

"Forgive me, my lord," she interrupted, a flare of disdain directed at him. "I had not realized the burden I was asking you to take. How thoughtless of me. Please forget I ever mentioned it."

"Dammit, Kyla," he swore, losing his temper at last. "You are so quick to offend and so slow to heed me! Listen to my words, my lady, I will not say this again! I promise you that you will not have to worry for your horse, because you will not be imprisoned, or beheaded, or whatever it is you fear will happen to you. Do you understand me now? You will be a free woman, as soon as the king has done with you. You are not the criminal."

If she was taken aback by his sudden show of anger she kept it well hidden. She let the silence rest between them, looking off into the horizon of rooftops. The noises and smells of the city surrounded them now. Babies screaming, merchants hawking goods, the sound of cheerful drunkenness from a tavern they passed.

"I do not like the dark," he heard her say once more, but under her breath, so he might have imagined it.

Chapter Six

———— ◦◦◦◦◦ ————

HE AIR IN HENRY'S private chamber was cold and thick and smelled of perfumed beeswax mingled with the spiced goose of his supper, the remains of which could be seen congealing in lumps on a golden plate by his chair.

Henry had not bothered to rise from his ornate seat by the fire when she entered, as he used to do. He had not taken her hand and held it a little too long, as he had before. And he did not smile at all as he surveyed her up and down, dressed still in the plain bliaut from the innkeeper's wife.

She had done her best to clean it, but cold water and rubbing could not mend the rents in the fabric, nor the wrinkles lining it. It was clearly a coarse peasant's gown, certainly nothing suitable in which to be presented to the King of England.

Yet it was all she had, and no one had sent her anything else. Kyla met Henry's gaze without flinching. Beside her Roland was rising from his bow.

"My liege," he said now, taking a step back to stand beside Kyla.

"Well, Strathmore, you have done it, We see."

Scattered to the corners of the room were clusters of Henry's most favored nobles, advisers, ministers, knights. They grouped together in jeweled shades, radiating suppressed excitement, an occasional glint of metal from the firelight glancing off a ring or a clasp, arms crossed, ears straining for every word that passed.

Kyla inched closer to the fire, trying to absorb some of the heat to take the chill off of her body. Both Henry and Roland paused to look at her and she stared back, unruffled, not wanting to say anything she did not have to.

It had been hard enough executing her curtsy to Henry. In a private compromise to the wild thing in her that had not wanted to move at all, she had made it less deep than it should have been to the sovereign, not quite dipping all the way to the floor. She wondered if Henry had noticed.

Her skirts grazed the edge of the iron grate; she twitched the hem away from the heated metal, now keeping her eyes lowered for fear he might see the wildness for what it was: disdain, humiliation. Anger.

Henry's left foot was partially in view, velvet-shod, ermine-trimmed, a tumble of royal robes almost covering it. The marble floor was slick, cream and white beneath it.

The floor in the room assigned to her was not marble, not at all. It was the same dull stone that had made up the floor of the room of the French man she had visited years ago, gray and dirty and worn smooth in a path in front of the meager window, a path that suggested endless pacing by its occupants.

There was a pallet, not a cot, and several brass braziers, not a lone candle. But the rats were still there. And the seeping smell of desperation lingered as well.

She thought of spending days there, weeks, but could not imagine spending even this night in that cramped little room. She would go mad with it.

Their arrival at the Tower had garnered all the attention of a royal entourage, with shouted greetings and trumpets announcing them in blaring bursts. There would be no cover for her, no privacy, Kyla quickly realized, and so set her mind to capturing the air of supreme indifference she had been practicing these past days. It was much more difficult here, in a place where she had been so often before. She knew these people, she recognized many faces, but still they seemed foreign—pale, shiny masks with glittering eyes and moving mouths. The babble of sound surrounding them had drowned out the actual words. She heard her name repeated, her father's, her mother's.

Roland had held her arm gently but firmly, guiding her through the steps she had often walked in eager anticipation as a girl. Kyla was grateful for his touch, enemy or not; it was warm and comforting, it was human and sane amid the chaos of the moment. He kept her close to him, pushing past the gathering crowd, smiling and not answering anyone, just moving them along.

Inside the hall the throng followed, lesser now in the imposing grandeur of the entrance.

A man had come to them in elaborate livery, a guard, who bowed to them both and then indicated Kyla was to come with him.

She had felt Roland's grip tighten then on her arm. He seemed to want to speak but changed his mind, releasing her, stepping away.

The guard bowed again, waiting.

Kyla had glanced up at Roland, who gave her that small, crooked smile. She couldn't tell what it meant, that smile. Be brave? Go to the devil?

She had turned away and followed the guard, not bothering to look back again. She heard Roland begin to speak to the remnants of the crowd but by then she was beyond listening, beyond caring what he told them. She was echoing the steps she had taken those years before to the darkest part of the Tower, and she was wondering when she might see daylight again.

Well, she was not seeing it now, that was certain, but that was because the inky-black night lay beyond the long glass windows of Henry's chamber. The darkness was punctuated occasionally by the glow of a torch. She could not tell if there were stars out tonight.

To her surprise, she had been summoned to Henry only a few hours after her arrival. To her even greater surprise— and secret relief—Roland was in the room with her, taking her arm once more as they advanced to the king together, pressing her fingers with the warmth of his, smiling down at her.

Kyla didn't know what he was smiling about. She certainly didn't feel that confident.

"It pains Us," said Henry abruptly, "to see you so plainly dressed, Lady Kyla."

Clothing! Of all the things she had been expecting to hear Henry say, she had never imagined that this would be his first concern. He would talk to her of clothing, stupid nothings, over all else that had shattered her life—murder and intrigue and betrayal.

Kyla frowned down at the skirts, trying to maintain her composure. "Your Majesty." She struggled to keep her tone even. "I regret it does not please you."

"Strathmore," said the king. "Give Us your report."

Roland released her arm. She listened to him recite the facts of the chase, from London to Scotland to England again, and of her own capture, told now in such a matter-of-fact way it felt more like a dry history lesson and not a chapter torn from her own life.

The iron grate was scrolled with an iron garden: iron roses, iron lilies, iron leaves, even a clever iron bumblebee hidden amid the vines. It was topped with iron strawberry leaves, an even row of them, one after the other from end to end. Kyla wondered at that, if it was perhaps a sly comment from the blacksmith, to have the row of leaves on a humble grate so clearly reflect those of the royal crown.

But perhaps she was the only one who noticed. There were plenty of other distractions in the room to draw the eye, richness well suited to the private chambers of a king: detailed tapestries, chests and chairs littered with gemstones, an enormous dark bed with feather pillows and brocade cloth-of-gold draping the corners . . .

Kyla realized the room had fallen silent again; apparently Roland had finished with his tale. A sideways look told her the king was studying her, rubbing his chin. She noticed his left foot was now tapping the marble floor, an impatient rhythm that made no sound.

She sighed a little, then looked up at him fully once again.

She kept her hands hidden in the folds of the bliaut, fingers clutching at the material.

"Now, Lady Kyla." Henry shifted in his chair. "Enlighten Us with your version, if you please."

She could not ignore a royal command. The image of the Tower room flashed in her mind, but she pushed it away, clenching her fists tighter.

"My father did not murder my mother, Sire." This statement brought forth bubbles of comment from the corners of the room. Henry raised one languid hand; the sound stopped instantly. He gestured for her to continue.

"He loved her, he would never have harmed her. He died with her name on his lips, calling out for her. He did not kill her."

She wanted to lower her eyes again but did not. Instead she kept her focus slightly off the king, more on the blackness of his hair, the richness of his gold velvet cloak. She felt Roland beside her, solid, strong, masculine.

"I convinced him to leave. I convinced him of the peril of staying. I planned everything."

She waited but no one interrupted her, no one called out their disbelief. Henry looked brooding. Kyla continued.

"After my mother was . . . found, it was as if the life had drained out of him as surely as it had from her. He would not eat, he would not sleep. He would not drink. He sat, day and night, in her chambers, sat there and wept."

The memory choked off her words and she had to pause, curling her toes in their thin leather slippers, concentrating on the feeling of the marble floor to distract her. Her palms were sweating. She felt Roland take her arm again.

She shook him off. "I knew what was being said, Sire. I knew what people were thinking. I knew he had no more awareness in him than a babe. He was just existing, not living. Not understanding. I had to try to save him."

"So you ran away," mused Henry, staring at the fire.

"I couldn't let him die like that, for something he didn't do. I couldn't allow that."

"Yet," said Henry softly, "he *is* dead, my Rosemead."

"Yes," she replied. "My *father*."

He didn't say anything to this for a while, just continued his study of the flames. The men in the corners of the room never moved now, never breathed, it seemed to Kyla. Only Roland was real beside her. How odd she should be grateful for him now.

"Tell Us how he died," Henry ordered.

"A fever, Majesty. He was not well after the discovery of my mother." Kyla made herself let go of her skirts, laced her fingers together to form a graceful cup in front of her. "He did not recover from that, I think. He died just a few weeks out of London. It was bitter cold, and he kept giving his blankets to my brother and me while we slept."

She didn't want to think of this, didn't want to lose her composure now, in front of these sickly eager men. She would not give them that satisfaction. She had not cried over her father's death, there had been no time for that. She was not going to cry now.

"My brother and I continued up to Glencarson, as you know, Sire. My father wanted us to go to my mother's brother."

"MacAlister," said the king, still pondering the fire, not looking at anyone.

"He took us in."

She didn't want to say the rest of it, it was still too raw, the uncertain hope that Malcolm had embodied, which had come tumbling down around their ears with the arrival of Roland and his men.

Surrender the Warwicks.

If they had searched for more provocative words to incite Malcolm they could not have found them. She would not now give them the satisfaction of knowing they picked out the singular glaring weakness of the man who had represented their shelter and survival.

Nothing she had said, nothing she had done could have changed Malcolm's mind, she realized that now. He had thrown his fate to the battle and cared nothing for all the good people he would drag down with him.

If God wills it, so be it.

And, she supposed, God had so willed it, for so it became.

What could she tell these fine court men about that day when he had locked her in that room, taking Alister with him?

She had screamed and cried, begging and demanding and threatening until her voice was thin and hoarse, getting nothing but silence from the other side of the door because they were all gone then, gone to the battle, and maybe she was the only sane person left in this whole wide world.

From the distance she had heard the war cries, and each one cut her to pieces, each one could have been Alister or the man who would kill him, and she was helpless to do anything about it.

Eventually the battle sounds had stopped.

Then came the fire.

Part of her wanted the end then, considered how easy it would be to lie down on the pallet and simply breathe in the acrid smoke, let it wrap around her lungs until there was nothing else.

But of course her body would not obey this half-hearted will, and it had reacted by taking a blanket off the pallet and covering her fist with it, pounding on the heavy glass window high in the little room.

It took forever to break, forever standing up on a chair, coughing, blind with tears, pounding and pounding until her fist was raw and she couldn't see the window any longer through the smoke.

Finally it had broken, but she almost couldn't reach up high enough to climb out. Kicking, pulling with all her might, heedless of the jagged glass that cut her, she made it out at last and tumbled to the ground only to be surrounded by flames. The fire was everywhere. It was everything.

Her dress had caught fire when she landed and she used the blanket to pound it out.

By then it was all over. It had not taken the smoldering remains of the village to show her who had won the battle of Glencarson. There was never any doubt in her mind who would prevail. She covered herself with the blanket, stumbled past the remaining English soldiers who were busy catching the serfs as they tried to run away. But she was running for the field, running for Alister.

Someone had grabbed her, one of the Scots, and taken her aside before she could be captured. Someone had held her still while she fought weakly, telling her to be quiet and wait, it was over now, she should wait.

She hadn't wanted to. But she had known he was dead by then, so what could it matter if she found him now or three hours from now?

They waited until that evening, all of them, mostly women, when the English troops had moved off, satisfied with their day's work. That evening the survivors went out together to the field.

Kyla never knew who it was that held her back, and probably saved her life. She never got to thank that person, though she had tried to thank them all later. It had been so hollow then.

The hollowness now emptied her, let her look squarely into the eyes of Henry. He was small and swarthy, a man who held the essence of a crown on his head even when it was bare, as it was now. A man who held the very fact of her existence in the turn of his thoughts.

She had nothing more to say. She could feel the looks of the men in the room: Henry, dark and moody; the nobles, curious, unsatisfied; and Roland . . .

She remembered his kiss that day in the forest. She remembered the way he avoided her eyes when he told her he couldn't let her go.

She wondered now if he regretted that decision and turned her head to look up at him, etched in amber from the fire. He was already staring down at her. Their look meshed and held, a strange heat between them.

"It is a heavy business," said the king into the silence. "We must think on this matter further. We will call you when We are ready to hear from you once more. Take her back to her quarters." He began to rise from his chair.

Roland saw Kyla's face go ashen.

I promise you . . . You will be a free woman . . .

"Sire." Roland very deliberately took Kyla's hand in his own, letting everyone see the move. "A word, I beg you."

Henry eyed the intimate gesture with the astonishment of a cat who had just discovered that the mouse it was chasing is really a lion. He slowly moved his gaze from their locked hands to the face of Roland. Then he sat back down.

Beside Roland Kyla was tense, wary, the instinct to flee so strong in her it hit him in waves—panic, run, hide. He kept his grip firm on her hand.

"I do beg your forgiveness, Majesty. In the midst of the haste and excitement over our arrival, it seems I have forgotten to mention that Lady Kyla has done me the honor of becoming my wife."

The shock of his words reverberated throughout the chamber, igniting a buzz of comment that even Henry could not suppress. He slouched in the chair, unblinking, lips slightly pursed. Eventually he raised his hand again and the noises stopped.

"I do humbly beseech you," said Roland, keeping his own stare pinned to the monarch's, steely hard despite his careful words, "not to separate me from my new bride."

A slight smile took Henry.

"I see," he said.

The tension in Kyla had turned to something else, something less defined, full of surprise. Roland brought her hand up to his lips and kissed the back of it, slanting a warning look to her.

She was stoic, only the storms in her eyes giving her away. He lowered their joined hands, looking back at Henry.

Roland was intensely aware that his spur-of-the-moment plan could explode in his face. All Henry had to do was order him to stay in the Tower with Kyla, instead of releasing her to him. Then they would both be stuck.

"I have promised, kind liege, to show her the sights of Lorlreau as soon as may be. She has had a hard winter and is in sore need of rest." He hurried on, realizing that perhaps nothing could be more restful than months confined to one room. "I have promised her the good air of Lorlreau will be all that she will need as a balm to her spirit, as she is a balm to mine."

Henry's smile vanished as soon as Roland mentioned Lorlreau, replaced now with suspicious consideration. He wasn't happy with this unexpected announcement. Roland knew the king was wrestling with the idea of letting Kyla go, and thus letting go of any hope of resolution in the deaths of Gloushire and the baroness. He decided to push his luck just a bit farther.

"My men are weary," he said indifferently, as if it meant nothing. "They are eager to return home to Lorlreau, and their families."

There, he had said it, the subtle implication, the gentle words really meaning nothing gentle at all. Henry understood him clearly, he knew. They had known each other too long not to pick up on the delicate messages in seemingly innocent words. Henry knew exactly what Roland was saying, but would never openly say.

Roland's men were many and fierce. They were also famous for their unwavering loyalty to him, just as Roland was known for his loyalty to Henry. The stories of the Hound of Hell had never been all that embellished. They had never had to be; the truth was staggering enough.

The loss of Roland's trust in his king could be a very damaging thing, indeed. Very damaging.

He was gambling with everything he had ever wanted in this moment, and for an instant wondered if he had gone mad to do so. If Henry didn't back down, Roland's life would be as good as forfeited, his lands lost, his people cut loose and defenseless. It was insanity to risk such a thing.

But in his hand was Kyla's delicate one, and she grasped him as if he were her only lifeline. He knew he was, and the urge to help her was overwhelming. Never had he known such an awareness of another person before she leapt into his life. He had never felt the desire she produced in him, nor the wonder at her hidden strengths, her sheer physical beauty.

She was staring up at him now, eyes shuttered, considering

him, calculating his risks. The edges of her hair hung down to tickle his hand where it held hers, a burning singe of awareness of the melting red of it. And that was just her *hair*, for God's sake.

"Married," said Henry at last, shaking his head, breaking off the challenge in the look he had held with Roland.

Roland knew in that instant he had won. He had seen that small shake before, though it had been seldom. It meant the king was stymied.

At least for the moment.

"Aye." Relief flooded through Roland. He tried to keep it out of his voice.

"We suppose, Strathmore, that We cannot make a liar out of you to your fair young bride by denying your promise to her."

Kyla's fingers trembled for a moment in his, just a twitch, then were still again.

"Very well. We will release her to your custody and allow you both to travel back to Lorlreau. Mind you, We may call you back at any time, no matter about the nonsense of the good air of Lorlreau."

Roland grinned. "You yourself called it thus, Sire, when you last visited."

"Aye, well, so I did," Henry grumbled, dropping his kingly manner for a moment. "Just make sure you are there when I need you, Strathmore."

"I always am."

"All right. Go on with you, then, both of you. Good journey and all that." Henry stood up and crossed to his bed. The clusters of men parted immediately for him to pass.

Roland bowed to the king's back, pulling Kyla's hand down to curtsy when she didn't move to follow him. She dipped down carelessly, and almost before she was finished he was pulling her to the door.

"Strathmore," called out Henry, as if he had forgotten something. Roland turned and Kyla edged closer to him. He put an arm around her shoulders.

"Buy your lady some proper clothing. The next time I see her, I don't want her wearing rags."

Roland bowed again, smiling, and this time he didn't have to prompt Kyla to follow. Together they backed out of the main doors and into the antechamber beyond.

Chapter Seven

*S*HE COULDN'T BELIEVE IT. How easy it had been for him, how smoothly the lie had slid past his lips, how totally convincing the words were, combined with the steady purpose of his gaze and that polished smile.

Henry had believed it! He had let her go!

Kyla had to fight not to pull her hand from Roland's and go leaping with joy out to the king's hall. They were not out of danger yet; there were still people everywhere, even here in the antechamber—guards and servants and nobles, all of them staring, whispering, beginning to come toward them. But she wanted to run and shout and laugh and keep running until she was home safe again, home to Rosemead.

Empty Rosemead.

Roland tucked her arm firmly under his, pulling her close, keeping his eyes ahead of them.

"We haven't much time," he said to her quietly.

"Time?" She had all the time in the world now, thanks to him, and so didn't understand his remark, the urgent undertone to his voice, but turned her head and smiled up at him.

"If Henry uncovers the deception, he will punish us both."

Kyla felt the slender pulse of joy drain out of her at his words; a new trap lay suddenly yawning at her feet. Some of the people were openly walking toward them now, full of false cheer, ablaze with curiosity.

Roland captured her gaze with his own, sober and bright. "Do you plight me your troth, Lady Kyla?"

She gaped up at him, the room began to spin, her feet faltered. Roland yanked her back up. He began to walk faster, away from the line of people edging closer who were now calling out their names in cultured tones. It would not do to shout in the king's antechamber, no, but they were close to it, these men and women.

"Say it now, Kyla, or we will both be lost. Neither of us will see home again."

"I . . ." Was he joking? Could he be serious, the lie suddenly transformed to truth, or else . . . what?

The Tower, the Tower for both of them, not just her, but this man as well, her enemy. Yet he had risked himself to save her. Good God, of course, it was so clear now, he couldn't let her go, not after that scene with Henry. She wasn't free at all. And now, neither was he.

With a few simple words from him to the king he had placed himself at risk to help her, and she had thought it so foolhardy, so obviously untrue, that her whole body had broken out in a cold sweat even next to the fireplace. She had been waiting for Henry to laugh at the jest, or to order them furiously back to the Tower, or to pick apart the lie and throw it back at their feet, defying them to prove it.

But no, Roland had judged well. Henry had swallowed his protests in that harrowing, endless moment and accepted the false fact of their union.

Now she knew the fact could not remain false, or the consequences could be unimaginable.

She faltered again, and again Roland pulled her up, his body warm next to hers, the doors still so far away.

They were well and truly snared in the net he had spun. If she didn't marry him, if Henry found out about the deception—

"Strathmore!" came a man's hearty tones, commanding, close.

"My lord!" came another voice from the other side of the room.

They were friends and acquaintances of her parents', some just a blur of faces, vague recollections from times past, and they were all converging on the two of them now, right now. They were never going to make it to the door leading out to the hallway.

"Say it," urged Roland under his breath, squeezing her arm.

A woman stepped in front of them, glittering in a crimson gown with gold edging, a billowing scarf surrounding her headpiece. She wore a puzzled smile, she was looking at Kyla, saying her name. She was almost upon them.

"I plight thee my troth, Lord Strathmore," Kyla whispered quickly.

Roland glanced down at her, the lines around his mouth loosening, something like relief in his eyes. "And I to thee," he said quietly, just so she could hear him, and then the others were there around them.

"My dear girl," said the woman, reaching out a hand to her.

"Strathmore," said a man to her left, a chorus of voices surrounding them, bodies crowding close, some clapping Roland on the shoulder, jarring them, taking careful note of her appearance—the plain gown, the rents, the stains, her loosened hair, what would they think?—then Roland's possessive hold on her arm grew gentler. He pulled her slightly in front of him, blocking her from the mass of people as best he could.

Kyla lifted her head higher. The lady in the crimson gown came closer, a swell of women behind her.

"Do you remember me, Kyla?" asked the woman, and the strangeness of her features blended into something more familiar. Her mother's friend, a lady-in-waiting, as Helaine had been, a kind face among the many.

"Lady Elisabeth." Kyla was surprised at how normal her voice sounded. "Of course I remember."

"Successful journey, then, eh, Strathmore?" said a man loudly, drowning out the other voices.

The crowd became quieter, the avid gazes landing first on her, then on Roland, who replied, "A great success, I should think, Jared."

There was something peculiar in the air, Kyla noticed, a subtle, grasping hunger she had not encountered here at court before. No one was pretending not to stare at her. There were no discreet whispers behind fans or hands now, but rather a more flagrant rudeness that went beyond even what she had experienced with the soldiers. These people knew better than to stare at her. She was to be protected. She was the daughter of a noble family. She was one of them.

But of course, she realized, she wasn't one of them any longer. It hadn't taken the ruined bliaut and wild hair to make them realize that. From the moment her mother's body had been discovered in Gloushire's bed, her family was disgraced, set apart from all the others, if for no other reason than that the transgressions of the Rosemeads had taken on such a public hue. Private sins, yes, were certainly allowable, but public ones were quite different. Kyla was open game to them now.

"Indeed!" said another man, leering. "You've caught the plum of the Rosemeads, by heavens."

"But now what to do with her, eh?" said the hearty-voiced man, standing by her elbow, reeking of perfume. There were several suggestions from the crowd.

"I'll take the plum, by God. I've got a pie for her!"

"Nay, she'll stay sweeter with me!"

Some of the women began to make fretful noises, feigning shock, but before anyone could say anything else Roland interrupted, his voice mild and carrying.

"I would take care with what you say of my wife."

In the ensuing silence he flattened his palm on her shoulder, then moved it openly across her collarbone in a disturbingly sensual motion, pulling her back to rest against the front of him.

Kyla fought the blush that rose in her cheeks.

Lady Elisabeth, directly in front of them, recovered first. She gave a strange smile, then deliberately separated herself from the crowd, leaning over and kissing Kyla lightly on the cheek.

"Congratulations. I am sure your mother would be most pleased."

Kyla thanked her, or at least tried to thank her, but by then the others were commenting, their rising disbelief and forced jocularity combining, the noise level drowning out her words. She could hear her heartbeat thudding in her ears, and she could feel Roland's pounding against her back. The heat of his body felt good, a solid calm amid the storm surrounding them, a focal point for her. She closed her eyes momentarily, blocking the turmoil, and then everything else faded away and all she could feel was his heartbeat, regular, strong, and the palm of his hand resting at the curve of her neck, his fingers light against her skin.

His arm rose and fell with each breath she took. She liked the weight of it on her, she liked the way he didn't crush her with his strength but rather kept her steady against him, allowing her to feel the reassurance of his body.

Part of her realized it was scandalous. She should open her eyes. She should smile at these primped gawkers as if it were the most normal thing in the world to be standing there at Henry's court with the Earl of Lorlreau stroking her softly, leaving pinpricks of heat wherever he touched her.

Her husband.

Her eyes snapped open. Roland was good-naturedly answering the barrage of questions.

"Well, yes, Lady Beatrice, it *was* rather sudden."

When she shifted, his arm tightened; the caress became a bond, holding her in place as he continued on in that affable voice.

"In fact, I myself feel as if it only just happened. No doubt it is the effect of my overwhelming delight that the lady would have me, unworthy as I am."

Uncertain congratulations echoed around them; a few more of the women moved forward to kiss her, all cool cheeks and rustling satins and velvets, the diaphanous worlds of the scarves enveloping her as they came close.

Kyla smiled tightly at each of them, attempting a normal stance even though she couldn't move; Roland's grip gave her no quarter.

"A most interesting tale you have to tell, I am sure," said Lady Elisabeth. "Perhaps one day you will share it with me."

Kyla didn't know what to say, what could she share with these people, even her mother's friend? But Elisabeth merely patted her hand and drifted off, signaling a retreat to the rest of the more polished set. Gradually the crowd thinned until Roland gave their excuses, saying they both needed to rest.

They left the room still arm in arm, with the dense knots of people staring after them.

He took her in a different direction from where she had been brought in, opposite the dank walkway that led back to the little room assigned to her. She followed without comment, trying to absorb the shocking changes the last hour of her life had brought, trying to find the glaring hole she was certain must exist in this bizarre plan he had created for them.

But she couldn't find the hole. There was no escape. He had told the king they were married, and in the minutes afterward he had made it a truth, and she had let him. Now everyone knew.

They were married. Those private vows were as legally binding as anything public, she knew it as well as he did.

Married!

Kyla swayed a little against him and Roland frowned down at her, wondering how long it would take before the feverish blaze in her eyes sapped the strength that let her walk now. He tightened his support on her arm and willed her to stay with him a little longer, just enough to get back to his chambers. Then she could faint all she wanted.

Roland didn't question the thing in him that had pressured her in that timeless moment back in the antechamber. True, his ruse to the king was a tricky thing, and certainly they could have been undone by the discovery of it, but such immediacy was not really necessary.

He could have taken her back to Lorlreau and married her there. Harrick would have performed the ceremony without a fuss, and never spoken a word of it again if Roland had asked him not to.

As long as he kept her with him, no one would have known if they were actually wed or not. It would not have mattered all that much.

But then, crossing that threshold from the private chamber to the more public beyond, riding high on his thrill of out-maneuvering Henry, Roland had looked down at the woman beside him, her hand still tight in his, the delicacy of her features turned up to him, the silver-smoke eyes, the sculptured curve of her cheek . . .

The *want* had come pounding back fiercer than ever, the urge to crush her to him, to overwhelm her with himself, to make love to her forever, drowning them both. It seized him with fire, mingled with the exhilaration already singing in his blood, and he knew then that he could have her the way he wanted, permanently, that his advantage was right now, and if he took it, the eyes, the lips, the hair, her body, all of her would belong to him. He could take his time dousing the fire that burned for her every day for the rest of his life.

There was no question about it. She had wavered as the crowd approached and he had pressed her, pressed her hard, exaggerating the danger until the fear he had built up spilled over her defenses. When she gave in, when she said the words he needed to hear, the satisfaction drenched him, the completeness of it searing his soul, and he had thought, *At last.*

She had borne up well against the assault, but he had known she would. Kyla Warwick—no, Kyla Strathmore—was no wilting flower, but rather something more sturdy. An eagle, a lioness.

A fox, beautiful and resourceful.

Still, he supposed it was natural that she might be feeling some of it now. The shock was wearing off. They were almost to his rooms.

When they reached his door she paused uncertainly in front of it, as if she was afraid he would leave her standing there in the hallway instead of ushering her in. But she entered the rooms readily when he motioned her to go before him, stopping a few feet inside with her arms crossed over her chest, looking distractedly to the window on the far wall.

It offered a view of the courtyard; nothing very interesting there. Roland had seen it countless times before. Henry always gave him the same set of quarters whenever he stayed in London. All too often there were things taking place down there in the courtyard he did *not* want to see, and he thought perhaps Henry knew this and kept him here on purpose, as a not-so-subtle lesson true to the monarch's style.

Roland shut the door behind him firmly, then threw the latch.

She seemed so alone suddenly; an isolated figure standing forlornly in the middle of the openness of the outer chamber. She had pushed her hair forward over one shoulder to cover her arm, so from where he was he could see that her back was slim and perfectly straight, he could follow the trimness of it almost down to her waist, until the bliaut faded the line with loose folds of cloth.

"Very impressive," Kyla said to the window in her husky voice, and he didn't know if she was speaking of the room, or the view, or rather of his own performance just now.

She threw him a look over her shoulder. "The rooms a little higher up the stairs, my lord, are not nearly so fragrant as this." A graceful sweep of her arm indicated the fresh rushes on the floor.

"I am sorry about that," Roland began, wanting to soothe the glimpse of pain in her.

"Nay, for what?" she interrupted. "There is no need for you to apologize. You were only doing what you had to do."

"That's right." He crossed to her, glossing over whatever hidden meaning she might have, then added emphatically, "Wife."

Her chin dipped down at his word, her fingers tightened on her arms. That little crease he had seen before appeared again on her brow, boding trouble.

"It cannot be. . . ." Her voice faded away, mystified.

"It is." Roland stood before her a little combatively, ready to battle for this unexpected union with a fierceness that surprised him. "You gave your vow, Kyla, and I gave mine. It is an honorable match."

She wanted to argue with him, he could see that she wanted to argue, but for whatever reason the words failed her, and she only looked searchingly across the room, as if the answer to her problem lay just behind a chest or tapestry.

He pressed his advantage. "You would not go back on your word, Kyla." He made it a statement, not a question.

"Of course not." Her arms uncrossed, the fire in her eyes sparking again.

"Excellent. I suggest we sup and then retire. Tomorrow will be a long day for us both."

Without giving her a chance to respond he took her hand in his and led her to the door of the adjoining bedroom. She followed him, stepping delicately around the rushes with the catlike dexterity he had first seen that night in the inn, when he had watched her and admired the skill of a thief. When they reached the threshold he stopped outside it.

"Why don't you take a moment to refresh yourself while I send for the food? There will be warm water in the basin."

"How do you know—"

Roland smiled. "There is always warm water in the basin here. Henry enjoys showing off as much as the next man."

And he was right. After he smiled at her again—tender and intense, a smile that set off a warning chime somewhere within her—and shut the carved wooden door between them, Kyla found the polished copper basin resting on an iron trestle near the fireplace, with enough heat collected in it to keep the water delightfully warm.

This was his bedroom. It was not so grand as Henry's chamber, of course. It was smaller, more comfortable, less imposing, and obviously much more easily heated.

A chest for clothing, several wood-and-leather chairs around a table, a painted wooden screen in a corner, and yes, a marble floor.

One bed. One not-so-large bed, more of an oversized pallet, really, certainly big enough for one person, even a large man like Roland. For two, it would be by force a cozy affair.

Kyla turned quickly away from the bed and cast about

rather apprehensively for some alternative place to rest. The chairs? Only if she wanted to remain upright all night.

This was absurd. She would simply take some blankets and put them on the floor, if she had to, or perhaps Roland would be willing to . . .

Sleep in the bed with her. He was her husband, Kyla realized with fresh shock, of course he would want to sleep in the bed with her, wouldn't he?

What an incredible thing he had done, that bluff. How noble of him. How completely unlike the Hound of Hell she had been expecting. Why on earth would he have done such a thing?

The heated water was invigorating, much better than what she had been given in her other room, earlier. She tried to concentrate on that and nothing else, the comforting cleanliness sliding over her face and arms, warming the tip of her nose and her cheeks, relaxing the tightness in her hands.

In a daring move she dragged the heavy wooden screen over to the fireplace and behind it quickly stripped out of the bliaut and slippers, standing shivering on the marble tiles until she wadded the cloth under her feet to block the chill. She bent over and twisted her hair into a rope, then tied it up high on her head, wrapped secure in its own coils.

A sea sponge was provided with the basin—all the luxuries for the favored guests, Kyla thought wryly—and with it she scrubbed away the last of the travel dust until her skin was pink and glowing and the crackling fire evaporated the drops of water decorating her that the squares of drying cloth had left. She would never have thought a sponge bath felt this good.

Kyla knelt, warm now and oddly comfortable, in front of the hearth of the fireplace, holding her hands out in front of her, letting her palms absorb the heat, watching the flames dance between her fingers.

The door to the outer chamber opened.

She stood up quickly, using the screen to hide herself.

"Kyla, something has just—"

Roland stopped when he saw the screen, the top of her

head just visible. She watched him nervously from the crack between two panels.

Her gown, ripped and dirty, was still beneath her feet.

"I, uh . . ." He seemed at a loss, staring at the top of her head, then moving down to catch the corner of the eye that peered out at him. In his arms was a bundle, a cloth sack of some sort, which he held motionless, as if forgotten. She saw that small smile coming back to him, curving his lips upward until it lit his eyes as well, so vividly sea-blue right now, and she felt herself respond with a slow inner heat.

"Yes, my lord?" She attempted a normal tone.

Roland shook his head, still smiling, and glanced down at the bundle in his arms.

"This has just arrived for you, from someone or another's maid. Lady de Corbeau, I think she said."

"Oh? Lady Elisabeth?" Kyla tried, without success, to maneuver so that both eyes could see through the slats. "What is it?"

"I don't know. Clothing, I suppose. It feels like clothing." The brightness in his gaze magnified. "Why don't you come out and see for yourself?"

"No, thank you. You may leave it on the chair, if you please."

Her body was warmer than the fire now from the blush that flooded through her. She quickly bent over and shook her hair out like a cape to cover her, and even though she knew he could not see her—it was impossible that he could see her—she could have sworn he followed the move as avidly as if the wood were clear glass.

"The chair, my lord." She prayed he would do as she asked, leaving her alone in her embarrassment.

For a moment he did nothing, seeming to debate something within himself, staring down at the material he held. But then he bowed to the screen—and if ever a bow could carry a sort of wicked sauciness, this was it—and placed the bag carefully on the chair nearest to her.

"Our food is ready, my lady. Please do join me at your leisure."

"Of course," she said, feeling ridiculous.

He shut the door carefully behind him.

She sagged a little against the screen, then gathered herself and darted out to the chair, grabbing up the bundle and taking it back to the fire. It was quite heavy, and she almost had to drag it instead of carrying it.

The flickering light revealed a sturdy cloth sack with a corded satin drawstring tied in a knot to keep it closed. Inside were, of course, gowns: lovely bliauts and underskirts, the fine, rich fabrics that she used to be so familiar with, months and months ago.

Lady Elisabeth, in her genteel way, had noted her problem and moved to solve it. A small note inside said she hoped that Lady Kyla would forgive her impertinence, but as Elisabeth understood that the nature of travel could be quite inconvenient and not so accommodating to the niceties of a lady, she hoped Lady Kyla would accept these few poor gowns as her own until Lady Kyla found the time to have some better ones made up.

It was signed, "Your Friend, Elisabeth de Corbeau."

Well, at least Henry would be happy.

She slipped through the adjoining door so quietly that Roland almost didn't hear her, not that it mattered. Before the sound came the awareness of her behind him, a provocative sensation pressing against his back, pleasurable and sharp. He was growing more familiar with it now, that intensity that only she could produce in him, and so when he turned to her he was still composed. The welcome on his lips died away, however, when he saw her.

Somehow he had not anticipated this. He had become accustomed to her in a more sensory manner over the past few weeks, noting the way of her more than the look of her. She had needed no enhancement to her beauty as far as he was concerned, and the state of her dress had never struck him in any other way than that the old bliaut was too large for her, creating some vague worry for her health.

But here now was Lady Kyla as others must surely have

seen her hundreds of times over, a glamorous flame of beauty so vivid it almost hurt to take it in.

The blue-and-gray gown was soft against her, hugging with startling clarity the figure he had been fantasizing about, outlining her breasts, clinging to her waist, her hips, to fall in secretive, feminine folds down to the floor.

His breath left him in an instant, he forgot to breathe, and then she walked toward him and the gown moved with her, showing him the curves and shadows of her body in a graceful flow of sapphire and pearl-gray, the silver links of a belt tilting low on her hips. The ends of the belt became lost in her steps, sliding and disappearing between her legs as she walked.

Roland felt himself begin to shake.

She paused as she reached the chair he had set apart for her, not meeting his eyes, then sat down, gathering the skirts around her.

It was as if he had never seen a woman before, never noticed how certain colors set off others, like the vibrant, deep blue to the burnished luster of her hair, the silken clarity of her pale skin. He had never before noticed that the squared cut of a bodice could frame so clearly the secret swell behind the cloth, suggesting what he had only dreamt of.

His wife.

Roland gripped the back of her chair, moving it courteously closer to the table. From his stance above and behind her he could see over the top of her dark red hair, directly down that low neckline. He could watch her chest rise and fall, straining the cloth, pushing against it. . . .

He closed his eyes and backed away, finding his own seat.

She was quiet, of course, keeping her head modestly low, thinking her own mysterious thoughts and surely having no inkling of the direction of his own.

"Are you hungry?" he asked, covering his disorientation with a gesture to the food in front of them. "I'm afraid it's mostly cold fare."

"I could eat this chair itself, my lord," she said sincerely.

She made him laugh, the unexpected humor in her

matching his own. "Perhaps we can find something a little more to your taste."

He began to pick and choose for her from the array in front of them, selecting the choicest bits for her plate. She let him, silent again, watching his hands as they worked, moving over the cheeses, the cold roast, the bread. It was all so ordinary, so deceptively normal, the two of them alone together, dining together. And after all, they had done it before. Several times on the journey here he had joined her for a meal, judging for himself the depth of her appetite, what she favored, what she didn't. Nothing so extraordinary in that, really, except that then he had been her captor, and she had been, in all honesty, his prisoner.

It had created a uniqueness to the scene, a grand pretense on his part that she was his honored guest and he was merely attempting to please her. Sometimes she had humored him, allowing him the game, but more often than not she had merely watched, an enigma to him, splendid in her solitude. And he had let her have her peace, though the burn for her would not dim.

Tonight was different. Both of them knew it, neither of them could acknowledge it.

She ate daintily, as was her wont, taking small bites. He found it difficult not to watch her eat; it was almost an art, the way she held the cheese between her fingertips, the way she closed her lips around the bite, the careful precision, the lowering of her eyelashes as she avoided his stare.

He ate almost nothing. He was not hungry, not in that way. His need was far deeper than that. Shadows from the braziers defined the valley between her breasts, sliding over the snowy skin, teasing him with light and dark.

"Everyone seemed very impressed with you, my lord," she said into the silence, dipping a corner of her roast in hot mustard sauce.

"Really?" He toyed with the cutting knife on his plate, trying not to gape at the illumination of her.

"Capturing the outrageous Warwick, bringing her back."

"Pay no attention to them, Kyla. They are fools."

"Are they?"

"You know they are. They simply want to feed the scandal." He shrugged. "They have little else to occupy them."

"They came to Rosemead in droves," she said. "Afterward, I mean."

He didn't say anything, so she continued, looking off somewhere over his shoulder.

"I would like to go back."

"To Rosemead?"

"It's my home."

He considered this, the delicacy of the situation. "I think it might be best," he said, attempting careful nonchalance, "if you were to stay away from Rosemead, at least for a while."

She looked surprised. "Why?"

"I have told Henry I am taking you to Lorlreau. It's what he is expecting. Rosemead is too close to London for him not to consider changing his mind about keeping you here."

He was making it up, all of it, and desperately hoped she couldn't tell. She scowled down at the table.

"You will see Rosemead again, never fear," he tried.

"When?"

Roland let out his breath. "Someday. Someday after the scandal has blown over. Until then Lorlreau is the safest place for you."

The scowl stayed; her fingers began to tap impatiently against the table.

"I am sending out men to investigate the death of your mother," he said quickly. "It would be best to be gone by then."

The tapping stilled. Finally she looked up at him, the light from the candles leaving her eyes clear and reflective, like mercury.

"I heard them congratulating you on your ruse."

"My ruse?"

He wasn't sure what she was talking about—his charade just now, or, for one heart-stopping moment, their marriage, that she thought it just a trick. But then she went on.

"Your letter, the one you sent at Glencarson. I believe they thought it quite clever."

"Oh." He didn't want to talk about this, their history. It jarred the mood he wanted her in. "More wine?" He poured her more without waiting for her answer.

"It was, you know." She looked at him thoughtfully. "Clever."

"Thank you." He picked up her goblet and handed it to her. "A toast."

She held it, waiting, and he picked up his own and touched the rim against hers. "To Lady Strathmore, fair and daring."

She gave a little laugh, disbelieving, but he didn't smile back at her this time, just drank his wine. After a moment, so did she.

He set down his goblet with a thump.

"Are you tired?"

She gave him a quick, nervous look—the teasing lightness banished in a second—then spoke down into her wine. "No." The goblet tilted, almost spilling on her. "Yes."

Roland stood up, closed the distance between them. He took her goblet and put it on the table, then bent over and cupped her elbows with his palms, pulling her out of the chair. "Which is it?" he murmured.

She tilted her head back to meet his eyes, her own wide and luminous, and he knew right then that he was lost, because she was so lovely, and she was his, and nothing could stop him from tasting her again, from mingling the wine on her lips with his, which was what he did.

His hands gripped her arms, holding her in place as he bent her farther back, then sliding down to support her waist.

God, she was so sweet, sweeter than he remembered, and it was like she was the air around him, he needed to breathe her in to survive, he needed her to fill his lungs, his mouth, or he would perish in this surging fire that enveloped him.

He pushed the chair behind her out of the way without stopping his kiss, pulling her closer, feeling that soft, slender shape through the gown, the crush of her breasts against his chest, her hips a tormenting heaven against his.

There was no chain mail between them this time, nothing to prevent him from feeling her fully, only the thin layers of her gown and his own woolen tunic.

She was trembling slightly, kissing him back, but when he began to move them both to the bedroom she made a small sound, gasping for air. He wouldn't let her protest—the wanting, the hunger quickening in him would not heed that—and so he swept her up in his arms and carried her to where he wanted her to be, the bed, laying her down and covering her with himself before she could move.

He had never wanted something this badly before in his life. Part of him was shaken by that knowledge, but the hunger devoured even that in the luscious curves of her beneath him, her hair spread like a sunset cloud around them.

He buried his face in it, the smooth, heavy silk of it, then moved over to her neck, stroking his hands down the sides of her body, lifting her hips to press harder against his, letting her feel how much he wanted her.

"My lord," she said faintly.

He leaned over and kissed her again, invading her mouth with his tongue, plunging in over and over, an echo of the rhythm his body wanted to match with hers.

The placement of her hands on his shoulders became a barrier. She was pushing him away.

No! his mind shouted, his body throbbed.

She began to arch herself beneath him, trying to get him off of her.

"Please," she gasped, and he heard the anxiety in her voice.

It shattered him. He fell into little pieces around her, breaking off bit by bit, loosening his hold on her until without warning he had to drop his head into the curve of her neck, clenching his teeth, biting off the hunger while he was still able to manage it.

She was still now, panting, fingers digging into his shoulders in a frozen moment of rejection.

When he could he rolled off of her and onto his back, staring up at the darkened ceiling with a gritted parody of a smile.

"I beg your pardon," he said.

Beside him she sat up but didn't leave. After a long moment she spoke, smoothing her hands repetitively over her skirts.

"It's just that . . . I don't *know* you," she said miserably.

He wanted to laugh at that but didn't. It was too painful. "I was doing my best to remedy that, my lady."

She didn't get mad at that; he thought she might. Instead she stayed where she was, a lush blend of colors from the corner of his vision, her hair tumbled around her.

"I don't know who you are," she said slowly. "Are you my enemy or my friend? When I think I know the answer to the question you do something to change my mind. I can't pin you down."

"I am your husband," he said carefully.

"Yes," she replied, and nothing more.

He twisted to gaze up at her, watching her bite her lower lip. "Some would say that was enough," he suggested gently.

Her head ducked down, he lost her face, the bitten lip, behind the curtain of her hair. "I know."

Roland reached out his hand and captured a shining lock, twining it around his fingers and then his hand and then his wrist, pulling her closer and closer to him, until her face hung over his and his hand cupped the back of her neck.

"Don't you think that's enough?" he asked softly, holding her there.

The sensual line of her lips flattened out. "No, I don't."

"Are you certain? Do you know better than the church? Than the law?" He began to lightly pull her head down closer to his, feeling her breath on him, taking in her scent again.

"All I know is how I feel, Lord Strathmore."

Her lips were almost on his, he held her in a steely grip but she would not go that last extra inch.

"I know how I feel, Lady Strathmore, and I feel that I have every right to get to *know* my wife better." He emphasized the word to make his meaning clear. "And there is really no one in the world who would think differently than that."

"Other than me."

It would be so easy to close that last inch with force, both of them knew it. She was no match for him. If he chose to consummate their marriage right here and now there was really nothing she could do about it.

Except hate him.

He released her hair. "Other than you," he agreed, and then sighed, tucking his hands behind his head, closing his eyes. There was even a shade of something like shame in him, that he would think of forcing her to please himself. Of course he wouldn't. Of course not.

"I'm sorry," she said, not sounding sorry at all.

"No more than I am, I assure you."

There was a long period of silence, of him trying to control the stinging in his blood and her still beside him, unmoving, thinking about her virtue, or this monster she had married, or God knew what, Roland thought acidly.

At last she moved. "I will sleep in the other room, my lord."

"No, you will not." He sat up abruptly and saw her jump back, a reflex. It fueled the irritation mounting in him all the more, and mixed with the shame and hunger, making his voice curter than he meant it to be.

"I'll sleep in the other damned room."

He took a handful of blankets with him and left.

Chapter Eight

ꙮ

*H*ER FIRST SIGHT of the island came on a day that at first seemed ill-suited for viewings.

To call the sea choppy would be kind at best, or else an outright lie. As far as she could see, which admittedly wasn't far through the mist, the water rose and fell in sickening rows, one after the other, foamy and high, rocking the small boat she sat in so much that as each wave fell, the bow would slam down hard against the bottom of the swell. Yet she wasn't about to let them know how she felt.

For Roland and his men seemed perfectly at ease in the topsy-turvy spin of the skiff. They must have made this crossing so many times before.

She hadn't been expecting an island; she didn't know why. Kyla recollected now that she was out on the ferociousness of the open sea, that someone had mentioned to her once that the Earl of Lorlreau made his home on an island. But the memory must have been buried beneath the quicksand of all that happened later in her life, and the fact that Lorlreau was the main island in a string of three that made up the earldom had completely slipped away from her.

She remembered now, of course. The sea wind bit into her cloak and made a mess of the simple braid she had attempted, scattering her hair in wild strings around her. She held on to the side of the skiff with grim fortitude, staring over the whitecaps, looking in vain for any looming shape through the sea mist that would indicate this torture soon would be over.

They had left London the dawn after their arrival there. A sharp knock on the chamber door had preceded her husband striding in, frowning down at her where she lay, still mussed in the covers of the bed. He had ordered her to prepare for their departure.

Perhaps he was poor-humored from the night in the outer chamber, where she had not noticed any visible signs of sleeping. Perhaps it was something else, that other thing that Kyla preferred not to think of just now because she was still embarrassed, and she didn't like feeling embarrassed.

Of course he was handsome. She had always thought that. Of course when he kissed her she would kiss him back. It was delightful, dark and delicious and unfamiliar, seeming to lead somewhere that she could not imagine but wanted to.

So yes, she had responded to him. She was helpless not to, just as she was helpless not to feel the fear and self-loathing that sprang forth from their lovemaking.

He was the Hound of Hell. How could she make love to him?

And she was his wife. So how could she not?

Kyla could not deny the part of her that was appalled that she would even think about sharing herself with this man, this murderer. The marriage was a sham, a sick joke they were now forced to play out.

Equally strong—as much as she hated it—was that other part of her, the corporeal part that cared nothing for either the marriage or the murders. Despicable, terrifying, but oh, God, still so true: She wanted him. She wanted him in a way she had never even known existed before he kissed her that first time. She craved his touch, she longed for his kiss, a million of them, another moment alone with him to press against him, to discover the end of the erotic journey he had taken her body on that London night . . . this murderer. . . .

It gave her a headache thinking of it and so Kyla dropped her focus to the sea itself, rushing past in hard steel-blue waves, and the steady dip of the oars as the men heaved and hoed their way across the water.

Roland, beside her now, was as coolly impersonal as he had been since that morning two days ago, back at Henry's palace. Not cold, not cruel, just polite. Distant. A stranger with the air of putting up with a regrettably rude houseguest.

A few errant strands of her hair would periodically whip up into his face no matter how she tried to contain them. He would remove them without comment and without looking at her. Other than that, nothing about this rather perilous voyage seemed to stir him.

She couldn't believe that they had wanted to sail this surly, writhing ocean when she had seen it from the docks, especially not in the rickety skiff Roland had pointed to. It was a joke, surely.

But no, they were serious, all of Roland's men, and all of them had piled into the four long skiffs that were now making their way to Lorlreau, except for a contingent that had stayed behind to wait for the larger boat to bring the horses across. Kyla thought the horses probably got the better deal.

They had helped her into the skiff courteously, big, rough men who called her Countess and handled her as if she were glass. The first time she heard her new title was from the maid in London who had come to dress her that morning. Kyla had let the word drift over her, just assuming that the maid, for whatever reason, was referring to someone else—until the conversation stalled, the girl waiting for acknowledgment, and Kyla realized it was her, she was the countess. It would have been amusing if it were not so strange.

She was becoming more used to it. Duncan, Roland's captain, would only address her by the title, thus setting the precedent for the others to follow. Now it was "Countess" this and "Countess" that. She thought a little sardonically that if she was ever in a room with another countess she wouldn't be able to figure out who was who.

Without warning, the sun broke through the blanket of clouds above. Through fate or coincidence, it was just as the fog bank reversed itself, dissolving in front of her eyes in pale, sparkling rainbows. And then there was Lorlreau.

A sort of cheer erupted from the men. She couldn't help but want to join them.

Like an enchanted promise Lorlreau rose from the sea, full of peaks and valleys, velvet greens bright against a pinkish-golden base, cliffs and trees and long beaches, and then there, in the distance, the outline of a castle in the hills. The sun gave a shimmering glow to it all, warming the landscape's textures in high relief, even allowing her to pick out what might have been people around the pier reaching out to the sea.

They *were* people, and they were multiplying. They were running out on the pier, waving and calling, a few jumping up and down with excitement.

The men around her seemed to put some extra effort into their already strenuous task, sweating against the wind, grinning like boys.

Even Roland's mood lifted. The sun kissed him with yellow gold, brightening the honeyed hair, turning the turquoise of his eyes to something as magical as the place, rare and gifted. He was smiling with his men, tacking the small sail, his movements quick and glad.

It was impossible not to get caught up in their enthusiasm.

As they drew closer she could hear the happy voices calling out to them, names being yelled across the water, children racing back and forth between the adults, everyone laughing or smiling. A cluster of men waited patiently near the edge of a reddish-brown cliff that formed the inner circle of a cove, and she didn't understand why until the skiffs veered off in that direction and she could make out the metal ladder bolted into the rockface.

The boat rocked violently as the men stood and tossed up the rope to the others to secure the skiff to the heavy iron pegs lining the top of the cliff. Water splashed into the bottom of the boat, soaking her hem.

Beyond the busy men were now the other people she had seen, calmer, waiting for them to begin the climb up the ladder. She was seated near the back, wondering how she was going to manage the climb in her skirts, when Roland began urging her up to the front, telling her to go ahead and he would be right behind.

"Just don't look down, and don't let go," was all he said, giving her a little boost up to the first rung.

Kyla closed her eyes, fighting the nausea rising up in her, clinging with one hand to the cold, wet metal while the other clutched her sodden skirts. Behind her the men were standing in the skiff, talking to the people up above.

She took one step, then another, then another. It wasn't a long climb but to her it seemed endless: grip, step, pause; grip, step, pause. The sloshing of the water below created a wet, slapping sound that reverberated around them.

When her head reached the top, eager hands were helping her up, pulling her to the safety of the solid ground.

She thanked them, straightening her skirts, tucking her hair back again, smoothing the cape, conscious that everyone was staring at her, quiet, even after Roland came up behind her.

She looked a mess, she was positive. She could taste the salt on her lips, feel the dampness in the curling tendrils of hair that wanted to float around her face. Her gown was splashed with water, spotted and streaked in blackish stains against what used to be the color of cinnamon.

All around her were the blank faces of strangers, assessing her, drawing their own conclusions in communal silence. Kyla didn't know where to look, at the carefully empty eyes of the people around her, the sky, the ground, her husband?

"Behold," said Roland to the people, breaking the pall of silence. He draped an arm around her waist. "The Lady Kyla Strathmore, Countess of Lorlreau."

Several of the women gasped out loud, covering their mouths with their hands. The men were less affected, a few exchanging looks, and the children didn't seem to understand at all, just catching the curious spell that hung over the crowd, pushing back into their mothers' skirts.

One man nudged his way to the front of the crowd with

unhurried ease, his face aglow with something like delight. He took her by the shoulders and kissed her on the cheek.

"Welcome, my sister," he said, and his words were the charm that freed the others to come forward, bowing, curtsying, some of them taking her hand.

By now the other skiffs were docking as well, a steady stream of men were coming up the ladder, and many of the folk broke away to greet their loved ones, the rising tide of voices mingling with the water sounds below.

The man who had kissed her also embraced Roland, both of them clapping each other on the back. He wore the simple brown robe of a monk, she noticed, which would perhaps explain why he had called her sister. Except that when both of them turned to face her she was struck by the similarity between them; not much, the shape of the jaw, the line of the nose. But where Roland's coloring was fair and bright, the monk's was darker, chestnut browns and burnt sienna. And while Roland was one of the tallest men she had ever seen, the monk almost towered over him, over them all, actually, a gentle giant of a man.

"Kyla," said Roland. "This is my brother, Harrick."

She inclined her head and dipped down to the best curtsy she could manage on her shaky legs.

"Oh, come, none of that," said Harrick, pulling her upright. "I'm only a half brother, you know."

Roland put his arm back around her and began to lead the three of them away from the dock, leaving the others to follow as they would. "Where is Elysia?"

"With Marla at Lorlmar. We've been expecting you for the past month, and she has been driving everyone to distraction asking them to go look for you." Harrick kept his pace slow and even, matching his stride to their shorter steps as they found a stone path that led back into the woods.

"We were delayed." Roland tightened his arm around her momentarily. Harrick nodded.

"Ah, yes. And congratulations on your marriage."

Roland laughed. "That was not the part that delayed us."

Again he told their story, abbreviated this time, and Harrick listened without interrupting, only once throwing a quick, astute glance to Kyla when Roland got to the part about their wedding vows.

The air was cool but not chilly here, much better than it had been at sea. She heard birdsong scattered around them, noted the little starlike flowers that decorated the path of stones in trailing bands of pink and yellow and white. The thick, old evergreens around them gave off a heavy perfume, adding to the mystical atmosphere.

Kyla wondered who Elysia was.

Harrick was telling Roland about the state of affairs during his absence.

". . . and Madoc has been complaining rather vigorously about what he terms the lack of manners from some of our pages, which may or may not have to do with the eel found in his pallet this Monday past. . . ."

Roland laughed. "I bet he put it there himself."

"I wouldn't be surprised," agreed Harrick serenely. "Or perhaps it was Seena."

"A novel idea for keeping him in line," said Roland.

"She is best at it. I fear we are being rude to your bride." Harrick turned to Kyla. "You will meet Madoc and Seena very soon, my dear. They don't leave Lorlmar much these days. They complain that they are too old, but the truth of the matter is the castle would fall apart without them."

Since Kyla didn't really know what to say to this she merely nodded, reflecting back Harrick's easy manner with her, taking in the newness of the surroundings and the surprising comfort of Roland's arm, still around her waist.

From the edges of the thick woods she caught a glimpse of something, a liquid refraction that was gone in an instant, then back again. It was the glancing beam of sunlight off the eye of a sturdy doe, so still she blended in almost completely with the ruddy lines of the tree trunks and the hovering branches. Without slowing her steps Kyla watched the doe, who watched back, unperturbed, from her forest cover. As they drew closer the deer even bent down and took a mouthful of something, then lifted her head up again, chewing, watching the trio walk by without a trace of fear.

The doe was long-nosed and elegant, a faint speckling of white dabbed across her backside. She blinked again in the sunlight, a creature of leaves and earth and peace, then went back to eating.

"Almost there," Harrick was saying cheerfully. "We don't usually take the horses to the pier, Lady Kyla, since the distance is so short and the walk is so pleasant. I hope you don't mind."

"Not at all," she said.

It felt good to walk after the ride on the skiff, to get her blood back into her toes and the tips of her fingers, to breathe deeply of the pine-scented air. The trees climbed high up into the sky, their pointed tips and arching branches with clusters of needles and cones interspersed with ash and fir, birch and oak, and some trees she had no names for. More than a few held flowers for the spring, some white, some peach, most pink and lavender.

It was like a fairy-tale place, not a real island but her imaginings of one: the tame deer, the hushed forest, the perfect flowers, and now, around a pair of twisted oaks marking a bend in the path, the castle itself, Lorlmar.

It must have been hewn from the same rosy-gold stone that made up the base of the land itself, a fairy-tale castle, of course, to match the island. There were high turrets, the crenellated edges giving them a fanciful appearance; long, tall windows with pointed arches, some with stained glass; a smooth, even line of stone from wall to wall, broken only by the towers of varying heights with a circular keep inside rising above the rim. No moat, but a gate, a heavy one; and new, she would guess, by the still-dark wood.

The gate was open now, and people were spilling out. Kyla wondered how many people the island could hold. It seemed impossible that there were more people than she had already seen, yet there were. Most were soldiers, obviously, dressed in drab but heavy outfits, but here also were the castle servants, she would guess, many women mingling with the men, all of them happy to see their lord return, most not noticing her at all.

How many serfs across England would be so joyful at the arrival of their master? Harrick read her thoughts.

"Your husband is a popular man here, Lady Kyla," he said as Roland was enveloped by the crowd. She almost couldn't hear him over the chatter, the many voices welcoming him back.

"He's been gone almost a year now. We were beginning to wonder when Henry would release him to us again."

"A year?" she said. "So long?"

Harrick contemplated the scene, the pushing people. "He is a favorite of the king's."

That she knew all too well. Roland was answering questions, throwing looks to her, trying to get back to her. An old man was talking to him, chastising him for not paying enough attention.

"The serfs love him," Kyla said, stating something obvious that still seemed so unusual.

"Lorlreau has no serfs," replied Harrick. "Everyone here is a freeman." He smiled at her open astonishment. "Roland granted them all their freedom when he became the earl several years ago."

"Kyla," called Roland, beckoning to her, since he couldn't easily shed the crowd. "There is someone I am eager for you to meet."

Harrick led her to his side, breaking past the lines of people that turned to her in surprise. Their passing excited a whispered hum, hands shielding mouths, darting looks. Roland was standing near the entrance to the keep now, past the outer walls and into the open bailey. Close to him was a tall, stately woman in her forties, with brown hair streaked with silver and light blue eyes. The woman was studying her curiously, her hand protectively on the shoulder of a small girl, about six, who was holding tight to her skirts. The child was almost trembling with excitement, staring up with wide, dark eyes. The hum died down.

"Lady Kyla," said Roland. "This is Elysia."

Kyla curtsied to the woman.

"No," that lady said with slow amusement. "I am Marla. *This* is Elysia." She indicated the little girl.

Before she could react the girl let go of her grip on the skirts and held out her hands to Kyla, not saying anything. As Kyla knelt down to her level she felt the crowd draw back, absorbing every moment. She took the small hands into her own and then Elysia closed the distance between them, walking up with clear, blank eyes, tracing her hands up Kyla's arm to her shoulders, and then her face.

Her touch was feather-light, birdlike, brushing her chin and her lips, moving over her nose and her cheekbones, then onto her eyes, her eyebrows, her forehead. Kyla held perfectly still, only closing her eyes when the touch brushed over them, opening them again when she felt the small palms frame her cheeks, paused.

"We've been expecting you," said Elysia gravely. "Why did you take so long to come to us?"

Her eyes were so dark that at first Kyla thought them black, but no, they were midnight-blue, fringed with brown lashes to go with her familiar honey-brown hair.

"Well," Kyla said. "I had things to do."

"Are they done?" the girl asked.

"Mostly, yes," Kyla replied, surprised at her own answer.

"Good. I'm glad. You'll stay with us now." Elysia moved her hands from her face and then stepped closer to her, embracing her. "You'll like it here."

Kyla held her close, feeling the delicate frame of her, the wet warmth of the kiss Elysia pressed to her cheek.

"The air is turning colder," announced Marla. "Time to go back in, child."

Without comment Elysia released her, leaving Kyla kneeling alone on the ground, watching the little girl turn and reach for Marla, who took her hand and led her back into the keep.

Roland helped her up. "Jealous?" he asked softly, with a sideways teasing look.

She realized he had read her mood earlier when he had mentioned Elysia's name.

"She is charming," Kyla said.

"Well, I like that," grumbled a new voice, the old man who had been scolding Roland before. He shook his head. "Lord of the estate, ignoring those what raised him from a puny tot and nurtured him all them years, not bothering to introduce his bride to them what—"

"Hush up, you old fool," interrupted a new voice, a woman's, aged and crackled to go with the man's. "Anyone could see he was gettin' around to it."

A tiny woman with a fluff of white hair elbowed the old man out of the way and then nodded kindly to Kyla, smiling.

"My dear, this is Seena." Roland's voice was dry. "And of course, her husband, Madoc, who did indeed raise me from a puny tot to my rather inglorious manhood."

"Tush," said Seena. "You're plenty glorious for us, I declare."

"A terrible lad he was!" Madoc had come up beside his wife to study Kyla, and despite his cantankerous words, she saw the twinkle alight in his eyes. "Almost killed me off more than a dozen times, milady, all by himself! Just the worry alone, milady!"

Kyla nodded, serious. "Yes, I can see what a bother that would be."

Madoc squinted up at her, looking her up and down. He and Seena might have been twins, small and silver-haired, bright-eyed.

"She'll do," he announced to the crowd in general.

"Thank you so much," said Roland calmly. "I rather thought so."

Seena winked at her, then she and her husband moved back toward the castle itself.

Roland told the crowd he was pleased to be home but he was starving in the meantime, bringing forth hurried comfort from the women, who claimed they would have a veritable feast ready within minutes.

The tone of the crowd was much the same as the one at

the docks; celebratory, slightly more restrained here in the shadow of the castle. Greeting her in the wake of Madoc and Seena, they were respectful, curious. They formed a lagging congregation behind them as Roland took her into the keep, now mixing with the folk who had come up from the pier, beaming women linked arm in arm with their husbands, or sweethearts, or brothers.

It turned out the claim of a feast was no exaggeration. Inside the great hall, cavernous and round, with three fireplaces and rows and rows of tables and benches, were already the beginnings of a large meal laid out, with people scurrying everywhere to add more.

The head table was close to the largest fireplace, which held a bright, snapping fire. Elysia was already there, seated quietly alone while Marla helped with the meal.

"She was born blind," said Roland as he escorted her to the table. "Marla made it her duty to look after her, after her mother's death."

"She is . . . different," Kyla said, struggling to find the right word. Elysia sat with her hands folded primly in front of her, her back to the fire, waiting patiently for the others to arrive. She gave her great, blank stare to the space right in front of her.

Kyla found the word. "She is sage."

Is she yours? she wanted to ask, but didn't.

It was more than the hair that matched them up, more than even the line of their eyebrows, both elegant and straight. It was Elysia's bearing that resembled Roland's most, which was peculiar, because there was no way for the child to have ever seen it in the man to mimic. Squared shoulders, the occasional, slanting tilt of the head, slightly mischievous. And oh, that small, crooked smile, which she sent now over to Roland, settling her gaze nearly upon him as they approached.

"Uncle, have you grown while you were gone?" she asked.

Ah, thought Kyla, and then wondered how the child had known Roland was near.

"No," Roland replied sadly. "I fear I shall never catch up with Uncle Harrick."

"Don't lose heart," Elysia said, sounding doubtful.

"You shall just have to settle for me as I am. It's not all that bad, is it?" Roland seated Kyla next to the girl, then reached out and tweaked one of Elysia's amber curls.

"I have grown," she said proudly. "Almost a whole hand higher than the last time you saw me."

"I see that. Soon you will be a colossus over all of us." Roland took the seat next to Kyla. "But I really think that depends on whose hands we are talking about."

Elysia laughed, then turned those midnight eyes to Kyla, ardent again.

"Do you like venison?"

"Venison?" The image of the doe flashed in her mind, so tame and wild at once, a moment of innocence in the woods. "No, not really."

"Good." Elysia burst into full smile, clapping her hands.

Roland leaned over and explained. "We don't eat venison here." There was a note of ruefulness in his voice.

"Oh." Kyla was left again with that feeling of strange displacement, of being in a situation where the rules and way of life were just slightly beyond her grasp.

"Do you like fish?" Elysia asked now.

"Well . . ." Kyla wondered what to say.

"We do eat fish," Elysia said. She sounded regretful.

"And chicken," added Roland firmly.

"Yes," agreed the child, now mournful.

"Stay away from the chickens."

"We do." Elysia sighed.

"We introduced a pair of wild deer a few years back, hoping they would breed on the main island." Roland picked up a fresh roll from the wooden bowl placed before them and put it on Elysia's platter, then put one on Kyla's. "But the children tamed them while we still had them here at the castle. They named them both."

"And now their children's children are here," exclaimed Elysia proudly. "There's Katherine and Francis and Jasper and Sammy and Hannah and Belle and Bancroft—"

"Thank you, Elysia," interrupted Roland. "Why don't you eat now?"

"I saw a deer," said Kyla to the girl. "I saw her on the walk over from the pier."

"Really?" asked Elysia seriously. "What did she look like?"

Roland was smiling down at his plate. Kyla ignored him, thinking back. "She was reddish brown, I think, with a very fine nose, and large eyes."

"Large or small?"

"Medium."

"Was she spotted?"

"Yes, she was. Little white spots, I believe."

Elysia placed a hand on her arm. "You saw Eleanor."

It was curious, the gravity of the pronouncement, the light touch meant to draw more attention to the moment. Even Roland seemed to be paying attention suddenly, pausing in eating as he listened.

The doe came again to her mind's eye, vividly this time, and she put the name to the animal, something to recall the stately calm surrounding the deer.

"Eleanor," Kyla repeated, wondering at her ready acceptance of this strange custom.

"She's my favorite," confided Elysia, who then went back to eating.

More food was arriving, grilled fish, boiled eggs, bread and butter, cheese, vegetable dishes of onions, leeks, and peas. There was plenty of salt in small silver dishes set about, something that had been considered more a luxury at Rosemead. But of course, Rosemead had not the advantage of the ocean at its gate.

The noise in the hall was not deafening but still loud enough to make soft comments impossible. Kyla took in the rows and rows of people eating, all of them Roland's men, their families, the castle servants. She did not miss the covert glances thrown at her, the tilted heads of people comparing opinions, mouthing speculation back and forth to each other about the newcomer, the outsider.

As the meal went on the wine flowed more freely, as well as stories from those who had been separated from their home for so long.

A whole year. Kyla thought about that, considered how hard it would have been on her to be away so long, and then had a painful moment when she realized she had been gone from Rosemead, her own home, more than half of that time. Roland had said that she would be safer here and logic told her this was probably true, at least for the moment. And though this place had its own elemental appeal to her, mystery and sorcery, she would not forget Rosemead, and she would not forget her family.

She was lost in her memories still when Roland stood, gathering the attention of all the people in front of them. He raised his goblet.

"To Lorlreau," he said, "the last spot of sweetness on this earth."

The crowd cheered and yelled, at last quieting when they saw that Roland was not finished.

"And to my wife." He looked down at her, unreadable, his true thoughts hidden behind the turquoise. "May she always add her own sweetness and *obedience* to the peace of our fair land."

Again came the cheer, a welcoming roar, leaving Kyla to nod her head graciously while her cheeks flamed. She hoped no one else caught the implication.

Roland threw her a rakish smile, then drank to her, emptying the goblet to the rousing approval of everyone.

Elysia touched Kyla on the shoulder, a small tug that pulled her down until Kyla's ear was level with her lips.

"He likes you," the child whispered. "I can tell."

———————⌒〰〰〰⌒———————

*T*HERE WAS LAUGHTER coming from behind the wall.

Kyla frowned and shook her head, certain she was imagining the sound. It had been a long, long day, and the fact that the sun had only slipped down over the edge of the sea a short while ago didn't mean she wasn't ready to fall asleep where she was standing. The journey in the skiff, meeting all of Roland's people, Harrick, Madoc, Seena, Elysia, the boisterous meal . . . The facts were blurred through exhaustion; it had taken the last reserves of her energy to follow the servant up the stairs to this room, short though the distance was from the main hall.

Roland had bidden her an even good-night, a stranger once more, polite and reserved. She didn't have the strength in her right now to care all that much. Murderer or lover, at the moment it really didn't seem to matter. She couldn't think anymore. All she wanted to do was wrap herself in blankets, hidden and secure somewhere in the immense iron bed over there in the corner, close her eyes, and just let it all fade away.

But there it came again, a high-pitched sound, yes, definitely a laugh, coming from behind the fireplace, followed by a muffled thump.

Kyla paused in taking off her shoes.

For a second more she doubted what she heard—it was a trick of acoustics, sounds from another part of the castle carried oddly to this particular room, she had heard of such things before—but no, not again, not when the voices were followed by a few more thumps, all most definitely behind the wall.

She walked over to the fireplace, feeling much more alert. The paneling surrounding it was actually a fine-grained wood, deftly patterned and fitted, leaving not even the smallest gap between the planks. She ran her fingers over it experimentally, up and down, across, not really knowing what she was looking for but knowing something was there. At the top of the wall was a carved row of oak leaves and acorns, weaving in and out of each other all the way across the length of the room.

The corner to her left was blocked by a sturdy, tall armoire. Kyla considered it, the weight and the height of it, a magnificent thing that reached almost to the ceiling and was pressed flush to the wall.

Fading now, the laughter came again, mingled with more voices, ghost sounds moving away from her. After a few minutes they were gone entirely.

She shook her head once more, the exhaustion coursing back in an abrupt wave. She was too tired to think about this. She had faced enough oddities today to surely last her the rest of her life. In fact, the sounds behind the walls were really just in keeping with the entire island—inexplicable, surprising—so the best thing to do had to be to go to bed.

She found the trunk with her clothing in it placed crookedly against the wall opposite the fireplace. The great leather straps had already been unbuckled for her. In fact, even from here she could see there was a corner of a gown mashed between the hinges.

A thoughtless maid, perhaps. But when Kyla opened it fully she was greeted by a jumble of color, bliauts and under-gowns carelessly crushed, strewn together in a chaotic mass. This was not the way she had left her new clothing when she had packed it away in London herself, no doubt about that. Someone had been through the trunk since then. Tonight. Not a maid. Someone who didn't care if it was discovered that her belongings had been disturbed.

Kyla felt an unpleasant coldness steal over her. Why would anyone do such a thing? Why go through her gowns, when there was nothing extraordinary about them?

She knelt and pulled them out quickly, one by one, and thought they were all still there. She couldn't be certain, of course. She didn't really remember them all but it seemed to her that nothing was missing.

So whoever it was, they were not after clothing. Then, what?

She had nothing else. And the sad irony was, even the clothing and the trunk were not hers. Both had been given to her by others. Most of her real belongings were still back at Rosemead.

Kyla rocked back on her heels, surrounded by a hill of fine cloth, even gemmed belts and buckles. All of them, still here. It made no sense at all.

She made a sound of disgust and stood up, tossing the clothing back into a heap in the trunk. She would sort it all out again tomorrow. It must have just been a maid, after all.

She was too fatigued to think of anything else. At least she was able to find the nightgown easily.

The blankets on the bed were warm and soft, the goose feathers of the ticking cushioning her delightfully. Oblivion came swiftly.

Later, much later, she felt another presence in the room with her, someone else in the bed. But rather than being alarmed at the heat of the body sliding in next to hers, she felt comforted, secure. And when his arms held her firmly to him she didn't resist, but instead fell deeper into her dreams.

Chapter Nine

*D*REAMS OR NO, Kyla awoke the next morning alone in the bed to the dazzling brightness of an unfamiliar room.

That by itself was not enough to startle her; none of the rooms she had been in for the last few months had become familiar. But there was something . . .

Lorlmar. She was at Lorlmar. She was at Lorlmar because she was the Countess of Lorlreau—

At the end of the bed, peering just over the edge of one of the soft brown blankets, were seven little faces.

Kyla sat up, pulling the cover closest to her up to her chin, then realized how ridiculous the move was. They were only children, four boys and three girls, with one set of eyes a familiar midnight-blue that looked right through her.

"She's awake now," Elysia said helpfully to the others. She reached out an arm and found Kyla's ankle, holding on lightly.

None of the other children seemed inclined to comment.

The room around them was large and brilliant. She hadn't taken it in last night but now she could see the richness of it for what it was: the master suite. It must be Roland's room. And that meant at least something about last night hadn't been a dream at all, the peaceful warmth of him next to her, the strangely familiar sensation of his body curled against hers.

Her audience watched as she turned her head to take in the surroundings. Light, sturdy furniture, set off with thick rugs in greens and blues and gold. Tapestries depicting fanciful sea scenes: mermaids, sea horses, dolphins dancing through the waves.

A collection of seashells scattered throughout the room on tables, on shelves; wild things she had never before seen or imagined, some thick and flat with stripes or spots, a few spiny and fierce with delicate pink undertones. Her eyes came to rest again on the children before her.

"Hullo," she said.

"Good morning," replied a towheaded boy politely.

Kyla sat up straighter. "Was it you I heard last night?" It seemed a good guess, especially when they drew back and exchanged slightly guilty glances.

"I *told* you that you were too loud," said one of the girls crossly to the other.

"It wasn't me!" A brown-haired girl of about seven looked indignant. "It was Ainsley!"

"It was not!" A little boy rounded on the girl, vehement. "It was Matilda!"

"Well," Kyla smiled down at the lot of them. "It really doesn't matter who it was. I'm just grateful you were not a bunch of ghosts out to get me."

Elysia laughed, a tinkling sound. "We couldn't get you, even if we had tried. That's what the armoire is for." She tilted her head over to the corner where the wooden closet loomed, thick and imposing.

"Can't get past that," said the towheaded boy.

"Uncle put it there on purpose." Elysia put her other hand on the covers.

Kyla remembered her trunk, still at its skewed angle to the wall, the gowns a colorful waterfall over the edge of it.

"So," she chose her words carefully, "were any of you in here last night, perchance?"

"Oh, no." Elysia shook her head. "We don't come in without Uncle's permission. That's the rule."

Of course they didn't. Kyla had no reason not to believe the child. There was an air of sincerity hanging off all of them, in fact. 'Twas a maid, she thought again. Surely just a maid.

"Does everyone know of the tunnels behind the walls?" she asked in spite of herself.

"Oh, yes." A new boy spoke up. "We all use them."

"Really?" Kyla looked over at the corner with the oaken armoire again. "Everyone?"

Elysia was attempting to climb onto the bed. "It's ever so much faster than using the regular stairs, sometimes," she said, sliding backward despite her efforts.

Kyla reached over and helped her up, which was the signal to the other children to climb up as well.

"Spookier!" added Ainsley.

"Ask her now," whispered the brown-haired girl.

"Yes, now," said a boy.

"Auntie Kyla," said Elysia, providing Kyla a whole new shock with the title, "would you like to meet the deer today?"

The sunlight made the room look celestial, highlighting the wood paneling, landing capriciously on a large, horned conch, casting a milky glow over it. The main window had a stained-glass edging of waves, starfish, and flowing seaweed. Kyla thought she could just hear the steady boom of the ocean pushing in past the glass.

"Uncle said it was fine with him." Elysia flopped back on the covers. "He said to tell you when you awoke that breakfast is nigh past"—she wrinkled her brow at this, then repeated it—"nigh past, but that he had saved a light repast for you, to be sent up when you requested. But I rather think it might be nicer to go downstairs."

"We could go the regular way. You needn't be afraid," said Matilda.

Elysia spoke again. "So, are you hungry?"

"I am," said Ainsley feelingly.

"By all means, let us break our fast." Kyla smiled down at the ring of faces, considering not only the message from Roland but also the messengers. Seven active children, unsupervised, one of them blind, yet they apparently roamed the hallways and tunnels of the castle with complete freedom.

And Roland had gone off, obviously, leaving her to keep her own company. Was she to be like the children, alone, left to fend for herself on this island that was supposed to be her new home? Was this to be the state of their supposed marriage, two permanent strangers encountering each other only in passing? Fine.

Or perhaps she was reading too much into an innocuous comment. Perhaps he hadn't meant anything at all.

"Look, is it yours?"

One of the girls had Helaine's dagger in her hands, holding it up to the sunlight to watch the sparks of color from the gemstones in the sheath.

"It certainly is." Kyla took it from the girl, hefting the familiar weight of it in her hands, frowning down at it. Roland had been keeping it somewhere these past few days, no longer wearing it at his waist as he had on the journey to London.

She had thought it a deliberate taunt, the way he had worn it, a cruel thing designed to remind her of her weakness, that she had lost and he had won. But those thoughts had not matched the moments of kindness she had seen in the man, and after their marriage he must have packed the dagger away for his own reasons. Until now.

"It was over there," said the girl, pointing to the short pine table by the bed. Kyla nodded absently, rubbing her fingers over the smooth warmth of the stones and metal.

Elysia, still lying flat on the covers, smiled up into the air above her. "You should take care of the blade, Auntie," she said. "I think it must be very keen."

AFTER BANISHING THE BOYS to the hallway Kyla had dressed quickly, encouraged by the girls, until a maid had come from nowhere, insisting on doing her hair. In her desire to be at home here Kyla had acquiesced to the deferentially worded demand. The maid's unrehearsed reaction upon seeing the mess of the clothing had banished the thought that this gentle girl had rifled the trunk. Indeed, when she saw the

disorder she had clucked her tongue in reproach, then threw
Kyla an abashed look.

Kyla realized with some amusement that the maid believed
her new mistress had left her gowns in this mess. And so she
had, she supposed. She made the mess the night before. Lovely.
She was building up a fine reputation already. Outlaw, vigi-
lante, and slattern all in one.

So it had not been this maid. But there could have been
another. A castle this size must have dozens of maids.

The children had not protested the delay, only watched as
the young woman's deft hands wound the long red hair up
and away in some style Kyla did not know.

It was unfamiliar to her, this binding of her hair, something like a shadow from that former life she had, something
she supposed she would have to become used to again. She
had thanked the maid most sincerely, and that girl had smiled
and curtsied, leaving as silently and efficiently as she had
arrived.

The looking glass that the child Matilda held up to her
face showed her a woman Kyla didn't know. That woman
might really have been a countess, with her fine gown and
elaborate hairstyle. But there—those were still her own eyes
behind the polished facade of the woman, a relief—and then
there was no more time to reflect upon her own reflection;
the glass was taken away and the girls pulled her out the door.

The boys were still waiting, all of them becoming her escort down to the kitchens. On the way they saw many adults,
all of whom greeted her respectfully as they passed, and none
of whom looked the least surprised to see their new countess
being led around by a circle of youngsters.

And it was a good thing they were there, thought Kyla as
they twisted and turned their way around the keep. Could
she have found the kitchens on her own? Probably not. Lorlmar seemed even more immense on the inside than it had appeared without. The passages and rooms became a blur as she
was tugged past each of them—sunlight and windows in
some; tapestries in more; once a cluster of women forming a

crescent-moon audience around a girl on a lyre; several groups of men; soldiers, servants, all busy with things she could not imagine as she was rushed by them. She captured all eyes as they went past, yet no one said a word to them.

Seena joined Kyla and the children on the long wooden-plank bench in the kitchen as they all ate hot oatmeal sweetened with honey. She seemed to be expecting them, directing them to the table with a welcoming smile, serving up the bowls of creamy oatmeal with good cheer before sitting down herself beside Kyla.

"I do like to dabble in the kitchen when Cook lets me," she said, handing Kyla a carved wooden spoon. "It isn't often. But Roland has a penchant for my oatmeal, you know."

Kyla hadn't known, and didn't really know what to make of the information now that she did.

"Uncle has gone off to Taldon today. Taldon is one of our other islands," said Elysia.

"Oh." Since they seemed to be waiting for more from her, Kyla added hesitantly, "There are three islands?" She felt a little foolish that she wasn't sure of this, obviously such an important fact, but Seena only smiled again and nodded.

"Lorlreau, of course, and Taldon and Forswall. You'll settle in soon and see them for yourself."

"Lorlreau is the nicest," said one of the girls thoughtfully, prompting a spirited debate among the children as to which island, indeed, was nicest and all the possible reasons that might be.

Kyla touched the tip of her tongue experimentally to the steaming cereal, then took a bite. It was hot and delicious. Perhaps she had something in common with her husband, after all, even if it was only oatmeal. She realized she was actually ravenous; her appetite seemed to have come winging back for the first time since she had left London.

"Ah, what is that wondrous smell drifting on the breeze, tickling a man's nose until nothing can be done but leave off his studies to come and find the source?"

"Uncle Harrick!" Elysia turned her head to the doorway

leading outside, where the tall monk stood. "Come and eat with us!"

"How could I resist such a charming invitation?"

Harrick served himself, then bent down and folded himself in between two of the children, who scooted over to make room without pausing in their eating.

"I understand you are going to see the deer today?"

Kyla looked up when she realized the question was directed at her, and that Harrick was waiting patiently for her response.

"Yes. I believe so." She cleared her throat. "That's what I've been told."

"Eleanor will be there," said Elysia.

Kyla saw the charged look that passed between Seena and Harrick, a flash of an instant, and then it was gone.

"Will she, now?" asked Seena nonchalantly.

"Aye. She'll be wanting to meet my new auntie."

"Of course she will." Harrick threw Kyla a warm smile. "See, my lady? On Lorlreau even the animals will come forth to greet you."

"Oh, Eleanor already knows about Lady Kyla," said Elysia, scraping the last bits from her bowl. "She told me to expect her. Remember, Seena? I told you so. But now she would like to meet her formally."

Kyla chose her words carefully. "Are we talking about Eleanor . . . the deer?"

"Of course." Elysia looked around innocently. "Eleanor the deer."

Seena stood abruptly, whisking away Kyla's empty bowl and that of the boy next to her, walking to the other end of the kitchen.

Harrick seemed troubled but said nothing, and soon the peculiar moment was swallowed up by the banter of the children.

It was determined that Harrick was vital to the success of the deer-viewing party for reasons that seemed to be clear only to the youngsters, and so he conceded that no, he had nothing really more important on his schedule this morning than talking to deer, and of course he would go. From this conversation wound the thought that by the time they actually reached the deer it would be afternoon, no longer morning, and they all might be hungry again. So Seena volunteered to pack together a makeshift picnic, and soon the informal excursion was taking on all the airs of a formal occasion.

Somewhat to her consternation, the children seemed to melt away into thin air after the meal, saying they were off to prepare for the journey. Elysia slipped away without a goodbye, there one moment and gone the next when Kyla turned to find her.

Harrick had left minutes earlier to tend to a few monkly duties, he had said, and now even Seena was nowhere to be found.

Strangely, Kyla found herself alone in the kitchens.

From the corner of her eye came a flash of movement, someone walking past the open door leading outside. Thinking it might be Seena, Kyla walked over to it, taking a few shy steps out into the cool, fresh air.

No one was there. Just the empty sky, trees, a path pointing off to what might have been a garden secured by a sturdy wooden gate.

When she turned around and went back inside she found, against the sudden darkness of her vision as her eyes readjusted, two serving maids bringing out pots and tongs, talking together in soft voices. They paused, carrying a heavy boiler between them, staring at her.

Kyla smiled but neither smiled back. Instead they ducked their heads and put the round, blackened pot on the floor, then curtsied to her, avoiding her face.

"Could you tell me," Kyla began, and then stopped. Tell her what? Where she was supposed to go? Where she was expected to be? What she was supposed to be doing?

Neither girl had looked at her yet. Kyla drew up her chin.

"Never mind." She crossed to what she thought might be

the door she had come in through, striving for an air of confidence she didn't feel, leaving the women to curtsy to her retreating back.

This did look somewhat familiar, the curving hall that meant she was on the outer edge of the keep. Of course, she reflected wryly, they probably all looked like this.

Unlike the warm walls of Rosemead, which were paneled with wood or whitewashed with crisp new paint, the stone structure of Lorlmar had been left mostly in its natural state, rough with chips and mortar, holding the chill of the night tightly in its crevices.

Kyla felt it keenly as she tried to trace her path back to her rooms. Every now and then she would pass other people, inclining her head to them when their eyes met, returning whatever sort of look she got measure for measure: curious stares from a group of old men, polite nods from some soldiers, shadowed smiles from several women, or nothing at all from most of the servants. But no one said a word to her. No one bothered to ask her where she was going, what she was doing. If she was lost.

The last people she had seen had been well over ten minutes ago, three noblewomen in tremendous headdresses, weaving a quilt of gossip together in a small room. Kyla wasn't certain, but she thought it hadn't taken nearly this long to find the kitchens from her rooms this morning.

As she crept her way around the castle the light seemed to grow dimmer and dimmer; she was circling, nautilus-style, toward the heart of the keep and wasn't at all sure that was where she needed to go. Passages that branched off from the main hall seemed to lead nowhere she could recall seeing before; there were endless stretches of closed doors, and now, flickering torches were needed to light the way, even though it was full daylight out.

Kyla finally stopped, trying to get her bearings. Impossible. It all looked the same. Dark and dank, salty air, uninviting passages, closed doors, closed faces—

She missed Rosemead with breathtaking sharpness, like

nothing she had felt before. She missed the openness of it, she missed the gentle green hills of it, the cozy rooms with great windows of leaded glass, the people she knew and loved, her maids, her friends. Her family.

"Oh," she said, a little catch in her throat, blinking down at the hem of her gown. She leaned wearily against the cold wall, closed her eyes, fought off the homesickness.

She was still tired. She needed a nap. That was all.

Down the hall behind her came the echo of footsteps.

For no reason at all she felt a prickle of warning at the shuffling sound. How silly. She should be grateful not to be the only person here after all. Now she could ask for directions to her rooms. To hell with her pride.

Yes, someone was coming, coming in a rather quiet way, a soft padding around the bend, almost as if they didn't wish to be heard at all. And here she was, alone in the massive, spiraling hall of a place she didn't know. Lost and alone.

Without thought she reached out and tried the handle of the door nearest her, pulling at the loop of metal. It was locked.

The steps had paused; Kyla could hear only her own breathing, heightened, abnormally loud to her ears. She kept her fingers curled around the solid metal of the door handle.

Seconds passed. A torch sputtered with a sizzling frenzy somewhere nearby, then died down.

She told herself she had heard nothing. She was jumping at shadows, her imagination—

And then she could make out the breathing of the other person, the one who had stopped when she had, waiting for her to move again, to cover the sounds they would make. Like a cat lying in wait for a mouse, Kyla thought with a tinge of panic. A macabre game. There was no reason for anyone friendly to toy with her like this. She tugged hard on the handle of the door once more, looking around for another escape route.

Another hallway, to her right, up ahead.

The shuffling sound came again, closer now, not bothering to be so quiet. Heavy, booted steps, coming right for her.

She sprinted to the corner of the hallway, used her hands to push herself off the side wall, and kept going down the new passage, not looking back.

A blur of doors and torches. She rounded another bend and then another, until she could see people up ahead of her, walking down the hall, leaving and entering the rooms.

When she was almost upon them she slowed to a brisk walk, smoothing her hair back, casting just one glance over her shoulder.

Shadows draped the edges of the hallway behind her, obscuring sharp details. But there was no doubt it was very empty.

───────── ⚭ ─────────

*T*HE SKY AROUND LORLREAU was a particularly bright azure later that afternoon, Kyla noticed, and the fact that on the far horizon there loomed a dark corner of charcoal clouds seemed to daunt none of the crowd that set out to find the deer.

She had been escorted both to and from her rooms by the same maid who had done her hair, a quiet girl named Meg who had hesitantly offered to show her the way to the master chambers when Kyla had crossed her path in the hall filled with people.

Kyla told herself she had suffered nothing more than an attack of nerves, imagining she had been pursued this morning. Of course it had been her imagination. There was no reason for anyone to wish to frighten her. She had probably heard rats in the walls, that was all. Every castle had rats.

Nevertheless, she was grateful for her demure guide this afternoon, who knocked on the door before entering, who smiled at her without guile, and who then led her down to the bailey, where the rest of the party awaited her. For a moment Kyla considered mentioning her adventure this morning to someone, perhaps Harrick, but then she shook her head and dismissed the thought. It had been nothing. She was going to forget about it. Everyone here was all smiles and welcome, making any lingering thoughts of persecution dwindle off to nothingness in the clear blue sky.

In addition to the children and herself, there was Marla again, hovering around Elysia, and a few other women, as well as Harrick. They were to walk to find the deer, it was explained to her on the way out by Joseph, one of the boys she had met this morning. Walking was best since some of the deer didn't like some of the horses, and it would be impolite to offend the deer in their own home, and didn't she think so?

Kyla replied that she did think so, it was always a good thing to be polite, and this satisfied Joseph enough so that he began to point out some of the more interesting sights to her as they walked: Over there, under that rock, he had once found the largest bug he had ever seen; over there, in that knothole, he had once found a nest of baby owls, all now grown up; over there, behind that group of trees, was a meadow, and in the meadow lived a family of rabbits; over there . . .

Up ahead the rest of the group was scattered in a crooked line between the bushes and the hills, Marla holding the hand of Elysia, Harrick leading the way.

The picnic was held in the meadow of the rabbits, thick with clover and wild grass. From what Kyla had seen of Lorlreau so far it seemed a fairly typical representation of the island: sheltered amid windswept hills, rugged cliffs not very far away, a gentle slope leading off into the darkness of the forest. The song of the ocean was a low murmur this far inland, but still it came, comforting somehow, refreshing.

They ate their bread and cheese mostly in silence, even the children relaxing enough to just watch the sky, or pluck a blade of tender grass, or examine the array of stones decorating the field.

It made Kyla sleepy, warm sunlight and a full stomach, and she would really have liked nothing more than to stretch out on the clover and close her eyes. And then she had to smile, because such a thought seemed so natural to her, yet of course a lady would never dream of sitting amid the dirt and grass in her fine skirts; a lady would never picnic under the sun without shelter and escort; a lady, in fact, would probably never even have accompanied this hodgepodge in the first place. A real countess—that woman in the looking glass, perhaps—would have stayed behind at the keep, sewing, playing the lute, being submissive and refined and genteel, all the things in life that seemed to elude Kyla.

She thought about those times not so long ago when she had just fallen asleep where she lay: in meadows, under scrub, behind rocks. The stars had been her company, and the ground had been her bed and all the nightsong of the king-dom's creatures had lulled her to sleep.

Or, alternately, jolted her awake, depending upon how close they were.

It was so strange. She would never have thought she would miss those moments. They had been filled with fear and pain. And yet, and yet . . . something in her did miss them.

How many other countesses in all the land could claim to have had what she did? Her freedom. Not for long, no. Just a taste of it, really, bittersweet at that. No one to tell her where to go, what to do, how to dress, what to say. No Conner or Helaine, no Alister.

Had her life continued the course it had been on just a year ago, she would have eventually still found herself in this very meadow. Probably not right now. Probably the wedding would have been a few months away still, to be held in Henry's own cathedral. She would have still ended up the Countess of Lorlreau, albeit in a much more conventional manner. Her parents would have attended, her mother smil-ing through her tears, her father beaming. Alister would have waved at her covertly when he wasn't busy fidgeting with his formal tunic. It could have been so lovely.

She shook her head at the sky, wanting to surrender this vision before it became too painful. It was not reality. Reality was harsh and bloody and unfair and confusing. It was brutal and violent, and she was helpless to understand it.

Yet despite all the madness she was still here, sitting in a meadow on an island belonging to the Earl of Lorlreau, still married to the man who had been promised to her. The man who was responsible for the deaths of almost all of her loved ones.

Kyla found a determined line of ants beside her, shiny-backed, marching through their jungle with tiny bread crumbs as their prize. It was something she would have shared with her brother, a common thing they would have found uncommon together, a moment of fascination with a miniature world.

Maybe someday she would have her own son or daughter to share the hidden secrets of this meadow with. Maybe. She couldn't imagine such a thing right now. But the everyday habits of life might again seep over her, perhaps, and she might start a new family. She and her husband.

Roland watched the party pick up the remains of their meal and begin the hike back into the woods. He lingered where he was, half hidden by the convenient trunk of a pine, reluctant to dispel the vision of Lady Kyla walking her graceful walk beside some boy, nodding her head at his comments, following carefully with her eyes wherever he pointed, providing the perfect attentive audience to her young admirer.

His meeting with the steward at Taldon had gone much more quickly than he had anticipated but still not as quickly as he had hoped. The crops looked good, the fishing was picking up, no one's roof had blown apart in the last storm, no one's pigs were dying off; in other words, no major complaints to deal with. The most time-consuming part of it had been greeting everyone again, seeing old friends, learning the faces and names of the new children that had been born on the island in his absence. It was an old, familiar chore, reminding him of how much he missed being here, yet comforting him with the fact that he was finally back, and back with a bride.

Aye, and everyone had wanted to hear of her. They stayed on Taldon for the most part, coming over to the main island only as they needed to, and so many had missed her arrival yet caught the gossip on the wind. Near the end of his visit most of the men and women were informally gathered in what passed as the common house, breaking bread and peppering him with questions.

He had answered as best he could, but couldn't hide the fact that he was eager to get back to Lorlreau. He knew there were plans to take Kyla to see the deer today. He knew also he had lists and lists of things to attend to, a myriad of pressing items that all seemed to call out for immediate attention from the lord.

And yet here he was, breathless from hurrying to catch up with the group, now paused just outside their circle, watching her. Watching Kyla, his wife.

She looked different from yesterday, when she had been windblown from the sea, polite and resolute despite the fact that she so obviously hated to travel by water. He had been very proud of her, that she kept her composure no matter her discomfort, and as always he had been entranced with her radiance. Sea salt and wind could only enhance it, as far as he was concerned.

Today, obviously, a maid had come and done her hair up in some intricate fashion of braids that disguised the uncommon beauty of it, tucked it away behind a translucent veil, and he couldn't help but regret the loss of that unusual sight. How well he remembered Lady Kyla, riding beside him with her hair loose by her waist, swinging in time to the horses' steps.

His druid was a true lady now. Or was she?

Roland left the shelter of the pine and moved to catch up with the party.

Kyla spied him first, turning to him from across the field, and he saw immediately that she still could have been that nymph behind the veil and the braids, that unconventional and natural thing in her unrepressed by a maid's ministerings. The woods and the fields suited her, they always would.

"My lord," she said. She seemed flustered by something,

seeing him, but then gathered herself and curtsied—in the middle of the meadow, she curtsied—not meeting his eyes any longer, the veil falling forward over her shoulders.

So of course he had to bow back, a great, flourishing bow, which brought laughter from the children and a most fascinating blush to the cheeks of his new countess.

He fell into step beside her, leaving her young suitor to begrudgingly fall back to her other side. Roland clasped his hands behind his back, admiring the day, admiring his wife.

"How did you sleep?" he asked after a while, willing her to look at him.

She didn't. "I . . . very well, thank you, and you?"

"Very well, indeed," he replied, a blatant lie. He wondered if he had slept at all, in fact.

For in spite of his resolution to leave her alone, to let her come to him in the natural timing of her own need, last night he had arrived at the bedroom that used to be his, and now was theirs, and she had been sleeping so sweetly in his bed. One hand had remained outside the covers, lax, fingers slightly cupped against her chest. And strangely enough it was just that vision of her hand that did him in, wrist slightly bent, delicate, perfectly feminine, a pale curve of skin against the darkness of the bed. Just her hand, because that was all he was able to bear to think of.

He had not meant to stay in the room with her. He had meant to check on her, make sure she was fine, that she had everything she needed, that was all. He was going to sleep elsewhere, he didn't know where, probably with his men in the great hall. Somewhere else.

Instead he found himself slipping out of his clothes and into the bed beside her, incredibly warm and soft, sheer torment. She slept in a thin linen gown, which had ridden up to her hips already. He felt her bare legs brush his as he came closer.

Roland had held his breath but she didn't wake up, accepting his arm around her waist, her back to him, with complete ease.

And he had watched the night sky spin by for hours, turning the stars away from his window until the dawn had crept with pearly fingers into the room, all the while holding her, breathing her, wanting her.

When the sun touched the curved stone of the windowsill he had made himself leave. Mayhap it had been a lesson in fortitude. All Roland knew was that he had never spent a more exhausting, and heavenly, night.

The party now entered into the heart of the forest itself, following a thin path worn in the grass and dirt, walking single file. Roland put Kyla ahead of him so he could continue to watch her, envisioning the form of her clearly even past the veil, past the bliaut she wore, the underskirt, perhaps a chemise . . . with eyelets, and ribbons. . . .

The interior of the forest was cooler than it had been outside the trees, or perhaps it was just that the clouds had begun to creep over the sun. Either way, Kyla felt the chill of it through the thickness of the trees, the unmistakable scent of the woods surrounding them all.

No one was speaking anymore. It might have been the stillness of the forest that influenced them, it might have been just that they were approaching the lair of the deer. All that she could hear were their footfalls, crunching through old pine needles, past fallen leaves, each step slightly springy on the mossy ground.

Right behind her, especially, she heard the steps of Roland.

The others were slowing, looking back at her, forming a cluster at the edge of a little glen, motioning her to come forward. They parted as she passed through, then the children immediately pressed in behind her.

The glen was small and lush, with tall, wild grass pressed down beneath the shelter of a prickly bush. Beneath its lowest limbs lay three deer, a male and two females, with another male standing alertly nearby.

Elysia, beside her, took her hand. "Who is here?" she asked.

"Bancroft, Belle, Sammy, and Eleanor," said Marla softly.

"Here she is, Eleanor," said Elysia, slightly louder. "I've brought her for you." She pulled Kyla a few steps into the glen.

The male already standing lowered his head at their approach, but one of the females climbed delicately to her feet and came over to them. She was tall, almost past Kyla's shoulders, with the same ruddy tone and pale white spots that Kyla remembered from before.

Elysia reached out a hand and the deer nudged it with her nose. Kyla found her own hand being offered to the doe, Elysia holding it in place for her. The deer's nose was wet and cold, but not unpleasant. Kyla saw from the corner of her vision that Roland was on her other side, silent, observing her. The doe began to lick her palm.

"She likes your salt," said Elysia.

It tickled. Involuntarily she smiled, looking up and meeting Roland's gaze.

The shadowed sunlight underlit his eyes, turning them darker, more like the depths of the ocean. He was not smiling but she felt his heat: the pleasure he brought her, the intensity of focus that marked his entire body. His arm grazed hers, reaching out to pet the doe, but he was still examining her, scanning her whole face with that darkened gaze.

She was helpless to look away, caught in a fantastic spinning web of the desire she felt from him, drawing her in whether she willed it or no, coaxing her, subduing her, sparking that hidden flame within her she wanted to deny but couldn't, holding her breathless and suspended in the heavy air around them, the thunderclouds, the fragrant leaves and crushed grass, the promise of rain everywhere.

Someone jostled her, one of the children pushing past to get to the other deer, and the spell was broken.

She saw Roland look down and away, the lines around his mouth tight again.

The doe was done with her hand and was nibbling now on the sleeve of her gown.

"I have something for you, Eleanor," said Elysia in a singsong voice, reaching into the depths of her dress to produce a red apple. Eleanor immediately turned to it.

The children were squatting by the seated doe and buck, stroking them, offering more treats, while the women watched. Harrick stood in the middle of them all, not seeming to mind the tree branches that brushed his head.

Roland walked in front of Kyla to reach Elysia, taking her hand and leading her over to the other animals, crouching down with the children, talking to them, answering whatever questions they came up with.

Kyla stood back, removed from the scene, watching with that sense of distance that was becoming more familiar of late.

It was really rather extraordinary. The famed and feared hunter, the notorious Hound of Hell, playing now with children and beasts, as gentle as a daisy. No creature showed fear of him here; the children climbed over and around him, the deer allowed his approach and caresses with calm spirits. Elysia stood cradled between his knees, chattering on about something, and he nodded and laughed when he should, handed out more apples from a bag for the children to feed to the animals. Never once looking over at her again.

Everyone loved him. It was so obvious, everything she had seen on this island—nay, even before, from his soldiers—had cast that love and respect he commanded from his people back into her face with indifferent vigilance. It baffled her, the contrast. Didn't they know about him? Had they no idea what he had done, what he might do? He was a ruthless killer, he was the vengeful sword of the sovereign, he had no soul.

So who was this gentle man now, talking kindly to children and animals? Basking in everyone's admiration?

Suddenly, irrationally, Kyla was angry. They had no right to treat him with love. He didn't deserve love, he deserved fear. Couldn't they *see*? Were they all deluded? How could anyone not hate the Hound of Hell?

She should hate him. She knew she should. She had that right, more than anyone, perhaps. She should hate him every single day for the rest of her life, she should make him feel her anguish, since he had handed it to her.

But as suddenly as the anger came, it was spent. The hatred that should have filled her, in fact, never had. And never would. Because threading through her pain was confusion and doubt. There were too many inconsistencies in the man before her. Too many contradictions to what she thought had been plain truth: a hunter but a savior. A killer but a protector.

Try as she might, Kyla knew she could not point to him and declare, "Yes, there is the villain. He fully deserves his title."

And then came a whispering voice in her mind, teasing her under that moral posing, the most troubling aspect of all. Had he the blackest heart on earth, she feared it would make no difference to her desire. Her body had a claim on this judgment of him. She wanted him, sweet heaven, she did.

The sky was taking on a peculiar greenish-silver cast, the smell of rain became heavy and strong. A breeze was picking up, pushing her skirts back and forth in teasing gusts, making the veil Kyla wore dance around her shoulders.

"Eleanor was her mother," said a quiet voice behind her.

Kyla turned her head to see Marla, who had approached silently on the grass.

As cryptic as the sentence was, Kyla pieced it together immediately. "Eleanor was Elysia's mother," she said. It made sense.

"Yes. Your husband's sister. Harrick's half sister."

No wonder Seena and Harrick had reacted so strangely to the child's talk of the deer. Marla met her look, then shifted her focus past Kyla, back to the children. Kyla followed her glance.

"She named this doe herself?"

"Yes. It worried quite a few of us at the time. The doe is young, and Elysia had never shown an interest in naming any of the others. Just this one. It happened about seven months ago. As soon as the doe was born, Elysia insisted upon coming here and naming her. She rejected any other suggestions."

Elysia was leaning back now in Roland's arms, still talking, staring up in her vague way at the treetops, and Roland was responding thoughtfully.

"He's like a brother to me," said Marla, nodding her head toward Roland. "I helped raise both of them, you know.

Madoc and Seena and I. Their father had his hands full all the time, it seemed. Such a busy man, was Harland. Always so busy, especially after his wife died. Roland was only nine when it happened, Eleanor had just turned one. A fever took Rachel." Marla looked down. "Such a simple thing to take a life."

Kyla frowned. "Where was Harrick?"

"Harrick is the natural child of the old earl, a by-blow from his past glory days with King William. He was raised in a monastery on the mainland. He only came to the island a few years ago at Roland's insistence. It was supposed to be a visit, but he has stayed on."

Harrick laughed out loud, a deep, bellowing sound, causing all the animals to twist their ears to him and several children to imitate him.

"You see the ragged end of a noble line, my lady," Marla said lightly. "An earl, a bastard, and a blind child. For a long while all had thought this would be the end of the family."

She turned her head to Kyla, her eyes filled with pale blue mystery. "Of course, you will change all of that."

"What happened to Eleanor?" Kyla heard the question leave her mouth but almost didn't believe she had asked it. Something told her she didn't really want to know about Eleanor, the missing sister, the mother. A woman whose daughter would memorialize her with the name of a deer, a pet.

Marla stared at her for a heartbeat, measuring her, Kyla thought, considering her response. Kyla felt the weight of her judgment, a baffling thing since she had no notion of its basis. But still she must have failed this silent test because the other woman only shrugged before saying, "She died."

Marla walked over to the children, leaving Kyla alone again.

Eleanor, the doe, was looking at her, being patted on all sides by small hands, immobile, a wild thing despite her human name, enduring the touch of the children. Her eyes were liquid blackness, endlessly deep, and though Kyla knew it was impossible, she had the impression that the doe *did* know her, that she really was looking at her, looking *into* her, seeing things, making her dizzy with the contact.

One of the women moved between them, and when she had passed the doe had turned away, nuzzling a child, and it was just a doe again.

Kyla heard the rain before she felt it, a fat plopping sound coming from above. The drops were hitting the leaves of the crowns of the trees, shaking them, spreading beads of water in diffused showers that landed gently on her nose, then her cheeks, and turned the ground to a patchwork of wet and dry earth.

Before she could fully take in the fact of the rain it turned to a downpour, pelting them all, making the children scream with laughter, the deer bounding up and away into the woods for deeper shelter. Harrick, Roland, and the women were attempting to gather the children, all of them running in circles, chaos in the storm.

A bolt of lightning split the sky with a mighty *crack!*, blinding her, making her squeeze her eyes shut as she stumbled backward. The rain had already drenched her all the way through. She was a waterlogged mass of skirts, the veil clung to her neck and cheeks with a clammy foreignness that made her skin crawl. There was more lightning, each bolt coming with a fierce announcement from the heavens, the howl of the sudden tempest filling her ears.

It was like being abruptly tossed into the middle of a hurricane, blinded, alone and vulnerable in the fury of the heavens.

Her arm was taken. Through the rain she could make out a woman beside her, guiding her somewhere, but she couldn't see the others past the downpour, she couldn't even see the trees any longer, so heavy was the storm.

The woman was making her run, she was pulling her along and Kyla was trying to keep up. It was Marla. If Marla was here, then where was Elysia? Roland had been with her last, surely she would be fine. Kyla was unable to go back to look now, anyway, she was completely turned around; but Marla wouldn't have left the child alone, Kyla knew that.

Through the rain, through the woods, Marla's grip on her arm shifted, until they were holding hands, running side by side, and suddenly something happened.

From nowhere came the feeling of freedom once more, a joyful, uncontainable thing, filling her up and bursting from her lungs with every breath she took. The rain was a liberating friend, it stung her skin but felt wonderful. The moss and the grass bowed before it, showing them the way home. Her legs were strong, she could run all day, she could run forever!

Kyla couldn't stop the smile that took her lips. Beside her, holding on with her cold, wet hand, Marla was smiling too, blinking up at the sky, matching the joy in Kyla as surely as she matched her pace.

All around them now Kyla saw the others, the children safe, frolicking as the rain lightened to gentleness, Roland carrying Elysia on his shoulders, Harrick guiding his flock of youngsters, all of them heading back to the keep without distress, the children skipping playfully.

Marla laughed out loud, a contagious happiness, her face still upturned, and she was singing as she ran with Kyla, the grip between them unbroken, Lorlmar waiting for them up ahead.

Chapter Ten

―――――――――――― ⚬꙰⚬ ――――――――――――

𝒯HEY WERE EXPECTED back at the castle.

As they approached, the children playing games around the adults, Lorlmar's occupants came out of the keep to meet them, not quite scolding, mothers and nurses and a few soldiers, as well. Everyone remarked on the storm, the brief flurry of tumult at midday, the loudness of the thunder, the closeness of the lightning. Soon the children could be heard describing the danger in great detail, how brave they were, how they rescued the others, each tale more expansive than the last.

Marla had released Kyla's hand and exchanged it for Elysia's as they reached the gate, swinging off into the interior of the keep with one last farewell smile and then a guiding glance over to Roland, who was with his men, laughing, brushing his wet hair out of his face.

The children were dispersing in twos and threes, going off to their nursery to get dry. It seemed a good idea. Other than one look on the way back—she supposed to ensure that she hadn't been left behind—Roland had not bothered with her again. In fact, he seemed to be going to great pains to avoid even being near her. He was standing now with his back to her as the people swarmed away, and after an uncertain moment, Kyla joined them and went inside.

Through sheer luck or just persistence she managed to find her chamber again, entering with relief that her memory had not failed her, and even greater relief that she had not heard any further mysterious footsteps trailing her.

The bedroom held the last light of the storm, blurring the edges of the shadows, darkening every color with misty illusion.

Off came the wet gown, the bliaut, everything, laid out to dry over a pair of chairs by the fireplace. She rubbed herself dry with a soft blanket from the bed, wrapping it around her, patting her still-braided hair with the trailing ends of it as she crossed the floor, intent on finding another gown.

But to get to the chest with her clothing—all neatly put away now, she noticed—she had to pass the main window, which held a view she had not yet examined. It arrested her, the tops of trees, emerald bits of the sloping hillsides, the jagged edge of a line of cliffs. Off to the right was the ocean itself, a pewtered sweep of water stretching away until it became lost in the horizon.

The clouds were rolling up into themselves, flat on the bottoms with puffed curlicues on the tops, the lavender of them now growing stained with glorious purple and scarlet and orange from the sinking sun.

She was leaning against the base of the windowsill, lost in her reverie, when the door behind her opened.

Roland passed through, almost having to duck his head down to clear the arch of the doorway. "Kyla? I've been looking—"

He stopped when he saw her and she stood frozen as well, half turned, both of them captured in the perfect harmony of the moment: her standing alone against the sky, barefoot, wrapped in the blanket; him amid the warming light of the sunset, turquoise and gold and masculine beauty, looking stunned to see her, immobile.

Roland didn't know what to do. He hadn't been able to find Kyla, he had seen her arrive with Marla but she wasn't with Marla any longer, and Marla hadn't known where she had gone. He had terrible visions of her lost in the castle. It was still unfamiliar to her, and there were so many dangerous secrets at

Lorlmar she could stumble across. Concealed doors, hidden passageways, trapdoors leading down to the depths of the dungeon . . .

But she was here. Of course she was here, this was the logical place for her to go. This is where he should have thought to look first. She was standing before him, his druid, just a blanket wrapped around her, the red satin of her hair still brighter than the sky behind her, tucked up and away, plainly showing him her bare shoulders, and oh, God, lower down the blanket lay open so innocently, exposing the line of her leg in teasing clarity.

He tried to look away and couldn't. He tried to turn around and leave but his body would not obey him. He was locked on the vision of her leg, long and shapely, he could see that now, and he could not move. No, he couldn't move to save his life.

She shifted, making some soft, dismayed sound, and the blanket shifted with her, opening up higher, showing him the creaminess of her thigh until she covered it in a hasty grasp, letting another corner go dipping dangerously low over her breasts.

Roland found he could move, after all. He turned around and closed the door behind him, slamming home the bolt, locking them both inside.

She stood still as he came over to her, tilting her head back to look at him. There was no trace of the fear he had been dreading seeing in her; the silver and black of her eyes remained calm, their seduction holding him as a pagan would worship at the moon. But she was the moon, and he was her vassal. He could just sink away in her eyes, lost in them forever, surrounded by her perceptive candor, living in the flicker of desire he found there now.

Slowly, slowly he placed his hands on her shoulders, testing her resistance, allowing her to break away if she chose. Her skin was warm beneath his, smooth, the bones so fine. Still she didn't stop him. Her lips parted slightly, a short intake of breath.

He spread his fingers out, sliding his palms over her back.

The contrast of her skin against his left him feeling slightly giddy, like drinking too much ale at once. He took a step closer to her, then another half step, so that the blanket she wore touched him lightly, and he could barely feel the rise and fall of her chest, more rapid now, grazing the front of him.

She let him, she let him do all this, so she had to let him kiss her too, because he would surely die if he didn't kiss her soon.

He bent down, still giving her plenty of time to stop him, and when she didn't he only brushed his lips against her cheek, closing his eyes at the painful pleasure of it; a half concession to the anxiety in him of her rejection.

But Kyla turned her head to meet his lips and in an instant the passion blazed between them. As one they moved together, she put her arms around him and he crushed her to him, mindless of any earlier thoughts to go carefully, to go slowly.

She wouldn't let him, anyway. She was a living flame in his arms, twisting up to get closer to him, meeting each of his kisses with a hunger of her own, that smoky seduction he had envisioned in her becoming so real so fast.

He let the blanket fall away from her back, caught between them both, and now his hands could fully explore the fine expanse of her, down the straight spine, the sweet dip of her waist, the tender curve of her bottom. He cupped her there and pulled her into him, lifting her, and she gasped against his lips, holding on to his shoulders. She was so light, yet real, solid flesh beneath his hands, and his body knew it perfectly well.

He pressed his lips to the hot line of her neck, tasting the dew of the rain still on her. Her hands clenched against him, knotting up the tunic he wore, pulling it tighter. He allowed her feet to touch the floor again—she was so much smaller than he, it was no effort at all to lift her up, one hand under her knees, the other under her back, the blanket trailing and trailing until it fell off of her in a whisper.

She shivered then, from the cold or the moment, he didn't

know, but they were to the bed already. He set her down amid the pillows and the blankets, admiring everything, it was too much to take in at once. His fantasy was engulfed by the reality of her, Kyla, here with him, in his bed. The shiver took her again and her eyes turned down, shyness now.

Roland took the fur nearest to them and turned it over, holding it so that the soft down skimmed her skin, heightening sensation, brushing over her thighs, her stomach, those perfect breasts. Now she looked up at him, at the curve of the smile teasing his lips.

One hand reached up and touched his mouth, lightly, and he was stilled, letting her trace the outline of his lips, his jaw, his chin. Her eyes were narrowed, concentrating, so serious now. He moved and kissed the inside of her wrist and felt her fingers tangle in his hair, pulling him down to her.

He wanted to stretch out beside her and only then realized he was still fully dressed, he hadn't yet changed from the rainstorm. His clothes were a hindrance, an unwelcome burden. He stripped out of them carelessly and she sat back and watched him until it seemed the embarrassment overtook her. Then she closed her eyes and turned her head away, licking her lips, that exquisite blush sweeping through her again.

"Kyla." His voice was hoarse and low. It was almost too good to be true; he had been wanting her for so damned long now, she had filled his dreams with hot liquid desire, she had tormented his days with forbidden thoughts of her touch, her taste, her wetness. He had to make it like this for her, no matter how much it killed him, he had to know she wanted him as he did her.

Her skin was hot now, she had tugged more blankets over her and he found her beneath them, warming himself with her heat, almost crazed with the sensation of her bare body rubbing against his. He had to stop and grit his teeth, he had to fight the *want* that throbbed through him and demanded satisfaction now, right now.

When he was lying next to her she turned her head back, though she still wouldn't meet his eyes, long lashes and that small pucker on her forehead, the first sign of uncertainty. He had promised himself he would wait for her, he had promised himself he would control the fever that wanted to consume him, to consume her, take her and overpower her until she screamed with pleasure. . . .

He made himself pause, running his hands over her cheeks, cupping her neck, driving himself to distraction as he tried to think of how to bring her back to him. The twists of her hair in its woven bonds were hard under his touch.

Roland lifted her until she was sitting and then moved behind her, not quite fully touching, his legs surrounding hers. Kyla turned her head, a perfect profile to him, a question on her lips. He silenced her by stroking a finger across her mouth, letting the words fade away, then tracing the fullness of her lips, her cheeks, and back to her hair.

The braids were lost amid themselves to him, he had to follow the strands in and out of each other until he found the end of one tucked under itself. Unwrapping it was like finding treasure, gently combing through the strands, letting the fire stream though his fingers, unfurling in splendid waves all the way down to her waist.

He was careful with each one, taking out the pins, stroking through the length of it, admiring the fall of color against the whiteness of her back. She stayed motionless for him, only ducking her head down now and again as he rubbed his fingers against her scalp, massaging away the tightness there, selfishly feeding his own craving for her with every touch, moving down to the slope of her shoulders, kneading her skin.

At last the braids were gone, there was only the thick mass of her hair between them, cool against his chest, his stomach, unbelievably torturous against the part of him that wanted her most, and he almost couldn't move from the unique sensation. Here was his wife in front of him, the softness of her overcoming him, the rich redness of her hair like satin, like the heat of a shooting star, inflaming him.

Roland leaned forward, sliding his hands down her arms,

slow at first and then ending with a kind of rough squeeze against him, taking his breath away as she was pressed into him, her face turning toward him.

"Kyla," he said again, into her temple, and it was a plea now, harsh and shaking.

Where was logic when she needed it? Where were revenge and justice now? She didn't know, she couldn't think. She didn't want those things any longer, they were just words, vague concepts she no longer cared about but knew she should.

Kyla tried to consider something, anything but the man with her, his touch on her shoulders, his lips whispering across her brow. Impossible. He was waiting for her, he was breathing into her hair, holding her against him. She felt the planes of his body pressed against her, that hard and exciting part of him against the small of her back, his arms secure around her, but she was not his captive. He would not force her, she knew it. The choice would be hers.

She wanted this. More than the aching inside of her, more than the hunger that saturated her and craved every part of him, more than even that she knew she wanted this fulfillment. She needed it. The girl she had been—immersed in virtue and righteous indignation—was gone, and Kyla was suddenly glad for it. She had rediscovered a woman's feelings in this moment and it suited her. She welcomed this change. She wanted this knowledge, this mysterious thing that was about to happen.

She wanted, with her whole heart, the answer to the questions Roland had unwittingly given her with that first kiss. She had been haunted for too long, her body would not allow this moment to go unanswered. Any regrets that might have formed were now just ashes in the wind. He was the gossamer thread that held her together, he was all she wanted, and the faint, faint trembling she felt in his arms while he waited for her matched the hot yearning inside of her that was pure desire.

Kyla moved up in his embrace, turning so that she could look at him. Her dark lashes swept up, revealing honesty, still holding that passion he had recognized in her before, a caught breath in her finally being released.

Her face lifted to his, unspoken consent. Her lips welcomed his and Roland's instant gratitude was boundless, exuberant. She turned all the way around before him now, almost kneeling on the bed, and he had to fight the urge to lay her down and take her now. Her hands on him heated the song in his blood, feather-light, tentative, exploring his shoulders, his chest, and then lower, when she stopped, shy again. With a great effort of will he guided her, let her feel his desire, encouraged her with a moan he couldn't stop, kissed her neck, the fragrant line of her jaw, then bit her lower lip lightly, prompting her hands to clench together in surprise.

He almost couldn't stop then, the unexpected agony of her pleasuring him in that abrupt burst, but he pulled away in time and rolled onto his back, taking her with him so that she lay across him. The cherry silk of her hair fell in waves around them, scented with rain and with her. How he had fantasized about this moment, Kyla beside him, around him, filling him up as he wanted to fill her.

Her breasts were crushed against his chest, it was killing him, and to preserve his self-control he allowed himself to look at her for only a moment. Druid magic, haunting and soft and firm and feminine, and his, his, *his.*

It was a mistake. He lingered too long on her sensual beauty. He was going to attempt to woo her further with words, all the elaborate compliments that she deserved. Velvet lips, silver-smoke eyes.

But she was here. She was his. That was all he needed.

It was too late for him, the want in him seared away all thoughts of caution and compliments, burned him inside out, ignited the part of him he had locked away all these years, that blackness, that loss of control he'd fought so hard to banish. And so now it was too late for her, as well.

Too late for remorse, because he was already pushing her off of him so he could cover her, he was already taking one rosy nipple in his mouth, so taut, while his hand found her sweetness, petal-soft and damp, and she was responding, she was lifting her leg, she was gasping with her head back amid the covers, with surprise or pleasure, he didn't know, but still he didn't stop, he couldn't stop.

She was the only thing in the world. She was the center of the universe, she was his essence, she was all of him, and everything in him told him that this was right. This was what he had been living for, right now, this moment, with Kyla beneath him, opening herself up for him, taking all of him in herself, her eyes wide with wonder and pain and shock.

He kissed away the pain, he moved to disguise it, to blunt it, to distract her because he had never wanted to hurt her but now, oh now, nothing could stop him from satisfying the darkness. For he was the darkness.

And their rhythm was the echo of the primitive force in him, driving him on, taking her with him. He shared it with her and she accepted it, the pain diminishing, her body changing from stiff resistance to something else, a recognition of this dance, her hands now clutching at him, pulling him closer.

He would die from this. He would splinter apart from the black bliss of it. She was doing this to him, his druid, her skin hot and moist, her legs coming up to enclose him, wrapping around him, her eyes like moonlight, watching him with awareness now, something new in her, sultry and alert. Full lips, her panting short and exquisite, and he moved in her, fascinated, her tightness taking him in, all of him, all of him, over and over.

The blackness was her spell, she absorbed it she spread her magic over it and gave it back to him until he couldn't hold any more, it was too great. It spilled over him, he lost the last of his control and surrendered to it with a hoarse cry, letting go of the pleasure until the sparkling blackness in him was spent, and there was nothing left of him, no pain, no guilt, only the end.

And her, Kyla, the touchstone to prove his darkness.

THE RAIN HAD CURLED his hair into shaded waves of amber and honey, flowing down with soft regularity to the pillow he lay on. It formed an incongruous halo around his sleeping features; instead of adding to the innocence of rest, the golden curls seemed to frame the roguishness she had come to recognize in him. Even with his eyes closed, Kyla thought, her husband possessed a certain deviltry, from the slanting line of his brows to the dimple that appeared when he smiled.

She looked up, and he was looking back at her, still smiling.

"You're not asleep." She couldn't keep the accusation out of her voice.

"Apparently not," he agreed, stretching his arms back behind his head.

Dawn had come and gone with both of them oblivious, but now Kyla could see it was well past that, past even the time she had awakened to yesterday—it seemed like months ago—when the children had come to escort her to a late breakfast.

They were alone in the room now. The sunbeams slanted just a little more over the walls this morning than she remembered, past the horned conch and over to the carved marble of the fireplace mantel, pure white.

Roland watched her drop her eyes, masking whatever she was feeling with the fans of her lashes.

While she slept he had watched her for hours again, well into the night, watched her until his vision of Kyla had become a dream of Kyla, a dream in which she laughed and danced beside him, living flame and storm somehow joined together.

She had been like that last night in his arms, she had scorched him. He took it willingly, whatever pain she inadvertently brought to him he would live through, because it meant having her here beside him in real life every morning, every day, every night.

Roland rolled to his side to face her and placed one hand tentatively on her arm. She didn't move to stop him so he slid it down to the curve of her waist, enjoying the delightful feminine line of her.

"Did I hurt you last night?" he asked.

"No. Yes." Her standard answer when he got too close.

The pucker between her brows was back, but he thought he knew what this was: the lingering shyness of a maiden. That she could still be shy after what they had shared somewhat surprised him, but then again, she was made of some magical element he might never fully comprehend.

He had to smile. "Then I am not sorry, and I am."

She watched him now, examined the smile suspiciously, then relaxed when she perceived his teasing. "It only hurt at first," she offered, then blushed, hiding her face.

Roland moved closer to her, pushing the blankets and furs out of his way until there was nothing between them again and he could cup her face with his hand. He had been going to say something silly to reassure her, something light to make her smile back and forget the pain, and then maybe something else, something sweet to feed the flame he now knew lived in her. Because he was ready for her again.

But instead Roland lay face-to-face with her, both of them resting on their arms, his hand still warm against her cheek. She looked back at him openly, the level of their heads exactly matched, the extravagance of her hair tumbling past her shoulder.

All the pretty words he thought to say were gone.

She was no tavern wench, to be tumbled and appeased, as he might have done in his very green youth. She was no courtesan, to be flattered and soothed, as he might have done in his early years at court. She was, in fact, like no other woman he had ever known, and she was also his wife. And he was a man now, not a youth. She was his responsibility. But there was more to it than that, so much more, because as he lived out the pattern of his life, all Roland could see now was Kyla in it, Kyla everywhere, day and night, tempestuous or fair. She blessed the ordinary man that he was, and she alone held the key to redemption that he might seek.

In some disquieting way he had known this from the very first night he had seen her, that fateful night at the inn, when she had fought him for what she believed he had done to her and her family, when she had stood before him and condemned him without fear, a shining angel of ruthlessness. And he had deserved it, yes, even as he had wanted to capture her for himself.

She was his forevermore, and he was hers, whether she wanted him or not. Mayhap if she had had more time to consider her fate she would not have married him. Mayhap she would have retreated to the Tower, to Rosemead, and eventually to some other man, had he not acted to bind her to him.

No other man on this earth, Roland was certain, would be able to fully appreciate the Lady Kyla the way he did. So although he had been selfish, and although he had acted on what he thought was just lust, he knew now that Kyla had captured him, not the other way around. He was her prisoner. She held his heart. And there still lived that weak part of him that wanted her to forgive him, that would have said or done just about anything to erase everything bad between them, leaving only today and all their tomorrows to look to.

So instead of some flowery nonsense, what Roland said was: "I want you to know something. I wasn't at Glencarson. I had not arrived yet when the attack came. If I had been there, I would have stopped it."

The impact of his words took a moment to sink in. He could almost watch the progression in her eyes, confusion to comprehension, disbelief to denial.

She pushed off his hand and sat up abruptly, a tremor to her lips.

"You would dare say such a thing to me now? After . . ." She trailed off. It seemed even in her anger she would not find the words to name their loving. "Don't lie to me! I was there! I know you gave the order to attack!"

He sat up as well, searching for reason where there was none to be found. He had started this and he was grimly determined to see it through. If it made her hate him anew, at least he would have the comfort of knowing she had heard the truth. She deserved the truth. "You were there, Kyla, but I was not. It wasn't my order to attack. I was still days away when . . . one of my subordinates took over. He was not even supposed to deliver my message to you until after I arrived. He sent it early."

She stared over at him, the tremor not leaving her lips until she pressed them together. Her hands were unconsciously clenched into the covers. He plowed on.

"I would not have assailed a village of innocent people just to get to you and your brother. I am not that kind of man."

Not any longer.

The ruthlessness in her was back with a vengeance, sparks and silver fire. "Oh, no, I see that. You are a man that lets his inferiors take the blame. Do you think I am *witless?*"

"No, no." He shook his head, smiling sadly. "You are the most far from witless person I have ever known. And you do have a point. Glencarson was still my responsibility, and therefore ultimately I am still accountable for the actions of my soldiers. But I did not give that command. I would not have."

He let her think about that a moment, hoping she would hear the truth to his words, discovering that what she thought of him meant more than he had even guessed before. She had to believe him.

Kyla looked away and shook her head, mouth downturned.

"I don't know what to believe anymore, Lord Strathmore. You keep me topsy-turvy. You say you didn't lead the command at Glencarson, and yet you hunted me and kept me prisoner. You dragged me to London only to save me from the king. And then, last night—"

Her voice choked off. She dashed away a tear that appeared in the corner of her eye.

That was what broke him, the lone tear, the only one he had ever seen her shed through all of her misery. Not once had he seen her cry, and God knew she had had reason enough to do so.

He gathered her to him despite her muffled protests, easily overcoming her halfhearted attempts to rebuff him, gathered her close and rocked her gently as more tears followed. He said whatever came to him, trying to help her, wanting to comfort her, wanting her healed from this terrible wound.

"You tied me *up!*" she sobbed into his chest, holding on to him now as they rocked. "You tied me up, you made me *parade* around like a criminal, *you* did that. . . ."

He was sorry, he was so damned sorry to have ever hurt this fragile girl, and yet he wasn't—because all of that meant she was here with him now.

If things had been different, if her family had lived and their betrothal had run the common course of betrothals . . .

But that was not what happened. So Roland whispered his apologies to her, he kissed her hair and her forehead and her temple, he cradled her and stroked her and apologized some more, all the while aware that some part of him wasn't sorry in the least. Some part of him, his own ruthlessness, was glad he had thought to tie her to him, was glad that she had not been able to escape after all. For then he would be alone again, his one chance at happiness having slipped away into the mists of middle England.

After a while she quieted, and his rocking slowed until he was leaning back against the iron headboard with her relaxed against him. He still held her with both arms, he let his lips rest against the crown of her hair. His eyes were closed, trying to judge the aftermath of the moment, trying to contain the feeling of triumph mingled with desperation that he felt now.

He had told her the truth and she had stayed. She had allowed him to comfort her. She had shed some of the bitterness, yes, but was it enough?

Her hair had become a mass of heavy corkscrew curls, delightfully whimsical, the opposite of her mood. He let one springy lock wind around his hand.

"Your hair curls from the rain, did you know?" he asked, mostly to distract himself from the uncomfortable feeling of vulnerability she provoked in him.

"So does yours," she said after a moment, her voice low.

"Really? I hadn't noticed."

She pushed back from him and he reluctantly let her, watching intently for any of the anger that might remain.

But it wasn't anger in her now, it was something else. Perhaps resignation, perhaps weariness. She was still considering what he had said. She was probably going to be considering it for a long while, he thought.

She looked blankly around the room, past him, on to the bits and pieces of things that he had surrounded himself with to represent his life.

The mermaid tapestry for his mother, who used to stay up late just to tell him stories of gods and beasts and magical creatures.

The horned conch for his father, a worthy bauble for the king of the seas.

A heavy tome on meditation from Harrick, the learned man.

Right beside that, lacy bits of moss from a nest Elysia had found and presented to him.

A small jeweled box, hinges broken, from Eleanor. Her childhood chest of dreams.

Kyla saw all of this but understood none of it, how could she? He hadn't told her. There was no reason for disappointment when she skimmed his few precious memories without pause, without thought.

"I need to be alone," she said. "Please understand."

"Of course," he replied, and held back the protest that wanted to stay her.

He gathered his clothing, putting himself together with slow movements, every now and again glancing over to her, solemn in the bed, watching him. Not angry, Roland told himself. She's not angry. She simply needs time.

When he was ready he walked back over to her, not saying anything, leaned over, and kissed her hard on the lips. He wanted her to think about that, as well. It wasn't all bitterness between them. There was hope, there was passion. What more beyond that, he wasn't ready to say.

She allowed the kiss, not rebuffing him, not quite kissing him back, but still her lips were soft and succulent, enough to make the aching blackness in him spring forth again. The want.

He repressed it by leaving the room, shutting the door softly behind him.

---

*S*HE HAD NO RIDING HABIT. Apparently even Lady Elisabeth had not been that farsighted. Kyla had made do with the regular gowns on the ride from London and they would do fine enough again right now. She was going for a ride. She would let the clear, fresh air and the galloping pace of Auster clear the cobwebs from her head.

She found the stables after walking somewhat aimlessly around the bailey, nodding greetings to the strangers that called out to her, watching from the corners of her eyes those who watched her. She passed squires and knights, laundresses and farmers, and then finally a stablehand, who pointed her in the right direction for the old stone building that held the horses.

She had been remiss. She should have checked on Auster sooner, but though he nickered and shook his head at her in mock anger, she knew he had been well treated. Clean, crisp hay, clear water in a bucket, and one of the largest stalls in the whole building, more than enough for him to pace back and forth, which was apparently what he had been doing before she came up.

"My boy, my darling," she murmured, trying to soothe her absence with words. "My great, strong boy. How dost thou fare?"

The black muzzle was soft; Auster curled back his lip and nipped lightly at her fingers, just for play, before allowing her to stroke him again.

"Careful, milady," came the sharp warning of a man beside her dressed in the stablemaster's garb. "Strong teeth is what he's got."

Kyla smiled. "You are correct. But we are friends, see?" Auster rolled his eyes fearsomely at the man, who backed up. Kyla laughed at his playacting. "No need to fear. His name is Auster, and he is a peaceful creature."

It was clear the stablemaster thought her either a liar or demented.

With a great deal of gentle persuasion and more than a little use of the force behind her new title, Kyla convinced him to saddle up her stallion, which was why she was now enjoying the sting of salt in her eyes and the whipping wind in the ragged tail of her hair, streaming behind her as she took Auster into a full run away from the castle.

She had not only refused an escort, but she had also forbade it, which didn't sit well with the stablemaster, it was obvious. From the loud muttering and the flat scowl on his face as she rode away, Kyla knew her time alone on Auster was limited at best.

The stablemaster would tell the steward. The steward would tell Roland. And Roland would, no doubt, send someone after her, if he did not come himself.

Kyla lowered herself closer to her mount, urging him on faster, faster. She was no longer the prisoner of the Earl of Lorlreau. He might think the chains of marriage would tame her; he might think, now that she had given herself to him, that he could control her. She would show him how false that was. He would never control her.

But someone would come after her, probably very soon, and she accepted this as fact; indeed, it seemed to lend this moment even more sweetness. She was sore in an unaccustomed place, sore even though she rode sidesaddle now—the stablemaster had been utterly aghast at the thought of the new countess astride, and she had to concede on that point. The unfamiliarity of the sensation brought back in vivid detail all the reasons she should be sore there, in that private, feminine place, and so mostly Kyla didn't see the landscape she passed. Not the people in the fields. Not the trees, the meadows.

Guilt. Horrible, crushing guilt, that she had acquiesced to the hunger for him, that she had made the decision to satisfy her own pleasure over the sanctity of her values, over what she thought she knew of right and wrong. She had melted into the gold and turquoise of him, she had felt alive and free and wild with happiness when he was inside of her, she had adored watching him, feeling him, moving with him. She truly was his wife now, in every sense. Yes, crushing guilt.

And it was the guilt that spurred her on, driving her farther and farther away from the castle.

She was at the cliffs now. Auster gave way to an easy canter along the top of a rocky wall of stone that plunged down to crashing waves.

It was a clear day, no trace of the clouds that had crept up yesterday. Coming back to herself Kyla slowed her mount, the canter to a walk to a stop. An upward gust of wind pillowed her hair in front her—she had left it unbound again—a mask of deep red blocking the sky, the ocean, until the capricious wind shifted again, showing her where she stood.

Across the flat waters lay two more isles, their outlines clear and sharp under the midday sun. Taldon and Forswall, no doubt. Not very far away, not nearly so far as the mainland, she was certain. In fact even now, what was that there on the crisp waves? At least two boats full of men, going from here to there or there to here, she couldn't say. Both rigs had sails out in full, white banners, cheerful and bright against the deep blue water.

Auster shook his head at her idleness, growing impatient. Kyla patted his neck, urged him to a walk again, loosely following the line of the end of the land, taking care not to come too close to the drop to the sea below.

Although the view was unfamiliar, although the land was strange, her thoughts were not on her new home but rather on the man who had brought her here.

It was hard to make sense of the confused swirl of emotions that had become her life of late, but beyond the searing guilt was something deeper, something calmer. Kyla tried to understand that. Last night had happened and she didn't want to regret it. She didn't want to rue her fate any longer, there seemed to be no point in that. That was one lesson that had been curling bitterly on her tongue ever since the murder of her mother.

She truly wanted to believe that it didn't matter that her

desire had overridden her common sense. That it didn't matter that Roland had made her his own with all of her apparent consent. That it didn't even matter that what she had felt with him had been the blossoming of that deeper thing living in her that she never had the name for: passion or infatuation or . . . love.

Of course that didn't matter. Love! The winds must have blown away her senses to even consider such a thing. She couldn't love him. How incredibly stupid.

The guilt rushed back, enveloping her. She fought it, pushing it away. Something more important was at stake.

It had mattered what he said afterward, about Glencarson. That mattered.

Because that would mean that the hatred she had been so carefully tending might just crumble to dust, might not have the will to survive after all.

Roland said he had not ordered the attack. If it was true, then Roland had not killed Alister. Not directly. Not really even indirectly. And the guilt would be meaningless.

Kyla brought a hand up to cover her eyes for a moment, trying to block out everything. But still came the raucous cries of a band of seagulls over the water, diving and floating on the currents. The incessant beat of the water against the rocks. The wind scraping past her ears.

The screams of the women pierced her. The mud was thick and dark, smelled of blood and earth. She tried to keep her eyes ahead of her, she tried not to look down, she didn't want to see what she was stepping over, stepping on, stepping in. She didn't want to know.

Alister was up ahead, Alister was lying in a twisted pile of men, just like a broken toy, one of his arms at an impossible angle. His blue eyes were sightless, his freckles stood out so clearly against the waxy hue of death. Odd how she never would have thought of that, that freckles would not fade even when the life force was gone, even when the blood had drained from the body in a puddle beneath him. She had to close his eyes, it wasn't right that they should stay open like that, she had to close them but she didn't want to touch them, she had to make herself touch him—

Her own scream bubbled up and she let go of it, facing the

wind, letting it snatch the sound away and carry it out to the infinity of the ocean.

She was crying again but it was all right now, because she was alone, there was no one here to witness her weakness.

When it was over she leaned her head wearily against the mane of her horse, exhausted. Auster took this as a sign to move on.

So Roland hadn't ordered the battle. It was just another trick, then, one of the many tricks she had endured. The confusion in her made her almost dizzy. Was Roland still responsible? He had been the one chasing her, he could never dispute that. He had lived up to his name, he had been relentless, and could she allow a small factor like timing to whisk away all his culpability?

Perhaps he would have ordered that attack anyway, once he had arrived at Glencarson. Perhaps he was just saying something he thought she wanted to hear.

Or perhaps not. She had to admit she wanted him to be a better man than she had believed. For whatever reason, she did want that. But she also wanted someone to blame, Kyla realized. She wanted to be able to focus her rage on *someone*. Otherwise, the random viciousness of this life was just too awful to contemplate.

She closed her eyes, keeping her head down, and when she opened them again she found Auster had wandered off without her direction and taken her around a hedge to an unexpected thrust of granite that jutted out over the sea. On the thrust stood a tower.

It was made of stone, but not the same stone as Lorlmar; this was gray with corners and curves of green lichen to outline every block. The tower was round and tall. She had to lean back in her saddle to view the top of it and even then she wasn't sure that what she saw was the end of it, or rather just her imagining of the end of it.

No, it was real enough. She dismounted to touch it, leaving Auster with a small pat to roam where he would. She knew he would not go far.

The rock was cold, hard, just as it looked. On one of the

blocks, the one facing directly out to the sea, was a cross carved deep into the stone, but that was the sole decoration. She found a door, plain wood, locked tight. Scraggly patches of grass and brambles hugged the base of the tower, as if to hide from the constant wind.

How strange. She supposed it might have had something to do with the other islands, both still visible from here. But there were better vantage points for Taldon and Forswall, both of which were a little too easterly now for the best sighting.

A snatch of breeze brought a murmur of conversation, low and unintelligible, feminine voices. They faded in a heartbeat, leaving Kyla turning in circles for the source of the sounds. She listened again carefully but heard nothing further, only the wind, the birds. There were goose bumps on her arms.

Around the far side of the tower she found the path to the beach below. And although the beach was empty of people, at least then she understood the odd placement for the monolith.

It wasn't much of a beach here, more of an inlet, the golden sand creating a meandering finger that zigzagged between huge, rough boulders pushing up from the waves, until it disappeared altogether in the dangerous froth of the waters.

And the waters were dangerous, they had to be, judging from the wrecks of the ships littering the shore below.

Kyla crept down the path carefully, mesmerized by the sight of the smashed wood, ribs and beams of ships caught on the rocks, impaled until they rotted or the surf tore them apart. There had to be the remains of at least four large ships there, and who knew how many smaller.

The timbers were shiny from the water, some bleached, some newer-looking, a few with even the planking from the hulls intact.

It was a death trap, this little inlet, as the men from these ships must have discovered. The current must suck them inward to the sharp black-and-gold rocks and crush them in the whirl like paper.

She didn't venture far onto the beach. It was too eerie, even in full daylight, examining the shattered wrecks, which had sent out stray beams here and there with almost wild abandon.

The sand was cool and wet, soaking her slippers immediately. She took them off and carried them instead, using her other hand to gather her skirts up to her knees.

A gull was perched on a thick, old plank of wood that had become wedged perpendicularly between twin columns of rock. It watched her movements curiously, following her with small black eyes.

Kyla paused with the water now pulsing over her ankles. There was no reason to go any farther. She had seen enough of the damage to understand what had happened here. Yet still her feet moved through the water, carrying her forward to the inverted shell of a medium-sized rig, its keel facing up to the sky like a knife blade.

Inside the shell it smelled strongly of salt and rot and birds. There was a tidal pool caught in there, she could see scattered orange bursts of starfish decorating the darkness. The gull that had been watching her suddenly gave a screeching cry and flapped up in front of her before heading up into the sky, causing Kyla to take several startled steps backward, dropping her skirts.

She ran into something soft—that wasn't right, there shouldn't be anything behind her—and opened her mouth to scream, but before she could came the slam of darkness, engulfing her.

There was only the ocean pounding at her, and the images of the starfish burned behind her lids. And then nothing.

Chapter Eleven

$\mathcal{S}$OMEONE WAS SHOUTING inside her head.

It made Kyla unhappy, the loud, angry voice, immediately covered by lower, calmer tones. The words were blended together, meaningless, shades of things she didn't understand. It didn't matter, anyway. She didn't want to understand.

The voice quieted and then her existence was black and endless, calm. Peaceful. Other voices began to speak to her, familiar ones, loving. Her mother's sweet tones, her father's, urging her to do something she didn't want to do. And Alister, even Alister, siding with their parents, telling her to go back, go back. . . .

When the darkness began to lighten she fought it, because it had been so long since she had seen her mother, Kyla missed her. She missed them all so dreadfully. How much easier it would be to go forward and not back. Easier.

But they wouldn't let her, knowing, perhaps, that what she really wanted was not with them any longer, but rather back with the body she had that was now aching with pain, lying flat on something soft. A hand was stroking her face, her cheeks.

And it was now Roland's voice saying her name, repeating it, hoarse and low.

She took a deep breath and the pain racked her further, clamping around her lungs, making her cough weakly.

Roland moved quickly to support her head with his hand, holding her, then letting her down gently when she stopped.

Her lips had been blue when they brought her back to the

castle. Blue, really blue, like no shade that should have ever touched the tender flesh of his living wife.

Someone had been carrying her. The watch, Roland supposed. Yes, it had been the watch. He had carried her into the bailey crying for help, and thank God Roland had been there supervising some of the squires on the quintain. He had heard the cry along with everyone else and had rushed to join the crowd that gathered to aid her.

He had grabbed her from them. There was no reason for that, Roland knew. It had been instinct taking over: *Kyla was hurt, his Kyla, he had to help her.*

Her gown was damp, her hair was stiffening to salty tendrils, he had seen this before. The heavy weight of her in his arms told him she was truly unconscious, perhaps dead—*No, no,* his mind had babbled—but he registered this as he was running with her to the keep, to their chambers.

Marla appeared from nowhere, running beside him, opening the door for him. The watch was trying to explain what had happened to everyone as they followed. Roland only heard snatches of his words.

Facedown in the water . . . Siren's Cove . . . Saw her horse, couldn't find her, had only just arrived . . . Footsteps in the sand . . .

None of it registered at the time. All that mattered was helping her somehow, wondering how much water she had swallowed, wondering if she was even still breathing.

Marla had been through this before, as well. When he laid Kyla down Marla took over, turning her on her side, pressing on her stomach.

Nothing happened. The watch was now telling them he had pulled her from the water and she had coughed, and when he had laid her across his horse she had coughed some more, the water leaving her.

Marla listened and nodded, her hands busy on Kyla, touching her skin, checking her eyes, rubbing her hands.

Now Roland hung back, allowing Marla to work, but his gaze was focused on Kyla's parted lips, the terrible pallor that had taken over her skin. She was stark colors, blue and white, only the red of her hair untainted. People moved in front of him, blocking his view, so he went to the side of the bed and stayed there, kneeling beside her, his thoughts running in circles.

Why? What had happened to Kyla between the last time he had seen her and now? Why was she at Siren's Cove? What was she doing in the water?

He rejected the first, most obvious thing that came to him. Rejected it soundly. Yes, she had been upset. Yes, she had been through so much. But there was no reason now for her to do anything drastic to herself. He could not, would not believe that she would harm herself after this morning, after last night.

It was the blackness in him, making him think of such a thing. It was the blackness throwing back the idea of something that had not seemed that impossible for he himself to do, six years ago. Kyla wasn't like that. Kyla was stronger than that.

Marla was the closest thing Lorlmar had to a doctor. She was midwife and dentist and healer wrapped in one, and Roland had seen her take care of countless people during their years together. He trusted her as he would never have trusted some supposed physician from the mainland. When she called for herbs and broth people instantly scrambled to get them.

When she began to lift Kyla's head, looking for wounds, Roland watched her pause and frown, fingers exploring beneath the mass of hair. She then let Kyla's head back down gently, throwing a warning look to him.

He didn't know what it meant but he knew that it was important. Marla ordered the room cleared when her supplies were brought, ordered everyone out, except Roland, of course, who would have refused to go anyway.

She showed him the lump on the back of Kyla's head; together they cleaned the cut that had broken her skin, leaving a thin, straight welt lined with blood. No accidental fall would have produced such a mark.

Marla didn't have to say what she was thinking. He knew

why she had ordered everyone from the room. But it sickened him to even consider it.

Someone had attacked Kyla. Someone had bludgeoned her from behind and then left her to drown in the waves.

Someone from Lorlreau.

Ah, yes, the blackness was coming alive once more. The anger. The fury, that someone—anyone—would dare to harm his wife.

And Marla, who had witnessed the blackness in him before, said nothing still, just handed him the bowl of broth to feed to Kyla.

So he crouched by the head of the bed and methodically began to spoon it past her lips, taking care that she swallowed each mouthful. A good sign, that she swallowed. He knew this. He concentrated on that, willing himself to think of nothing else.

And now, hours and hours later, the sun was gone, the room was glowing with candlelight, and he was still with her, taking care with the wound on her head as he supported her cough, anxiously noting every little thing she did. A platter of cold food someone had brought up was pushed to the side of the room, ignored.

When her eyes opened he almost did not believe it was true, he had been willing it for so long now. He was imagining it.

But then the silver and black settled on him, the haze of confusion disappearing as she blinked once, then again, and Roland knew this was not the creation of his mind. Kyla was awake.

Curious, the numbness that immediately took over his hands and legs. A new weakness, he supposed, preceding the overwhelming sense of thankfulness that left him swimming for words, fumbling to touch her, to confirm her awareness of him.

She was going to be all right. She had to be.

One of her hands stirred; he found his own clenching it, holding tight to her fingers, looking down in wonderment at their locked hands. He wanted to say her name. He had been saying it for hours now, a sort of chant of late, under his breath, feeding the vague notion in him that somehow if he said it enough she would have to respond. She would have to come back to him.

And so she had.

She was looking at him, really looking at him, and Roland could see she was struggling to say something.

"Relax," he said, leaning over her. "You're going to be fine." Amazing how calm his voice sounded.

She frowned up at him, not so pale as before. Not so pale, her lips now the faintest pink against the whiteness of her skin. She took a deep breath, grimacing only slightly as she slowly released it.

"Starfish," she said. And then, as if the word itself exhausted her, she closed her eyes again.

A woman's hand came down upon Kyla's forehead. It was Marla, slipping into the room unnoticed, now smiling down at him.

"She's better."

"She's feverish. Did you hear what she said?"

"I heard." Marla took a cloth and dipped it in the basin of water by the bed, wringing the excess out. "She's not feverish, my lord, rest assured on that. She has awakened, she has spoken. All will be well now."

Marla took the cloth and, to his surprise, placed it upon his forehead, taking one of his hands and making him hold it there. "You are the one who needs to sleep. You'll do no one any good by falling ill yourself."

"No." He pulled his hand away, letting the cloth drop. "I won't leave her."

Marla shook her head. "I am not suggesting that you leave her. But I am ordering you to rest." She picked up the cloth again and beat it against her hand impatiently. "Stay here beside her. There is room enough for both of you in this monster of a bed. Lie down."

She stood there, stubborn as he knew she could be, tapping her foot.

Rest was not such a bad idea, Roland thought reluctantly. With a sigh he kicked off his boots and carefully laid himself down on the covers beside his wife, taking her hand again.

"Good." Marla slapped the cloth on his forehead. "Duncan is outside the door, standing watch. You needn't worry about anything. If you want me, just call. I am staying in the chamber next to this tonight."

Roland lay back against the pillow, watching Marla with half-closed eyes. The gratitude in him was still alive; he needed to share it with her before she left, she had earned it. "You are a good woman," he said as she was exiting.

Inadequate words, and she merely waved a hand of dismissal without turning around, leaving the door open slightly behind her.

Beside him, Kyla's profile was etched clearly against the flickering shadows on the walls. Was it his imagination, or did she look more peaceful now? Her chest rose and fell with deep, regular breaths, steady. And her lips, were they not a deeper pink than before? More of a sort of rose color now . . . petals . . .

Kyla opened her eyes again, momentarily disoriented.

Roland was beside her, sound asleep, fully clothed. How odd. Why were all the candles still lit? Plainly it was nighttime, what extravagance to waste all those candles for two sleeping people.

The sense of displacement vanished as soon as she moved, however, replaced by a stabbing pain in the back of her head running all the way down her spine.

Roland began to snore.

She remembered the cove. That strange cove with the skeleton ships, the lurid orange of the starfish. The gull, screaming at her.

Or was it her who had screamed? No, she had tried, but nothing more came after that memory. She didn't know what had happened next. How did she end up here? Why did her head hurt so horribly?

Tentatively, she reached up with one arm and felt for the source of the pain but encountered only a great deal of material bound to the back of her head. She was bandaged. She must have an injury of some sort.

She remembered the gull again, bright black eyes, smooth white-and-gray feathers, darting in front of her, she had backed up, that's right, and then . . .

Roland turned to his side in his sleep, threw one heavy arm around her waist before settling down again.

He looked scruffy and ill-kempt. Even with his eyes closed she could make out the dark circles beneath them; the lines in his face seemed deeper.

With great care Kyla began to sit up, sliding under Roland's arm very slowly until she was able to lean back against the headboard of the bed and the room stopped spinning.

The window showed her a moonless night, a field of stars winking with diamond brightness. How long had she been asleep?

A connecting door swung open soundlessly, Marla's head peeked out. Her eyes widened when she saw Kyla sitting up, staring back at her.

Marla approached, looking over at Roland and then placing the back of her hand on Kyla's forehead.

"Headache?" she asked, and then nodded before Kyla could respond. "I'll be right back."

She disappeared behind the door, leaving Kyla to once again contemplate the room, the sky outside, her sleeping husband.

A thin ribbon of melted wax coursed down the side of a candle near the bed, joining a growing pool of droplets on the stone floor.

Roland's hand was a clenched fist in her lap, a frown creased his forehead. He seemed disturbed. Bad dreams, no doubt, and without thought Kyla touched her fingers to his face, tracing the lines until they vanished, leaving his expression peaceful once more. His hand relaxed slowly. She moved her own to cover it, noting the difference in the color of their skin, how much bigger his hand was than hers.

It was a man's hand, toughened and callused, tanned with

a life led outdoors, away from the shadows of domestic life. Her own was actually not much better. The months outside had darkened her skin only slightly, but her nails were still short, useful.

Experimentally she spread her fingers out over his, matching the curve of his palm, interested in how much longer his reach was, how much thicker his wrist. Her head tilted for a better view. What she saw pleased her in some indefinable way, the contrast between them that still suited their symmetry.

Marla was back. She entered the room with uncanny silence, a trait Kyla had noticed in her before. In her hands was a mug of something, coils of steam escaping from the top. She gave the mug to Kyla, who took it gingerly.

"Drink," she said. "It's a tisane of willowbark. It will help with the pain."

The hot liquid was bitter, and she sipped it slowly while Marla looked on, sitting down on the stool by the bed, silent and calm.

The moment stretched on, companionable, both of the women lost in their own thoughts, the candle steadily dripping in languid plops to the floor, Roland lax on the bed. Her left leg was growing numb from the weight of her husband's arm but Kyla didn't move it, preferring to know the feel of him even as he slept.

"Did you see who hit you?"

Marla let the question float out softly into the room, unaccusing, almost serene, and so Kyla just shook her head without surprise.

"No. It happened too quickly." Her voice was scratchy and thin; she cleared her throat lightly before saying again, "No."

"I thought not. From the mark on you, I thought your back would be completely to him."

Or her, Kyla thought, but didn't say.

"What were you doing at Siren's Cove?"

"Siren's Cove? Is that the name of it?"

Marla nodded. "It's said that from a certain angle at a certain distance, the rocks appear to hold the shape of two mermaids. One of them combs her hair, the other beckons you close with her hand." She shrugged. "I've never seen it, but I've heard men bet their lives on those two sirens, always the same, combing and beckoning. Once the ships come close enough, of course, the current takes them in. There is nothing to be done about it."

Kyla thought about that, the black and gold of the rocks, trying to twist them in her mind into the shape of anything even remotely favoring a mermaid. All she remembered was the rough outline of them against a hard blue sky. Nothing resembling either a woman or a fish creature there, real or mythical.

Another memory surfaced, the strange sounds she had heard before at the top of the cliff, the haunting echo of feminine voices. Had that really happened? Probably not. Probably it was either her imagination or her attackers. No reason for those goose bumps to come back, though they had.

"All those ships," said Kyla. "All those people."

"They were mostly pirates, anyway," Marla answered indifferently. "Pirates or smugglers."

The candlelight picked out the silver in Marla's hair and burnished the brown, creating an interesting effect that reminded Kyla, for some reason, of fairy dust. Another silly idea to go with her already fanciful thoughts. Kyla shook her head, then winced at the pain that shot through it.

"I had no intention of going anywhere," she said after a while. "I was simply taking my horse out for a ride. That was where we ended up, that little cove." She took another sip of the tea, wetting her lips. "I saw the tower and dismounted, then I saw the beach and went down the path. There was a ship's hull there, close to shore. Inside it was dark. I saw . . ." She frowned, trying to remember.

"Starfish?" suggested Marla gently.

"Yes. And a bird, a gull. It flew in front of me, I stepped back. And then . . ." She frowned again, squinting into the bottom of the tea, at the swirl of leaves and curled bark.

"And then someone, perhaps more than one someone, hit you on the back of the head," Marla continued matter-offactly. "I would suppose they used one of the old planks littering the beach there, which would mean they had picked it up only moments before. Perhaps they hadn't planned to hit you but the opportunity presented itself. Who knows?"

She locked her hands around one raised knee and leaned back, continuing in that calm voice. "The blow would have knocked you forward into the water, where you floated for not more than a few minutes, I would think. Any longer than that and even I"—she gave a self-deprecating smile—"would not have been able to revive you."

The tea, almost finished, sat in the mug forgotten as Kyla listened. Marla leaned forward and lifted it back up to Kyla's lips before continuing.

"During that time, while you were unconscious in the water, several things could have happened. For some reason your assailant, or assailants, left you alone. Mayhap they thought you were already dead, or were about to be. Or mayhap they heard the watch approaching. He would have been calling out a warning, that is our way. If they heard him, they would have run away in order not to be seen near you.

"The watch had found your mount, you see, and although he didn't know it was yours, he did know there was no reason for any horse but his own to be there. So he came down to the beach, saw you, plucked you from the water and—this is the part that actually saved you—placed you facedown across his horse to bring you back here. That got rid of the water in your lungs." She paused. "Perhaps we should employ this method for the next drowning," she added reflectively.

Kyla said nothing. She was watching Roland's hand again, curved in her lap.

"It was Roland who took you from the watch," Marla continued. "He carried you up here, he tended to you. He fed you and helped me bandage you. He has stayed with you from the moment you were brought back."

"He has?" His forearm was sprinkled with golden hairs, crisp and light against his tan. She blinked down at them; they were growing hazy, blurred in the warm candlelight.

Marla was moving around the room; everywhere she went

a cloak of soft darkness trailed her, absorbing the light. She extinguished the candles one by one, saving the dripping one for last. It had burned down to almost a nub. Deft fingers pinched out the last glow from it, a sizzle followed by a swan song of smoke.

Marla touched her fingers to her lips, then blew on them lightly. "There was henbell in the tea as well, to help you rest. Sleep now, Countess. Sleep well."

She smiled at Kyla in the gathering gloom, then walked out through the connecting door.

Kyla slid back down the headboard until she was flat in the bed once more. She turned onto her side to face Roland, so that the last thing she saw before falling asleep was the strong beauty of his face.

$\mathcal{D}$UNCAN WAS VISIBLY UPSET.

"I don't understand it, my lord," he kept saying, scowling at the horizon of hills and thatched rooftops, a line of fishermen mending nets next to the ruined pier by the castle wall. "I don't understand."

"How many new men?" Roland asked again patiently.

Duncan, who had fought beside him in countless campaigns, an invaluable strategist and armsman, now gnawed at his beard, still staring into the distance, not meeting Roland's gaze.

Roland sighed slightly, more like a sustained exhalation. He didn't wish to push his captain. It was plain to see he was taking the attack on Kyla as a personal affront to his station. He knew as well as Roland that he had been the one to screen the new men in Roland's ranks.

"Two dozen, no more than that. One fellow dropped out in London. Fleming, I think it was. So, two dozen."

"Two dozen men," Roland repeated, turning the number over in his mind. Twenty-four new men added to his army, men picked up here and there from their campaigns for

Henry, men without outstanding prospects from their families, no lands to speak of.

Lorlreau was short of men, it was a sad fact. The main island stood well enough in population—he had ensured that several years ago—but both Taldon and especially Forswall had acres and acres of empty fields with not enough manpower to go around. So when a recruit expressed an interest in staying, Roland had always liked to consider it. He had passed that duty on to his captain as the years had wound on, fully trusting Duncan's decisions.

There was no reason not to trust them still. He needed his captain's cooperation now, not his sticky pride.

"Talk to your lieutenants," Roland said. "Ask them if they've noticed anything odd about the new men. Anything. Be discreet."

Duncan nodded, his green eyes faded and shuttered. The fishermen mended on, repairing the endless holes in their nets, a timeless occupation done with gruff talk, pipes, and a few hours of relaxation under the sun.

It was so normal, exactly what he would expect to see this morning, the bent shapes of the old men hooking and knotting, dark spots against the sparkling water. No intrigue there, he would think. The same old men he had known all his life, friendly faces, nut-brown and seamed with wisdom.

His people, Roland thought, and then felt the hardness in his throat at the thought of a betrayal festering among them. It would not come from his people, it would not. He had two dozen chances to prove that.

Duncan nodded again, looked down at the ground. "How is she?"

"Better. She'll live."

"Quick thinking from the watch. Bright lad. Might go have a talk with him."

Roland already had. "Good luck."

Duncan straightened with a resolute look, then headed off for the soldiers' quarters, his burly form mingling and then disappearing with the usual crowd in the bailey.

The watch was a young man by the name of Lassen, and he was indeed bright. It was one of the reasons he had been chosen as watch, which—although the tower was lonely, although the work grew dull—was seen as one of the most coveted positions in the earldom. Roland had made it very, very clear that he expected the tower watch to be the linchpin in the security of the islands. The tower itself had been built tall enough to see almost three-quarters of all the islands, and most especially the strait. Most especially that.

Lassen had come to the castle without complaint at dawn this morning, summoned by the lord. He had kept his eyes pinned manfully somewhere in the vicinity of Roland's left shoulder throughout almost the entire interview, respectful, thoughtful.

Now that the shock of seeing Kyla unconscious in his arms had faded, Roland recognized him immediately. Younger son of McDermott, a solid man, a horseman with sharp skills in battle. He had his father's look completely, even down to the sunburned bridge of his nose. Roland racked his thoughts for other clues.

"And how is your wife . . . Isabel?" he asked, snatching a name from the mists of his memory.

Lassen relaxed slightly. "Very well, my lord. Asked to send her regards to you and your lady, my lord."

"Yes, well, and thanks to you, I shall be able to do that," replied Roland mildly.

Lassen looked down, reddened with pride or chagrin, Roland couldn't tell. He stood up from behind his father's desk and walked over to the window. "Where was the other watch, the man you were to relieve? Where was Dedrick Farrow?"

The young man cleared his throat but said nothing. Roland waited, unmoving, his back to him. Outside a yellow dog ran across the outer field, two boys right behind him. He heard Lassen shift in his seat.

A group of adolescent girls carrying baskets of something sauntered by, throwing giggles at a cluster of young soldiers pretending not to watch them.

Roland waited.

"I'm sorry, my lord," Lassen burst out.

Roland turned his head slightly. "Oh?"

Again, the uncomfortable silence.

"You do realize the punishment for missing duty, don't you?" Roland asked idly. "Of course you do. And since you were not the one to miss your duty, it need not concern you at this time." He turned around, allowing the full force of his gaze to fall upon the troubled soldier. "But where was the man you were relieving?"

"It wasn't his fault, my lord." Lassen wiped a hand across his brow, then caught himself, snatching the hand back.

Roland let the silence drift free again.

"Dedrick's horse threw a shoe, my lord, and came up lame not two miles from the castle. He had to walk her back, my lord. His horse."

Roland turned back to the window, considering this.

"As soon as he arrived he asked me to cover for him. Found me straight out, and I went. That was all."

"How much time, do you think, did the tower go unguarded?"

"No more than twenty minutes, my lord."

Now Roland turned and looked him in the eye.

"Thirty," Lassen amended, looking down again. "No more than that, I am sure."

He was telling the truth, Roland thought. Thirty minutes. And somehow Kyla managed to slip right through that window of opportunity for someone, slipped right past all his guards and defenses to the most dangerous spot on the island. And she had paid the price for it. Before he was through, someone else would be paying much more dearly.

He had dismissed the watch without reproof, knowing that whatever the young man felt had to be agony enough. And he had, after all, saved the life of his wife. For that Roland was almost willing to promote him.

Careful questioning had revealed nothing of real help. Lassen had arrived at the tower and found a great black stallion wandering free. He had immediately drawn his sword and called out a warning, but heard nothing in response.

Investigation showed him a set of footprints running down the path that led down to the beach. No, he couldn't tell how many. It was windy, and the prints had already blurred together in the fine golden sand.

He had seen the countess immediately, of course, a splash of bright green and yellow from her gown billowing in the waves. He had not seen anyone else. He seemed to recall other footprints in the sand, but then again, he had his attention on the countess by then so he could not be certain. He had been concentrating on attending to her, and Roland could not fault him for this.

Perhaps he would give Lassen a promotion, after all.

Duncan would take care of the other watch, no doubt, after he had talked to Lassen McDermott. He would find out the details of the horse with the lost shoe, the amount of time it had taken Dedrick Farrow to walk her back to the castle, anything else that might be of interest.

So Roland was left with a multitude of unanswered questions, a seething dark suspicion, and a tight, unpleasant band around his chest that seemed to smother his breathing.

Before him now the fishermen nodded and talked, their hands busy, their pipes glowing.

Betrayal. Kyla in danger. And he would do anything to protect her.

$\mathcal{S}$HE WAS SITTING UP in the bed now with the peevish expression of someone who wanted very much to get her own way, and was encountering resistance at every turn.

"I feel fine. I want to walk around."

Marla, measuring sprinkles of something into a cup as she stood beside the bed, tapped her foot. "Later."

"But—"

"Later."

"That's what you said before." Roland smiled at the sulky tone of her voice, then made his face as bland as possible as he came into the room. Kyla frowned at him.

"My lord, I greatly desire to walk about the room. I fail to see what possible harm might befall me. Lest some stone drop down from the ceiling upon my head, or one of your swords on the wall come suddenly flying off to impale me."

"A grave possibility," he allowed as he crossed to her. "I'm afraid I cannot permit you to take such a risk at this time."

Before she could retort he had bent over and brushed her forehead with his lips, causing her eyes to widen and her mouth to snap shut.

"No fever," he noted.

"Plenty of spirit," Marla added wryly. She had finished mixing her mysterious brew and handed it to Kyla, who, Roland supposed, at least knew better than to argue with that. She wrinkled her nose and began to drink.

Roland sat down on the edge of the bed, watching her sip the brew, watching the way the sunlight made her hair almost shimmer with colors, a long fall of darkest red to curl past her shoulders.

When she had finished, Marla took the cup away again and left the room, only the sound of her skirts swishing marking her passing at all. She shut the door.

He had come up here with no real thought except to see Kyla again, to satisfy the underlying anxiety that still lived in him. Now that he was here he seemed to lose his tongue, all he wanted to do was look at her. He thought he could do that forever.

She met his look with a hint of defiance, still smarting from the restriction on her, he knew. After a moment, that melted away—he could see it go, could almost mark the exact second when it turned into something else—and she looked down at the layers of blankets, a troubled curve to her lips.

"I must teach you how to swim," he tried.

She looked up in an instant. "I can swim," she said disdainfully.

He took one of her hands between his. Her fingers were cold.

"Then I must teach you not to let people hit you over the head when your back is turned."

The troubled curve of lips turned into, amazingly, a reluctant smile. He felt something in him dissolve with it. He took a deeper breath than he had been able to before.

"Perhaps you could grant me eyes in the back of my head, my lord," she suggested courteously.

He gave an exaggerated shudder. "I think not. You will give me chills of horror."

She relaxed a little against the pillows. He seemed so quiet now, so thoughtful and considerate, lost in contemplation of their intertwined fingers. She didn't know what to make of him. *As usual,* she thought with a sort of helplessness.

"Don't leave the castle without an escort," he said to their hands.

She thought she hadn't heard him correctly. "Don't leave...?"

"Without an escort."

"That's ridiculous!"

"In fact, I don't want you going off alone anywhere, not even within Lorlmar. There will be someone with you at all times."

Kyla let out a huff of air. "I am not your serf, my lord!"

He looked determined. "No. But you will do as I say."

She tried to snatch her hand back but his fingers tightened, keeping her immobile. He lifted his gaze to meet hers, brilliant blue-green, intent, unyielding. She saw him take in her face, lingering a moment on her lips, then down again.

"I am not jesting, Kyla. You are not to be alone, even within these walls, save our chambers here. If you wish to leave the castle you must come to me first and ask." He spoke over her gasp. "And I will determine if it is feasible."

"You cannot be serious!"

"I think you know me better than that."

"It was," she groped for words, "an accident! Or some strange chance. A stranger, a thief, perhaps."

"There are no strangers on Lorlreau. And this was no accident. No one accidentally picked up a beam of wood and clubbed the Countess of Lorlreau."

It was so obviously true that she had nothing to say, try as she might to think of another plausible excuse.

"We don't know how or why this happened, Kyla. Until this person"—he allowed himself the slightest sneer—"is apprehended, you will follow my orders. Your safety is my responsibility. I needn't remind you of what happened to your mother."

He let that hang vaguely in the air, having no idea what he meant by it but knowing it would affect her.

Emotions slammed through her, she couldn't find the words for them: *No, no, I won't be stifled like this, I won't live in fear like this.*

"You cannot make me," she finally said, her voice flat.

He lifted his brows, amusement and arrogance.

"Yes, I can." As simple as that.

"But what if you never find this person? What then?" Desperation lent her voice a sharper edge than she intended.

"Well, then. I would hope you may grow to like the company you will be keeping."

Roland let go of her hand and stood, once more kissing her forehead before she could react. She sat back, mute, thunderclouds gathering in her eyes. He left before she could put voice to them.

She heard him confer with the guard outside their door—there must have been a guard all along, she hadn't noticed—and then there was silence. She was alone.

Marla's tea was making her sleepy again. She devoutly wished she had not drunk it. There was too much to think about to fall asleep. She wanted to be angry now! She wanted to be resentful!

Roland still controlled her, still exerted his will upon her with effortless ease—a command here, an order there. He was used to it, no doubt; indeed, she could not imagine him without that invisible mantle of power he seemed to carry. He was the overlord of a remote island fortress, and even on the mainland he had an influence with the king that left common people bowing and scraping in fear.

She was not common. She didn't fear him. And he was not her master, no matter what the law or the church or even *he* said.

As the languid haze of sleep crept up on her, though, Kyla had a last thought, one that overrode all the others: Roland wanted to keep her safe. He was concerned for her. There was worry in his look, she was certain of it. Genuine worry. He cared about her, even if it was just a little.

A part of her felt lighter for it.

Chapter Twelve

⬡

HE ARMOIRE TURNED OUT to be much heavier than it looked, so much so that Kyla had to shift it in tiny increments, grunting with the effort, pulling with all her might, taking frequent breaks to let her head stop spinning.

Fortunately, it turned out she didn't need to pull it out far at all in order for the hinges in the wall to spring open, aided by Elysia and Matilda on the other side of the tunnel.

The panel opened not quite smoothly, more with a grinding noise and a shudder from years of disuse. Kyla paused, listening carefully for any sounds of alarm from the guard standing outside the main door.

After four days of confinement to the chambers she was ready to leave. She didn't care where, it didn't matter, she just wanted out. Marla had finally allowed that she was ready to leave her bed—two days after Kyla had been secretly stumbling around the room to practice her normal walk—but Roland had shaken his head, scowling, declaring her unfit yet to leave even the bed. The bed!

It was intolerable. They treated her like a child, a simpleton unfit to see to her own well-being, while she had crossed mountains and rivers on her own, had watched the magnificence of the sunrise over the Highlands in lasting solitude for weeks, had hunted and fished and survived without help from anyone.

Now they thought to hold her down with sheets and furs,

with fine linen nightgowns and long ruffled cuffs, tisanes
swimming with sleeping potions.

And Roland at night, holding her close, holding her gently, as if he feared the slightest move would shatter her like a
glass figurine.

The guard beyond the door was silent, apparently unaware
of the mutiny taking place inside his lord's rooms.

"Are you there, Auntie?" Elysia's voice crept out of the
darkness of the open panel. "Can you fit through?"

Her only visitors had been Marla and some of the children, and once Seena and Harrick. Roland thought it too
early to subject her person to the well-wishes of his people,
even though at this point Kyla would have welcomed a conversation with the devil himself to relieve her boredom.
Elysia had come every day, at least twice a day, and when she
had expressed a wish to come more often Roland had forbidden it, declaring he didn't want his wife tired out from childish antics.

Kyla had a very good idea about who was being childish,
and it certainly wasn't Elysia.

He would come into the room with distraction hovering
around him, his gaze wandering above and below and all
around her, seldom straight to her. He questioned her about
that day at the cove until she threw up her hands in exaspera-
tion: No, she really did not remember anything further. She
had already told him everything she could recall at least thrice
over, and she truly wished he would just leave her alone!

That, of course, was not what she wished at all, but it was
too late to take it back. She watched as he turned away from
her again, frozen silence.

Last night, late, late into the night, as he had held her
in the bed, he had begun to kiss her slowly, with drowsy
warmth, cupping her chin with his fingers, holding her still
for each slumbrous kiss, waking that fire in her that lived for
him. She had turned into him, enraptured by his touch, the
way his leg slid over both of hers, hooking behind her knees
to pull her closer to him.

He was heated and solid, a fragment of a dream made suddenly real for her, that he was kissing her again, that he was leaning over her with mounting intensity, an increasing purpose to the pressure of his mouth against her, his hands skimming her breasts.

She had arched into him, wanting more, knowing now what would come after and wanting even that, the pain through the enchantment. He moved down to take her nipple in his mouth through the cloth of her gown and she had tilted her head back and given a soft cry of pleasure.

And then he had stopped.

As if the sound of her voice had shattered the dream, he had stopped, lifting his head, staring down at her as if he had never seen her before, faintly puzzled. She stared back at him, her breath coming in staccato bursts, unwilling to believe that the moment had ended. But it had.

Roland had shaken his head—an answer to some unspoken question in his own mind, perhaps—then released her, rolling over and onto his side, keeping a civil distance between them.

She was too proud to ask him to continue. And she was too miserable to forget everything she had felt with him. Eventually, after a long night of stifling stillness beside him, she had fallen asleep once more.

It had been this morning that he had ordered in that remote voice that she should not yet attempt to leave the bed, right before he left the room, gone for the day to whatever he pursued out there, in the normal world. If anything on this island could be called normal.

Marla, who was there at the time, merely looked down at Kyla and shrugged.

So, this afternoon when she lay in the bed and stared in frustration for the thousandth or millionth time at the wall across from her, counting seashells, Elysia had come and patted her on the hand and said that Eleanor had told her that Auntie wanted to have an adventure just now. She then whispered an invitation to join her band of outlaws behind the walls of the castle.

And Matilda, on the blind girl's other side, mentioned

quite nonchalantly that the armoire didn't look nearly so big as she had thought before. In her desire to do something—anything!—Kyla had to agree.

Both she and Matilda had been wrong; it took her a good half hour just to shift the armoire the few inches she needed. But now it was done.

"Auntie?" Elysia's voice was thin and spectral, floating out of the blackness.

"Yes," Kyla replied, low. "I'm coming in now."

She gathered her skirts and squeezed behind the wood backing of the wardrobe, realizing that if—when—the next person came into the room it would be the first thing they would notice amiss. Fine. Let them wonder. She wasn't actually running away. In fact, she technically wasn't even going to be by herself; so there, that was at least one of her husband's irrational edicts she would manage to meet.

She made it through the opening in the wall and almost fell on top of her rescuers, both of them standing too close as she popped through.

All three of them collapsed against the farthest wall a few feet away and then burst into smothered giggles.

"Let's go," said Matilda.

The thin flame from a tarnished brazier lit the narrow, crawling path of the tunnel, held aloft by Matilda with practiced ease. Elysia took Kyla's hand.

"I'll guide you," she said.

The stones were cold to the touch, the ones making up the top of the tunnel blackened with years of soot from torches. Yet there were no cobwebs, no dust. Of course not, Kyla realized. The tunnels appeared to be in full use.

In fact, she could almost make out the sound of voices up ahead, adult voices, echoing against the stones.

Elysia and Matilda heard them as well, pausing uncertainly. "Um, this way," said Matilda, taking a sudden turn.

The walls got, if possible, even closer, forcing Kyla to walk with a stoop so as not to hit her head. The smell was damp and musty; beyond the light from the lamp there was infinite darkness. The children seemed completely unafraid, both still smiling, Matilda often turning around and checking to make sure she was still enjoying the adventure.

"Where are we going?" Kyla finally felt forced to ask, after the fifth turnoff into the bowels of the castle.

"To the nursery, of course," Elysia responded. "Almost there."

They still heard voices, but now they were muffled, not echoing; they were coming from beyond the walls. A man and a woman, the woman bursting into laughter; a chorus of women, teasing one another over someone called either Hamish or Hamlet. Men, arguing. They said her name. . . .

"Wait," Kyla whispered, pulling both girls back to the spot where she had heard the men. She placed a finger over her lips for Matilda's sake, indicating silence. Matilda nodded. Elysia was already avidly listening.

". . . cove. You made a mess of things. Impetuous . . ."

Another voice, fainter, carrying a whine all the way through the wall. "He said so! She was alone, I saw my chance . . . the watch was so near! It was just bad timing. . . ."

The other man's voice interrupted, deep with anger or disgust, Kyla couldn't tell. They had moved away from the wall, obviously, their voices growing fainter until they could not be heard at all anymore.

Kyla stood frozen, heart in her throat, trying to quickly sort though her options for the best thing to do. She remembered so clearly the trunk that had been searched, that morning she had been lost in the maze of the keep, the footsteps stalking her, the menace she had felt. The faceless enemy who had struck her from behind. Well, now she had found a voice—two. What she needed were the faces.

Matilda was staring up at her. Elysia was touching the tunnel wall, running her hands over it until she found the stone that moved. Belatedly, Kyla realized what she was doing.

"No," she hissed, but the door was already sliding open. This one made no noise.

She pushed both girls back into the tunnel, away from the

bright slice of daylight that now scored down the back wall. There was no sound from the room. She bent down, pulled both of their heads close to hers.

"I want you both to stay here, do you understand me? Promise me you will stay here in the tunnel."

Matilda, reacting to the authority in her voice, nodded wordlessly. Elysia looked past her, seeing her own darkness.

"Did you bring your dagger, Auntie?"

No, she had not. It was wrapped in cloth, stuck beneath the ticking of the pallet on the bed back in her chambers, useless.

"Don't worry," Elysia said now, as if she could read her thoughts. "You won't need it just yet. We'll wait here for you."

Kyla let out her breath, frowning down at them. "I'll be back soon."

Before she could lose her nerve she stood up and turned her face into the light, squinting until the glare became normal to her and she could make out the outlines of thick wooden furniture in the room, a round table with high-backed chairs, a small table next to the wall, a fireplace with ashes in it. The daylight was coming from a pair of high windows facing her.

The room was empty. Kyla slipped past the opening in the wall—a silk panel, her mind registered, a leaf-green silk with a lighter green pattern banked against the stones—and into the room, looking around once more to confirm she was the only one there. She was. In fact, there was no sign of anyone else having been there at all. Nothing looked out of place. No empty cups on the tables, just a chessboard left out, ready for a match. Even the ashes in the fireplace looked pristine, a perfect pile of feathery flakes.

Of course, if these men were meeting clandestinely, they would not leave any traces of their presence. And she would think that the men who were trying to kill her would wish to be clandestine.

The thought was so strange, so alien, that as soon as it came to her she pushed it away. It was too complicated, too bizarre to think about right now.

The hair on the back of her neck stood up; cautiously she walked farther into the room, toward the only door leading out. It was still ajar. Her fingers itched for the dagger she should have been carrying. Why had she left it behind now? When she had had it with her for years, it seemed, so naturally did it fit into her hand. Cursing her own stupidity wouldn't help now. She picked up a marble chess piece from the game displayed on the round table: the queen, the heaviest piece there, about the size of her hand.

A paltry defense, and she knew it. Better than nothing, however. It felt thick and solid in her palm. Her fingers wrapped around it, settling into the carved grooves of the marble gown, the waist, the neck.

No voices now. The door tempted her, invited her out into the hallway. Perhaps it would show her the way to go. She felt strange, almost out of her own body, as if she were watching herself cross the room and press against the wall, waiting, watching. Still listening.

What was that? She heard it again, the whining voice, it carried farther. Down the hall. Kyla narrowed her eyes and leaned her head out the door. Gloom, typical of a windowless inner hallway. Faint light ahead of her, perhaps a main room connected up there. Shifting shadows—

There they were, two men walking away from her, the other one speaking now. She recognized the deeper voice, although the words were indistinguishable.

The marble queen slipped a little in her hand. Her palms were moist. She transferred it to her other hand and then rubbed her palm on her gown before grasping it again, edging out the door into the hallway.

Up ahead the two men marched on, matched in height, but both were shadows to her, blots against the light they were walking into.

It would not do. She had to at least get a good look at them. Dear God, if she were to see them again tomorrow, tonight, she had to be able to recognize them.

Her skirts were almost no hindrance as she ran lightly down the corridor. She had deliberately chosen a gown of thin wool, lightweight for easier mobility; she had thought it would be best for exploring the tunnels. But she had not imagined she would be chasing a duo of men who wanted her dead.

Why? What had she done to deserve death? From the moment she had arrived on the island she had been threatened. Her clothing had been searched, she had been followed down halls when she was alone and struck on the head from behind, a coward's act. All along they had been waiting, obviously, for the right moment to kill her.

They walked ahead of her, oblivious, and she followed with a rising sense of anger—her old ally coming back, filling her with stealth and cunning. Who were these men who would arbitrarily seek to harm her, when all she had ever done was try to avoid conflict, to protect her family, to enact justice for outrageous wrongs?

They had reached the end of the passage and turned left, into the light. She had a brief glimpse of them then, one with black hair, the other brown. She couldn't make out their faces.

As silently as she could Kyla ran the rest of the way down the hallway, lifting her skirts up to go more quickly. When she reached the end she stopped, flattening herself against the wall to peer around the corner.

What she had thought was a room was actually just another hallway, an entrance to the bailey, where the light spilled from. There were people everywhere, of all heights, all colors of hair, all of them on their way to some business or another.

She turned the corner completely and leaned against the wall in disappointment, scanning the crowd, looking in vain for any sign of the two men.

They could have been anyone, there was no way to pick them out. They were most likely gone already.

Kyla closed her eyes and tightened her grip on the chess queen, willing the anger to go. It would not serve her now.

She had to get back to the girls. When she opened her eyes again she saw that she had already attracted notice. People were beginning to stare at her. She supposed she looked completely odd, the countess with her hair wild and her face flushed, no doubt, holding on to the chess queen.

Abruptly she turned around and went back down the hall before the pitying looks she had received turned into solicitations for helping her back to her rooms.

The hall seemed much longer now, with closed doors she hadn't really noticed before, and for a moment she grew confused—which one had she come from? Had she passed it already?

No. Clearly not. Because now she heard a voice that sent shivers down her back and brought forth a throbbing headache she thought she had forgotten.

"When?" Roland was demanding, his stern tone coming from the room just to her left. "How long ago did she leave?"

"She's coming right back." That was Elysia, sounding confident. "She just went to chase the bad men."

Kyla actually hesitated just outside the doorway, actually thought about turning around and going out to the bailey, after all, just to get away. She didn't want to face Roland right now, not in this mood. But then she heard a forlorn sort of sniff, and a tiny choked sob. Matilda, of course.

"I'll see to her, my lord." Another man's voice. Duncan, she would guess. "I've got men all over. We'll have her back in no time."

"No need, as you can see. I am already back." Kyla fought to maintain the coolness of her voice as she stepped into the room with the green-silk paneling. Some cowardice made her linger by the doorway. "Pray do not torment the children any longer, my lord. They are not at fault here."

Roland straightened slowly from where he had been on one knee on the floor, holding the hands of both girls. He had the look of being rusted into place, jerking up in controlled bits of motion before turning to take her in. His face was a mask, she couldn't read whether he was angry or relieved to see her. Only his eyes seemed alive, vivid in color, an icy blast to her soul.

Kyla took an involuntary step back.

"I told you so," said Elysia calmly.

"Yes, you did," Roland replied. Nothing in his voice reflected that look. But Kyla was not fooled. She realized she was still holding the marble queen and tucked it into the folds of her skirts.

Duncan, standing next to the paneling, cleared his throat.

"Take them back to the nursery," Roland instructed, without looking away from Kyla. Duncan moved to obey, gathering both children and leading them away into the tunnel.

She didn't know what to do, she didn't know what to expect. There was a heated sting to her eyes, she had to blink and look down to clear it. *Fear is doing this,* she thought. *I am afraid.*

As soon as the words formed in her mind she straightened her spine, made herself look up squarely into the gaze of her husband. The fear was irrational, based on nameless dark things her imagination dredged up. Fear was her enemy, and she would not succumb.

Roland dropped his look at last, moving over to the table with the chess game laid out, tapping one finger on the king with the missing queen. She followed the move with unwilling fascination, watching the way his fingers skimmed the rows of stone figures, pawns and knights and bishops and rooks. And then back to the king, to the glaringly empty black square where his queen should be.

Roland looked up. "Game?" he asked.

"I beg your pardon?"

He took one of the seats around the table. "Will you have a game with me?"

He seemed perfectly serious. She approached him slowly, half thinking him or herself mad. He waited, indicating the chair opposite his. His expression now was one of only remote courtesy.

She sank into the chair, keeping far back from the table.

"Black or white?" he asked politely.

She looked blank.

"I suppose you should be black, since it is already on your side." He straightened the board between them, finely fitted tiles of soft onyx and pearl-white, exquisite, heavy figures lined up neatly on its surface. He tapped his finger once more on the empty square.

"I'll need my queen," he said.

She realized he knew she still clutched it, half-forgotten. Kyla looked down at it now, the perfect marble features, and then handed it across the board to him.

"Thank you."

"You're welcome." Her voice wobbled just a little.

He put the queen back in place, then moved a pawn forward.

"Not much of a weapon, my lady."

She realized he was talking about the queen, noted the complete lack of accusation in his voice. It gave her the courage to look at his face.

He was studying her, still remote, as if he had found an interesting and slightly strange new species of animal suddenly sitting across from him, playing chess. Kyla sat up taller.

"It was all I could find on short notice." The wobble was gone.

"Of course."

She stared at him still, trying to decipher whatever hidden meaning she could find in his mild comment, his veiled demeanor. He raised his eyebrows.

"Your move, my lady."

She moved a pawn to match his. He considered it, rubbing his chin. The light from the windows in the room highlighted the slant of his brows, the devilish handsomeness of him. His fingers, long and elegant, toyed with a bishop.

"I suppose you are feeling well enough, after all, to get out of bed." There was a slight, dry twist to his lips.

"I suppose so."

"I am glad."

She looked up at him suspiciously but could detect nothing but truth behind his words. He released the bishop and advanced the same pawn as before.

She hardly knew what to think. She had been expecting anger, perhaps even fury, at having his orders disobeyed. The

look he had first given her as she entered the room had done
nothing but confirm that fear. But now he was calm, a different person entirely from that man who had scorched her with
his eyes, who had made her want to run and hide.

"Your move again, my lady."

She moved another pawn, then looked up to find him
staring at her once more. She tried not to look away but then
felt completely foolish to be caught in some contest of wills.
Instead she glanced down at her lap, marshaling her thoughts.

"I am impressed"—Roland leaned back in his chair—"at
your resourcefulness. The armoire was chosen specifically for
its weight."

She plucked at the hem of her sleeve.

"I ought to have that damned thing bolted to the ground,"
Roland continued pleasantly. "But I simply never had the will
to shut the tunnel access forever. I thought perhaps one day it
might come in handy. I suppose for you, it did."

Her sleeve had embroidered leaves on it. Ivy, she thought.

Roland picked up his knight and shoved it across the
board, knocking over two pawns, startling her with his sudden force. One of the pawns—a small marble peasant with a
scythe—spun in a lazy circle, caught between two squares.
Roland was contemplating his own hand, still on the knight,
dark and inscrutable.

"I had some"—she could see him search for the right
words—"*concerns* when I entered our chambers and found
you missing."

His fingers were whitening around the knight from the
strength of his grip. Kyla swallowed nervously.

"All for naught," she said.

"Really?" The pawn stopped spinning, leaving it slanted
across the board, head to her, the white tip of the scythe
pointing up to the air. "Was it indeed all for naught, Kyla?
This afternoon not only do I find that my wife has deliberately disobeyed me, but also that she has dragged two children
into a very dangerous game. My wife, who, as you know,"—
he gave her a feral smile now, and she saw again that blazing
cold in him unveiled—"has recently suffered a severe blow to

her head. She might not be thinking clearly. She might have gotten lost in the labyrinth of tunnels. Some of them go all the way down to the ocean, down to the caves under the castle, did you know that?"

"No, I—"

"Of course not. Or perhaps my wife hadn't gone off on her own, after all. Perhaps she was taken. Perhaps the man who hit her before had come to finish the job. Perhaps he had found the tunnel and pushed open the door, heavy as the wardrobe was. Perhaps he had killed her while she was sleeping and hidden her body behind the walls."

She sat up in the chair, shaking her head in denial, eyes wide. "You don't understand—"

The knight shattered into pieces behind her, an explosion so unexpected that she cried out, then covered her mouth with her hand. It took her a moment to realize that it had shattered because he had thrown it, hard against the wall behind her.

He was staring down at his hand. It was trembling slightly. He blinked down at it, as if it had done something astonishing all on its own.

Kyla had shrunk back into the chair, hand still over her mouth. Roland looked up at her slowly. "You don't know what it's like," he said. His words were thick and slurred, as if he were talking through a mouth full of wool.

She shook her head at him. Her hair fell down around her eyes.

"You don't know," he repeated in that strange voice. "The blackness. It's empty."

She was caught in a peculiar world—part of her was terrified of him, part of her wanted to comfort him. What was he talking about?

Roland paused, bending over at the waist as if in pain, hiding his face from her. But as quickly as the moment came it was gone; he seemed to come out of his trance, standing up, walking briskly to the panel that was still open in the wall.

"Come," he said in his normal voice. Another command. He held out his hand.

Kyla made her decision. "I will not stay trapped in that room any longer." She folded her arms over her chest, hoping she looked more certain than she felt. "It is plain to see that I am not ill. I have not gotten lost in tunnels, nor killed by . . . by anyone!"

He waited, saying nothing, leaving her to feel slightly silly at her own stand. But she had come this far, she wasn't going to give up yet. "I saw them, Roland. I saw the men. There are two of them."

"You saw their faces?" She felt his attention hone in on her with sharp speed, pinning her in place.

"No, not that," she admitted. "But I did see them from a distance. I saw them walking. I know their height, I know their size, their hair color. I know their voices."

"I see." Roland took a few steps toward her, leaning his arms over the back of the chair facing her. "And what do you propose to do about it?"

"When I come down to sup I will have an opportunity to look for them again. Everyone will be there for the evening meal, isn't that right?"

"Everyone but you," he said, unsmiling.

Something in her, that last bit of willpower to maintain her dignity, splintered apart.

"I am coming down for supper or you will have to tie me up to keep me away," she snapped.

"Don't tempt me!"

She stood up, pushing the chair out of her way. "You can't stop me!"

"You have no idea what I can do," he said coldly, towering over her. "As a matter of fact, I can stop you. I can do anything to you that I want."

"Why?" she burst out. "Why are you doing this? Why are you so—" Before more words could come tumbling out—or worse, the tears clogging her throat—she clapped her hand over her mouth again, appalled at herself, at her loss of control.

Roland watched her, unmoving, then bowed his head and rubbed at his eyes. "Why indeed?" he muttered to himself, sardonic.

She deliberately pulled her hand down, controlling the tears, clenching her teeth together.

"All right, you win," he said, sounding weary. "Come to dinner with me. Why not? Let the whole world take aim at you."

Kyla shook her hair out of her eyes. "Don't worry. I'll be taking my own aim first."

"Wonderful," he replied, but his tone said *catastrophe*.

⸺⸺⸺⸺⸺

*T*HE COOK, NOT ANTICIPATING the arrival of the countess at the dinner table, had nevertheless scrambled to serve something special to please her.

"Gruel." Kyla lifted her spoon up to let the thin, gray liquid dribble back down into the bowl. "How thoughtful."

"Your delicate appetite, you know." Marla took a hefty bite of the roasted chicken seasoned with thyme and rosemary, then actually smiled at Kyla's envious look. "If you don't eat it, Cook will be so disappointed."

On the other side of her, Elysia tugged at Kyla's sleeve. When Kyla looked down, the child casually rested her hand on the top of a mastiff's head. The animal was drooling happily under the table between the two of them.

Kyla looked around from under her lashes. Marla was talking to Harrick. Roland had gone to Duncan's table, where he was leaning over and talking. His back was to her.

Without looking away Kyla took the bowl and lowered it under the table, holding it steady for the dog. Thank goodness the head table was not on a dais.

She placed the now-empty bowl back up on the edge of the table.

"More chicken, please," said Elysia brightly.

The great hall was as crowded as Kyla remembered, people gathered together on the long benches, loud conversations, laughter. So many people. How was she ever to find the men she sought?

Roland finished talking and turned around to seek her

out. She met his look just as a platter of chicken was set before her. She shook her head slightly to indicate she had not
yet spotted the men. He turned away again.

She, apparently, was not the only one looking. Careful ex-
amination revealed two or three soldiers near all three of the
entrances to the room, all standing around while they ate or
drank, talking, laughing just like everyone else. Yet she noticed how they covertly scanned the room as she did, how
they periodically looked to Duncan or Roland, and then to
the other men on the other sides of the room.

There were so many men with black hair, even more with
brown. Since almost everyone was seated it was impossible to
tell anything from height. And the din of voices drowned out
any individual sounds save those very close at hand, such as
Harrick leaning around Marla to offer Kyla a serving of stew.

She took it with an absent smile, her eye suddenly on one
particular man—not a soldier, from the dress of him; a farmer,
perhaps. Rough tunic, nothing unusual about him, except that
the way he turned to speak to a woman beside him sparked some
recognition. It was so uncertain. His features were plain, his hair
was black, true, but so was the hair of each of the four men next
to him. She might have met him when she first arrived, she
wasn't sure. But something about the way he moved . . .

No. Impossible to tell. She could hardly condemn a man
for the way he shrugged his shoulders, an awkward sort of
heave beneath the tunic. If only she could listen to his voice.

She had half risen from her seat with the unformed notion
of strolling over there when a commotion erupted near the
far entrance, the soldiers there abandoning their pretense of
jocularity to surround the person who was trying to come in.

After a moment they let him pass. He went straight to
Roland and gave a deep bow.

Naturally Kyla didn't know him. But he was dressed
warmly for the weather, his tunic and hose spotted and
stained with what might have been water, perhaps from the
splashings of a boat.

Marla put a restraining arm on Kyla, pushing her gently
back into her seat, mistaking her reason for rising. "No need

for alarm. It's John Campbell, one of the lieutenants. He must have news from the mainland."

Roland and the lieutenant were joined by Duncan, and then the three of them walked out of the room.

Marla put a hunk of bread on Kyla's plate; the chicken and the stew were already gone. "Interesting," she said. "I wonder what has happened."

Harrick smiled. "No doubt you will find out one way or another soon enough."

"No doubt," Marla agreed.

Elysia bent her head over her plate, unusually without comment, Kyla thought. She felt a tingle of alarm creep through her.

All three men reentered the room and split in different directions, Duncan going back to his table, the lieutenant joining another group of young men. Roland headed purposefully for the main table. The volume of noise dimmed for a brief moment, then swelled anew.

"What news, my lord?" asked Marla, all poise and steadiness, after he had taken his seat.

Roland took Kyla's hand, reserved but with that glimmer of concern she had come to recognize in him. The alarm curling in her chest grew stronger.

"What news?" She echoed Marla's words.

"My man has just come from London. There have not been any significant revelations in the case of your mother." He looked away, lost in thought. "But something of some importance did happen, something I think you would wish to know. It seems Lady Elisabeth de Corbeau has taken her life, my dear."

Kyla stared at him, the words spinning around her. Lady Elisabeth? Dead, by her own hand? She found herself shaking her head.

"It's true." Roland frowned across the expanse of the hall. "A few days ago. She seemed somewhat despondent before, I am told."

Kyla flashed on the image of Lady Elisabeth, congratulating her on her marriage, smiling with polished grace in the face of the unusual circumstances. Lady Elisabeth, sending over an entire wardrobe of gowns for her when she realized she had none. Lady Elisabeth, with the kind eyes and the concerned questions, her mother's dear, dear friend.

It was a strange kind of a shock, losing someone who actually had not been all that well known to her. To Kyla she had been more of a living extension of the life Helaine had led, another person who had known her mother and loved her. Now another person gone from this world.

"Took her life." Marla repeated the words sadly.

"No." Elysia spoke for the first time, drawing the attention of all of them. "What the lady took was her peace."

And then she bent her head down again and continued eating.

Another baffling riddle from this fey child, one that no doubt made sense on some obscure level—Kyla was learning that all of Elysia's comments had some hidden truth to them, no matter how innocently presented—but this time she didn't know what to make of it, and knew better than to ask. Elysia would only widen her eyes and smile, or shrug, or turn away. Kyla couldn't focus right now on anything but the awful fact of it. Lady Elisabeth, dead.

The meal was ending, and by the time she had gathered herself enough to recollect the man with the black hair, half the hall was empty, everyone else milling around, servants cleaning up.

Harrick had left, Marla had taken Elysia back to the nursery with the other children.

Roland, of course, had stayed with her, no longer eating but slowly drinking his wine, silent in the ornate chair next to hers, staring out at nothing she could see.

She didn't wish to go back to her rooms yet. It might have been that this was her first taste of freedom in almost a week and she was loath to give it up so readily. It might have been she felt a little too shaken still to spend the rest of her evening alone in quiet contemplation.

It could have just been, surprisingly enough, that she wanted particular company right now. That she wanted to be with Roland.

Yet her goblet was empty; her plate was already gone. She debated whether to interrupt Roland's thoughts with her discovery of the man who might or might not have been part of the duo they were looking for, but before she could, Roland slanted a look toward her.

"Care to see the stars?"

She did, very much.

He took her out of the great room to one of the many side rooms lining the main hallway. This one looked much like the rest, with a bit more decoration—a large, square-paned window with fragmented reflections of the two of them against the twilight; tall tapestries with tiny stitched people and long fringes; a checkered, tiled floor of granite, she would guess, white and blue-gray, immaculate.

Roland went to the fireplace and pushed a booted foot against a particularly vicious-looking black-iron dragon on the grate.

A section of the checkered floor opened up, magic in the dusk, revealing a set of stairs descending to blackness.

He smiled at her look. "One of my ancestors had a penchant for backup systems, apparently."

The stairs were steep and narrow, she had to place each foot carefully for fear of a misstep leading her to fall into her husband, below her. When they had both reached a sort of plateau he stopped, turning to aid her down the last few steps, then pushed a knob on the wall beside them.

The opening above slid shut on ancient runners, plunging them into complete darkness.

Roland moved, she sensed him somewhere lower than she was, perhaps kneeling. There was a scraping noise, then the sharp sound of stone hitting stone. It came again, this time with a small spark that showed him for an instant, an arrested image against the blackness: hair loose, a look of intense concentration directed at the ground. The spark came again and this time caught, creating a small flame that grew as it fed off the oil in the brazier at his feet.

"You wished to see the tunnels," he said.

He put the flint away in the small crevice in the wall

where, she assumed, he had found it along with the lamp, giving her a conspiratorial smile. "Follow me, Countess."

The weak light from the lamp showed her only more steps leading down.

"I thought we were going to look at the stars." A feeble protest.

"We are."

With that cryptic comment he moved on, leaving her to follow.

Although the walls became a little higher, the stairs remained as narrow, causing her to almost take them in half-steps, her skirts held up immodestly high, one hand on the wall for balance. Occasionally Roland would look back at her, still with that mischievous look, another aspect to the man she had married. Another completely different side to him.

It was becoming decidedly cooler now as they went lower and lower, the rush of salty air on her arms and face. Finally the descent became more normal but she found that by then her legs were growing tired from the strain. When the stairs ended at a level, stretching corridor she was silently thankful.

There was a moistness that clung to the stones, that tightened her hair into those unavoidable curls about her face, even when it was put up and away, as it was now. She was listening to the sounds before she realized what she was hearing: the boom of the surf, crashing to shore.

Faint purple light ahead indicated the end of their journey. Roland became an outline against it, warm yellow glow against the coolness of night.

When the end came she was still unprepared for it. One moment they were surrounded by the rough stone cavern that the tunnel had turned into, the next they were at the mouth of a cave, looking out into the liquid silver ocean, the vast blue night.

She joined him as he pulled her closer, both of them stepping onto the smooth-packed sand of the beach. Roland tilted his head up to the sky and she followed suit. An endless stretch of stars, pinpoints of shimmering light, a milky band striping the middle of the sky, all of it dissolving and blending into the edge of the sea before them.

The breeze was surprisingly pleasant, not too cool, a welcome complement to the water, the night.

It came to her that out there on that sheltered beach they could have been anyone, anywhere, not two people joined together under the most tenuous of circumstances, not two people who seemed to be always at odds with each other despite their best intentions.

They might be happily married, for example, Kyla thought. They might be an ordinary couple, a farmer and his wife, who married for love and were sharing their hardships together. They might be anyone. . . .

But looking at his face, the hard, clean lines of his features, the purity of the honey hair, the mystery in his eyes, she knew this was a fantasy that she could never sustain. He would always and only be Roland, Earl of Lorlreau. Who she was, however, was more of a quandary.

Was she Kyla of Rosemead, sworn enemy of the Hound of Hell? Was she the woman who had vowed to hunt down her nemesis and make him suffer for the pain he had brought her?

Or was she really the Countess of Lorlreau now, his wife, the woman consigned to support him, to be obedient to him, and perhaps, someday, to care for him beyond a mere ordinary feeling, to reach that plane that she almost didn't dare to name.

Was she supposed to love him?

The stars had no answers for her right now. It seemed to Kyla that she remained a painful blend of these two women, caught between two worlds that could not agree. It was a hardship, one that she suddenly grew tired of, here on the water-smoothed beach, watching the lip of the ocean come again and again to shore in sugar-white waves.

So that when he carefully set the brazier down in the sand and reached for her she didn't resist. She didn't think about her conflict, she didn't want to hear the two sides of her heart argue her fate.

When he cupped both hands to her cheeks she faded into him; when he scorched her with his kiss she reveled in it, she returned it to him ten times over. When he moaned and let his hands slide down her body, her breasts, her stomach, her bottom, her thighs, she held on to him, let him guide her, allowed him whatever he wanted, because that meant that she wanted it, too.

Somehow it didn't matter that the sand was cool against her skin, it only heightened the sensation of him touching her. It was a potent contrast to his hands, his body pressing her down into the softness of it. They were both lying down; she didn't remember it happening, it seemed as natural as the moment itself, inevitable that he would be on top of her, that her gown would come loose, that his tunic was off, he was bare-chested against her. It felt strange and wonderful at once, the hard planes of him rubbing against her breasts, her stomach.

He was all muscles and masculine scent, warm and pleasing in every way, supple and strong above her. His mouth was stroking her, his hands were exploring her, and she was wild for his touch, she was holding him closer, knowing that despite everything he would always have the power to make her feel like this—make her care about nothing except his touch.

She knew where they were going and braced herself for the pain of his entry, but to her surprise there was none, only a faint, stinging stretch as he slid into her, his expression closed in concentration, eyes shut.

He was immobile for longer than she could count, both of them breathing hard, both of them lost in the completion of the movement. After a long, long while he began to move, slowly at first, a rhythm that came back to her as if she had always known it, building heat and something else, something she had no name for. . . .

He whispered her name into her ear, a blended pulse with the ocean's ballad. She turned her head to his, their lips met and clung, her hands found his shoulders and held on, she was going somewhere else, he was taking her to a place she hadn't thought of, could not have dreamed of.

There was an almost-pleasure wrapped around her, blooming from the joining with him, spreading to every inch of her, an urgency. She was reaching for it, she wanted more and more and more of him and he knew it, he was showing her how to find it.

The explosion was a sudden starburst that shimmered and fell in long, glinting trails of light, streaking through her, leaving her gasping.

He said her name again and shuddered above her, finding his own release, tucking his face into her neck, holding her tight.

Kyla, my love . . .

And then they really were just another couple out in the apex of the night, discovering the cadence of life that had always existed around them, simply another small part of the greatness of the universe.

Chapter Thirteen

─────────── ତ୍ୱୠୠ୭ ───────────

*T*HE HERB GARDEN was already showing every indication of a healthy summer, with tender new plants reaching for the sun everywhere Kyla looked: in patterned beds, around wooden stakes and terraces, even creeping down in graceful fronds from special pockets of dirt in the garden wall.

Cook had appeared extremely pleased with herself as she had opened the waist-high gate to allow Kyla into the enclosure. The gate, it was explained, was to keep the deer out.

Kyla had not really desired a guided tour but felt obliged to at least meet the woman who kept sending her gruel for every meal, to attempt to explain as diplomatically as possible that she now felt ready for something a little heartier. She really couldn't find that many dogs who would eat gruel.

Cook—who, unlike what Kyla had been expecting, was not at all jolly or plump, but rather a tall, thin woman with a serious mien—had listened gravely to Kyla's request as they sat across from each other beside a chopping block. Then she scowled.

"Did Marla approve this?"

"Yes," Kyla lied. It wasn't really a lie, since Marla had not exactly disapproved of it, either.

"Well, then," said Cook.

That had left the two of them to look at each other, both itching to escape the other's company but with no polite way to do so. In the background a flurry of women moved back and forth, stirring kettles, kneading dough, dicing vegetables and meat. One of the women called out for a pinch of basil, allowing Cook to gratefully leap to her feet.

"Seen our garden, milady?"

And since she had not, Kyla was seeing it now. Cook had gathered her leaves of sweet basil, curtsied, and then rushed off. She reminded Kyla to shut the gate behind her when she left.

Kyla walked past the dark, curled leaves of the basil nodding in the breeze, past chamomile and thyme and rosemary, mint and mugwort, yellow bedstraw and a small bush of bayberry. The garden was crowded but not too much so, filled with plants and trees that Kyla mostly had no names for. The sky became a blue thread knitted through the leaves and branches above her as she walked deeper into the grove. She stopped beneath an arbor supporting a vine with white flowers. There was a stone bench there, a perfect hideaway.

She sat and rested, inhaling the scent of spices and new growth, closing her eyes, leaning back on her hands in the secret alcove. This was the first time in days, it seemed, that she had been alone at Lorlmar. No matter where she went she had a shadow, a soldier or a maid, all of them apologetically deferential as they dogged her steps. She had given up trying to fight it, but this morning the soldier with her had some urgent something to attend to, and Kyla had said she would wait for the maid to come.

She *had* waited, in fact. She had waited a good three minutes, enough time for her to be certain the soldier would be out of sight of her door, before leaving for the kitchens to have a word with Cook.

How delightful to find herself here, amid solitary peace again, surrounded only by plants and birds. Kyla leaned back farther, resting against the leafy green behind her, stretching out her legs.

Roland was avoiding her again.

It was astonishing, the swings of his moods, how he could be loving and tender one moment and a caustic stranger the next. For the past week or so she had been trying to convince herself that this truth lived mostly in her mind, that he was merely very busy, or tired, or distracted by his duties. And although all those things were most likely true, as well, they were not at the heart of her perception.

She barely saw him at all, except during the morning and evening meals, and sometimes not even then. The only thing she could count on was that he would eventually come to her at night, share the bed with her, and—twice now—make love to her again. Passionate, forceful lovemaking, laying waste to all of her defenses, making her crave him more and more as time wound on.

Kyla didn't want to care about any of it. She didn't want to nurse hurt feelings over the fact that her husband seemed to care more for fields and fishing than he did for her. She didn't want to wake up each morning feeling disappointed that he had already gone, knowing it would be another long day without him. She didn't want any of it! What she did want was to harden her heart until nothing could penetrate it, not his turquoise looks, not his charming smiles, not his hands on her body, mastering her, showing her how sweet it could be between them.

Why wasn't it working?

She sighed, kicking her feet through the small pebbled stones that made up the garden path. A red squirrel darted up a tree in front of the arbor and began to scold her.

A small sound came then from off to her left, a voice? Kyla sat up, suddenly alert, and it was there again: a wisp of song carried over the green tops of the herbs, a child's voice.

She found Elysia alone in the middle of the path, just past an old well caked with ivy. The child sat in the shade, a princess presiding over a court of dolls, all of them arranged with apparent care in front of her.

"Hullo, Auntie," she said without turning around. "Will you play with me?"

"Are you here by yourself?" Kyla was surprised.

"Oh, yes," Elysia replied. "I come here all the time. It's quite nice, isn't it?"

It seemed the squirrel had followed her; it leapt from

branch to branch until it was just above her again, still muttering.

Kyla sat down gingerly on the small stones, settling her skirts until she could sit cross-legged, as Elysia did, in the dappled shade. Elysia smiled, looking through her, and picked up the doll nearest her.

"I have a story. Would you like to hear it?"

"Of course," Kyla said.

The doll was cloth, with tiny sewn features, a flat nose, a rosebud mouth. It had long yellow yarn for hair, fraying at the ends. Elysia picked up another with her other hand, this one carved from wood, with a cleverly painted face and a gown of pink.

"There once was a queen," Elysia began. "She was good and kind. Everyone loved her."

This, apparently, was the yellow-haired doll, which bowed to Kyla.

"The queen loved everyone, too. Even the king would tell her not to love so much, not to trust so much."

Kyla felt her breathing begin to slow, the shade grew cooler. Elysia's hand moved, making the doll's head shake back and forth, just once, almost coy.

"But the queen didn't listen. She believed everyone was good like her. She thought the king was mistaken."

The painted doll moved over to the cloth one, dipping down in a parody of a curtsy until the wooden joints clacked against the gravel.

"Dear Queen!" Elysia's voice grew high. "You may trust me!"

The cloth doll pressed against the wooden one, an embrace.

"I know!" The voice lowered slightly. "I know, dear friend!"

The tips of Kyla's fingers were tingling, her toes were cold and numb. She found herself unable to look away from the scene played out before her, the small hands manipulating the dolls, their awkward movements. There was something almost grotesque about the way they looked to her right now, not quite human, a mockery. The queen's sewn eyes even had little black eyelashes spiking outward.

Elysia discarded the cloth doll, laying her down, picking up a new toy now, some sort of knight or soldier.

"Oh, no," said the wooden doll, seeing the soldier. "Oh, no, oh no oh no oh no."

"Quiet!" growled the soldier. "Do as I say!"

"No," cried the wood doll. "No, I can't! I won't!"

"Do as I say and they won't have to die." The soldier pushed against the wood doll, chest-to-chest.

"Noooo," moaned the wood doll, but it was too late. She was thrown to the side and the soldier slammed against the reposing queen, coming down on her again and again, making the yarn hair fly in all directions against the gravel, the rosebud mouth unchanged.

Kyla watched in horror, breathing through her mouth, wanting to shout *Stop it! Stop!* but unable to say anything at all, only watch as the soldier pummeled the queen, kicked her over and over until she skidded across the path and came up against a leafy fern.

The soldier was done, limp in the childish grasp now, folded over. Kyla slowly looked at Elysia again, white-faced. Elysia looked back at her, right into her eyes this time.

"Betrayal," the girl said in her normal voice. "Betrayal and death. That's what happened to the queen."

Helaine's crypt, a shrouded body on a slab of marble, not her mother, oh, surely not, the frail shell of a woman lying there, her beloved face almost normal, almost asleep, surely not dead—

"Betrayal," said Elysia, the shifting sunlight making the blue of her eyes bright for once.

She was worried that her mother couldn't breathe past the shroud, fine as it was. She was going to smother. But of course she couldn't breathe, because she was dead, dead, dead—

"Death," said the child.

Conner's hands, the last thing to disappear beneath the earth in the shallow grave she had scratched out for him, covering him with fistfuls of dirt. Alister silently weeping, her nails black from scraping at the hard winter mud of the ground. Conner's hands folded across his chest, speckled with the dirt she threw on as fast as she could, it wasn't fast enough—

"Bloodshed," chanted Elysia.

Alister, now looking so like their father, both of them in the broken earth, both of them buried through her sweat, no tears, not now, bury him deeper, deep as you can, try not to think about how the dirt shouldn't be on him, a sacrilege to put it on his face, but she had to, there was only her to do it—

She was stumbling backward in her haste to get up, scoring the tender flesh of her palms on the gravel, slipping.

Elysia almost seemed to watch, the dolls mute and still now around her.

"It's done now," she said. "It's over. This part of the story is over."

Kyla barely heard her. She was kneeling in the path, fighting the memories.

"The queen is in heaven now," said Elysia in a strong voice. "All the good people are in heaven. They are happy now."

Kyla stood up and turned away, walking aimlessly down the path. She found the garden gate somehow, worked the latch with unfeeling fingers, and still remembered to shut it behind her.

A normal thing. Shut the gate. Shut the gate behind you, so that the deer won't come in. Of course, the tame deer. Eleanor. Don't let them in.

She walked until she saw something familiar, a corner of the bailey, a smooth expanse of grass, the weathered walls of the keep.

She focused on the keep. She should be inside, that's right, there was some reason she was supposed to be inside, and Roland was going to be so mad at her. She really hated it when he grew angry, it seemed to shrivel something in her, something vital that she needed to keep going. She didn't want him to be angry again. She missed him. She did.

A man came up to her, took her arm. She allowed this; it must have been a soldier. Perhaps the steward. He looked familiar. He would guide her back inside, back to Roland.

"Countess," the man said, and again came that chord of

memory. The interior of the keep was blessedly cool, sooth-ing dark. They walked past the main stairs, they walked down a narrow corridor she didn't know. The man's grip on her arm was too tight. He kept her close to his body, she didn't like that, there was something wrong with the way he was pulling her along, down this strange path.

Kyla came back to her senses abruptly, painfully. She turned her head to look up at the man. Who was this? Not a soldier, not the steward, a stranger to her. Coarse, black hair, a hard profile—

Kyla twisted her arm from the man's grip, yanking back-ward with as much force as she could muster. The man re-sponded by pulling her easily back into him, covering her mouth with one hand, using the other to twist her arm be-hind her back and pin her body against his.

He smelled of dirt and old leather, and something else. Desperation.

"Lady," he said, a hoarse whisper, moving them both back and through a door, into a blackened room without win-dows. Kyla writhed in his hold to no avail, kicking at his shins, wanting to scream but unable to manage anything be-yond a muffled whimper.

"Don't fight me, my lady," growled the man. He let go of her arm; a sudden pinching of her waist made even the black-ness grow faint, sparkling dots of blue bursting on the edges of her vision.

"Don't fight," he said, but his voice was far away. She couldn't breathe. The dots grew bigger, multiplied. She sagged in his arms.

He shifted, loosened his hold. She felt one hand roam up her body, a rough palm against her, back down to her hips.

"Where is it?" he barked. "Where?"

She took a shuddering breath around his other hand still over her mouth, clearing her vision. His heavy touch roved upward now, over her stomach, across her ribs.

With a strength born of fear and fury Kyla joined her hands together in front of her and then jabbed one elbow backward into her assailant's stomach, making him lose his breath with a sudden *woosh*. His grip on her slackened enough so that she could turn and without thought she slammed the flat of her palm into his throat. She felt the flesh there collapse under her blow, a sickening crunch.

He released her with a strangled gasp, sinking to his knees. Kyla ran for the door but was plucked backward, making her stumble. A wild look behind her showed the man stretched out flat on the ground, one hand clenched on the hem of her gown. He was dragging himself up, using her to do it.

Kyla pulled with all her might and was rewarded with the sound of stitches popping free, and then all at once he lost his grip on her skirt.

She fled through the door and straight for the bailey.

⎯⎯⎯⎯⎯⎯⎯⎯ ⟨ꙮ⟩ ⎯⎯⎯⎯⎯⎯⎯⎯

*R*OLAND HEARD THE NEWS when he first docked after his trip to Forswall. If he had come back even an hour earlier, he might have prevented it. Less than an hour. Half of that.

Half of that and he would not have experienced the sick slam of his heart in his chest when Duncan met him at the pier and told him she had been attacked again. Half of an hour and he would not have had to fight the void that wanted to eat him whole, ready, jabbering darkness suddenly flowering to life again in the pit that was his soul. Madness eager to embrace him.

He found her in Marla's room. She had refused to go back to their own, he was told, no doubt fearing being confined there for the rest of her life. Which wasn't such a bad idea.

She sat in the chair that had been his mother's, the one Marla had claimed as her own as a girl. Portions of her hair had come loose from its bonds, silky red strands floating to her shoulders, making her look ridiculously young and vulnerable.

Her knees were drawn up to her chest, she was shaking her head at Marla, refusing the tea that was offered, a mulish set to her lips.

The door hit the wall with unnecessary force when he opened it. He hadn't meant for that to happen.

Kyla jumped in place, turning stricken eyes to him, and so

help him it was all he could do not to fall at her feet, not to bury his head in her lap and weep for her, for the bruises he could already see around her mouth, the mussed hair, the defensive posture of her curled up in the chair.

Instead Roland walked calmly forward, made himself take her hand, examined it, ignoring the silence around him.

Slender, delicate. Short nails, no wounds. Her fingers closed tight around his. He lowered his lips to the smoothness of her inner wrist, tasted the warmth there, felt the blood beating through her veins in rapid thrums.

"Can you speak?" he asked.

"Of course." Haughtiness, perhaps to mask her fear. "It was the black-haired one. Not the other."

He had already heard the details from Duncan. But hearing the words from her seemed to solidify the unthinkable thing in him, set the pulse of it to life again.

Destroy, destroy, destroy . . .

"What were you doing out alone?" he asked, keeping that pulse from his voice.

She looked away, stubborn, sulking, a trace of guilt in the angle of her head.

He waited, then: "No matter. It won't happen again."

He let go of her hand and turned to leave.

"Roland, wait," Kyla called, but he didn't pause, gave her no indication that he even heard her. He walked out, leaving the guard to close the door.

Marla sat down on her pallet, stared down at the mug of brewed herbs she still held with a look that Kyla could only describe as bitter resignation.

--------------------◎⟋⟍◎--------------------

*T*HAT NIGHT HE did not come to her, nor the next, nor the next. And although she found she was not to be held forcibly in their rooms, Kyla had now not one guard, but two.

They became her steady companions, Thomas and Berthold, both dark and massive, with grunts for yes or no, taciturn and firm as they watched everything that occurred around her. She remembered them from the journey from Scotland, two of her husband's most trusted men.

She should be honored, she supposed, except that with them she felt even more exposed than before. No one could mistake her presence any longer. No more slipping into shadows to spy on a world that would have spied on her, no more entering a room with quiet plans to assess whatever circumstances she was about to walk into. No more sneaking off into the tunnels of the castle, even. Roland had made good on his promise to bolt the armoire to the ground.

Now wherever she went people parted like a school of flounder for a shark that slid into their midst. Thomas and Berthold on either side of her, or in front of and behind her, emanating unspoken malice for so much as a stray thought that might wish to harm her. She was surely going to stifle from all this protection, go starkly insane with it.

The mood of the entire castle seemed to grow dark. To match the ambience of gloom inside, nature conspired to croon in sympathy. The skies grew cloudy and tarnished, a brisk wind off the sea chilled everything it touched, coming and going in howling shafts down the bowels of the keep. Conversations among the inhabitants of Lorlmar had become scarce and muttered. No one smiled anymore during meals. Men stood with arms folded grimly across their chests, women hovered with their heads ducked down. Even the children seemed to have vanished into the cracks of the walls, gone off to a nursery Kyla had no invitation to visit.

And whenever Roland was nearby, everything just seemed to cease altogether, even the wind. Everyone paused in what they might be doing and watched him, watched her, waiting for something. Kyla had no idea what.

She did know, however, what *she* was waiting for. She was waiting for Roland to come back to her. She was waiting for him to meet her eyes without that blank glaze over them, the once-tropical warmth now a cold glimmer. She was waiting for him to address more than a few perfunctory sentences to her.

But what always happened was he would pinpoint her

with that look, check her from chin to toe, then turn away, as if the mere sight of her pained him. It became another secret ache she tucked away behind her own careful facade of blankness. At least he wasn't as short-tempered with her as he seemed to be with everyone else. That was something, surely. When he had questioned her in detail about the attack, all she had felt from him was infinite placidity, only patience on his face. She told him everything she could think of save the moment in the garden with Elysia. That was too raw yet, that mesmerizing tale. Kyla could not speak of that to anyone. But she readily told the rest—where the man took her, what he said, how she escaped him.

When Roland asked what she thought the man might have been searching for she replied she honestly had no idea, provoking only silence from her husband, and a glacial look out a window. That marked the end of the longest conversation between them.

The third afternoon after the attack she was in the stables with Auster, talking softly to him, apologizing for not taking him out. Auster was expressing his unhappiness, snorting and pawing the ground, even nipping at the hilt of the dagger she had taken to wearing at her waist again; Thomas and Berthold—banished to either side of the line of stalls by her insistence—eyed the horse grimly.

The stalls were set up so that only wooden slats separated the uppermost portion of them. Behind Auster's stall was another, facing the opposite side of the stables. Through the slats she could see movement, a pale horse, men around him, working on his foreleg.

Kyla tilted her head into Auster's neck, stroking his nose, listening to the words that slipped between the gaps in the wood.

"Smith said he had just shod that mare. Just shod her."

Another man grunted in agreement.

"Now, I ask you, what's a horse doin' throwing a fresh shoe? Smith's shoe, which you know never come off till it's time to pull 'em?"

"I heard the nails were pulled straight out. Castor's lad found 'em. New nails, marked like Smith does for the horses. These were plain marked for that mare that Dedrick rides, three hash marks. Castor's lad found 'em thrown behind a stump."

The pale horse moved, let out a squeal of dissatisfaction. The men shifted and then continued talking.

"Aye, the lad took them nails to the captain right off. I was there for that. Never seen such a look on Duncan before. I heard that when he went and told his lordship, he like to blew the roof off. Had a fit."

"I heard he busted the furniture. Sent for poor Dedrick right then and there, wantin' to know how in blazes he could choose to ride a horse with no shoe."

"Nay." A new voice, quieter, more serious. "I heard it different. I heard his lordship didn't say nothin' at all. You know how he gets. Didn't say nothin'. But they found them nails all twisted and bent up the next morn. Twisted up like with his bare hands."

Silence settled on the men, and even the horse seemed lost in thought.

Kyla closed her eyes, continued stroking her stallion's coat.

$\mathcal{O}$N THE NIGHT of the fourth day she awoke suddenly, startled by the sudden dipping of the bed beside her, the glow of candlelight.

"Don't be afraid." Roland held the candle, sitting on the bed beside her. It seemed so unlikely that she did nothing for a long stretch of time, only stared up at him, waiting for the dream to change, for him to transform or vanish or, like the vision she had last night, to bend over and sweetly kiss her. But he did none of these things. He sat there, perched on the outer edge of the feather mattress, and slowly she realized she was not dreaming. Roland was actually here.

Kyla sat up, dazzled by the relative brilliance of him, the

soft gold of his loosened hair. Although his face was cloaked in dim starlight, she could feel the way he watched her, the intensity of him taking in her movements.

"My lord?" No, it wasn't a dream, not this. The candle flame shivered in a draft blowing in from the open door, letting her see his eyes for an instant before they grew shrouded again.

"Are you awake enough? Are you listening to me?"

She nodded.

"Get dressed. I need you to come with me."

"Where?" she asked, unable to quell the hope that sprang forth in her heart, thinking of the beach far below them, the soft sand.

Roland stood up, turned away from her. His voice was remote. "I need you to identify a body."

She dressed hurriedly, tossing whatever underskirt was nearest her over her head, then the bliaut, struggling with the buttons running up the back until Roland said something under his breath and strode over to help her. His fingers were swift and efficient, totally impersonal. When they were through he took her arm and led her out, both of them immediately surrounded by her two guards.

No one said anything as they paced through the shadowy halls of the keep, past sleeping pages and squires, soldiers sprawled out on benches in the main hall, outside to the murky night. Clouds gathered and scattered along their celestial paths, some so low they looked like they might melt into the dark earth.

They walked along the bailey until they reached the stables, but instead of going in, Roland took her around the side, over to a group of men standing near the wall. The men were obviously waiting for them.

They stood aside silently as she approached.

It was the man with the black hair, of course. Kyla only needed a glimpse of his face, his body lying lax in the grass and dirt. His tunic was slashed, a dark stain of blood crossed over half his ribs. One of the soldiers bent down and held a light closer to the form. She looked away, then nodded in answer to the unspoken question.

"Are you certain?" Roland remained standing behind her. She heard no inflection in his voice.

"Yes," she replied.

She backed up, clutching the long, trailing sleeves of her gown in both hands, a nervous reflex. Roland made a gesture to his men. As one the soldiers surrounded the body and hefted it up, moving off into the night until the darkness swallowed them whole.

Roland and Kyla watched them go, only Berthold and Thomas remaining beside them, silent as always. Kyla made herself look up at her husband, searching for a trace of warmth, a trace of concern from the man she thought she had begun to know.

"A pity," he said. Roland tilted his head down to her, gave her a mirthless smile, faint silver against the black night. "I would have preferred to kill him myself."

And she believed him.

Chapter Fourteen

───────── ⟨ഝ⟩ ─────────

*B*Y THE END OF THE WEEK Kyla could stand the pall on the castle no longer. After the body of the black-haired man had been found, Roland's mood became, if possible, even more dangerous. Now she didn't even see him at meals, and each night had become an empty stretch of time that melded into empty days. People shied away from her as if she carried a hex. Even Marla was nowhere to be found.

Kyla needed the solace of the one person on the island that she thought might be willing to guide her out of this strange maze of bleakness she was following her husband into. She needed to speak with Harrick.

Lorlmar had no chapel. The single mass Kyla had been allowed to attend had been held in the great hall of the keep, and so she had to seek out Harrick in the most likely places she thought a monk might go.

Not the kitchens, filled with shiny-faced women who had no time for idle inquiries.

Not the great hall, either, which held people only as they went to and fro. It was not time for meetings or meals.

Not the stables, since Brother Harrick, she was told, did not ride.

Not the bailey, large though it was, for Thomas and Berthold would have spotted the tall monk even from a distance.

Not even his own quarters, small and sparse by choice—
and completely empty, according to Thomas, who went in to
be certain.

She found Harrick in the nursery, a place she would not
have thought to look and discovered only by accident, as it
was in the same portion of the keep as the monk's rooms.
There could be no mistaking the deep, calm tones of his
voice behind the closed doors.

Kyla paused uncertainly in the hallway, wondering if she
should intrude. Berthold solved her problem by opening the
door for her.

Harrick sat in the middle of a circle of youngsters, hands
in the air, fingers splayed.

" . . . with wings bigger than three men, and eyes of fire,
and a string of pearls decorating his beard."

The children leaned back farther to watch his hands, now
flapping back and forth in unison.

"Tell us more!" cried a boy.

Harrick had seen her. The dragon wings came down,
transforming into mere hands again. The children let out a
collective sigh.

"We'll finish the tale tomorrow. Saint George will wait."

There were loud protests as Harrick rose to his feet, stepping
carefully around the clusters of children. "Tomorrow," he said
firmly, and like magic the protest died down, the children
jumping up and scattering to different corners of the room. A
few came over to Kyla, led by Elysia, an ordinary little girl once
more. A great deal more of them stood and stared in awe at
Thomas and Berthold.

"Hullo, Auntie," Elysia said, tugging Kyla's skirts with
both hands. "Are you feeling better today?"

Kyla reached down and touched the girl's cheek, smooth
and fresh. "Yes, thank you," she replied.

"Good." Elysia hugged Kyla's knees, then moved away
with her friends.

Women were taking the children's hands, making them sit,
be quiet, the countess was here, behave. The wind, so con-

stant of late, shook the windows of this tower room, rattling the panes, a whistling song brushing against the glass and the stones of the keep. Otherwise, the chamber had grown completely silent. Children and adults alike stared at her.

"Shall we walk outside?" asked Harrick.

"Yes," Kyla said.

The wind was calmed to almost nothing in the bailey, allowing the drift of conversations to wash over them as they walked: squires standing in a clump around the quintain, stableboys leaning on pitchforks by a loose stack of hay, five young women with baskets and pails, walking slowly around the bend.

Harrick had said nothing further and Kyla was trying to think of how to approach what she wanted to ask of him. They were headed out of the main gate, she saw now, and to her surprise neither of her guards protested this move, both of them still flanking her, Thomas allowing Harrick the privilege of being on her immediate left.

Harrick took them off the path that meandered to the pier, onto a barely trodden line through the ferns that led to a sort of natural cupola amid the trees, a circle of evergreens placed almost evenly every four feet apart.

He smiled when he saw her look up, searching the sky for the centerpoint where the branches met, a green star for a roof.

"Unusual, isn't it? I discovered it on my daily hike a few years ago." He turned to the other men. "Please wait over there. The countess and I desire a moment of privacy."

She expected the soldiers to growl a protest, to edge even closer to her, but to her amazement both men merely nodded, stepping back into the boughs of the woods, blending in with the forest cover.

"And how is your husband, my lady?" Harrick looked down at her, folding his hands together in a posture of serenity.

"I—" She could hardly say she had no idea. It was what she had been seeking to learn from Harrick, anyway. He had cut off her mental preamble with his own words, direct and to the point.

"I believe he is well," she tried.

Harrick raised an eyebrow, the resemblance to his half brother suddenly eerie. "You believe?"

"Well, I have not seen him much of late—"

"And why is that?"

"It's not that I have not wished to do so. He is simply not around for me—"

"Have you sought him out?"

Kyla was beginning to feel somewhat ill-used. "No," she said crossly, picking up a pinecone from the ground. "I have not."

"Why not?"

"Because he does not seem to wish for me to." The thick tips of the pinecone felt sharp against her palm, her fingers.

"How would you know? If you have not seen him to know if he would like to see you?"

She found the question nonsensical and ignored the flash of guilt it provoked. "If he wished to see me, I am not difficult to find." She pointed the cone in the direction of where her guards had disappeared.

"I never meant to suggest you were difficult to find, my lady." Harrick's voice was laced with amusement. "I would lay odds the entire castle would know your position within a half minute of your moving, so closely are you watched."

Kyla expelled her breath in frustration. "Exactly!"

"It seems to me"—Harrick looked up at the star of branches above, his voice low, his hands cupping emptiness—"that the one who is lost is not you, but Roland."

She opened her mouth to reply, then shut it. Harrick looked down at her again. "Exactly," he said. "I believe you will find him becoming acquainted with too much wine in his study right now."

"His study?" She shook her head.

"Thomas and Berthold will show you." Harrick placed a hand on her back, pushed her gently away from him, out of the circle.

OLAND WAS SITTING behind an enormous desk in a
room with a heavy brocade cloth draped over the battlement
windows. The cloth was purple and teal, creating an odd
glow where the sunlight tried to pierce it—muted, stained
colors that spilled at random across the rug.

The desk was littered with a strange assortment of objects.
A horseshoe, slightly warped; a thin golden necklace with a
locket; a jeweled box, perhaps to hold the necklace. A goblet
of something that left a daisy chain of sticky rings on the
wood. No horseshoe nails that Kyla could see, bent or
otherwise.

His head was bowed. He did not look up when she opened
the door, nor when she entered one slow step at a time.

"Not now," he said, and his voice had that strangeness she
had heard before, that time over the chess game. "Get out."

Kyla stopped, throwing a glance at the door behind her.
One of the men had already closed it, both of them waiting
out in the hallway.

"Dammit, Marla, I said I didn't want any of your infernal
brew. Leave me—"

Roland broke off when he looked up and saw her standing
there, curves and outlines of a dream he remembered, a
woman with autumn hair and moonlit eyes, a woman he
could not bear to even think about right now, but of course
he did, because she was all he ever thought about anymore,
she was his obsession, she was his life. Kyla.

She moved forward into his dream, gliding steps, her gown
spilling down to pool at her feet, a trail of silk or velvet or he
didn't know what.

Flowers to bloom beneath her steps. That was what should
happen. She deserved for flowers to bloom to life from her
touch, a trail of them to mark wherever she went; she deserved
a crown of stars, a staff of gold. . . .

He moaned and buried his head in his hands again. She
would be gone the next time he looked up. And then in her
place might be the blackness.

"Roland." She made his name soft, lyrical. He gritted his teeth against it.

Time spun out. Minutes. Seconds.

He was thirsty again. He needed another drink. He reached for the goblet but it was still empty. Why the hell was his goblet empty? He was the earl around here. That had to be worth something. He should have some more wine.

Roland looked up, and she was still standing there, exactly the same as before.

"My lord?"

He bowed his head and laughed into his hands. Perhaps she really was here. Certainly. Of course she was.

"What?" he said.

She floated over closer to the desk. One pale hand reached out, lifted the goblet he had knocked to its side, set it upright. Behind her trailed not flowers, not stars. No, no. Behind her came his nightmare. He could see it so clearly.

The blackness was fading. And what was taking its place was even worse.

She moved in flawless beauty in front of him now, blocking the visions, teasing him with flashes of what might have even been redemption: steady hands, eyes like truth. But that had to be the wine singing to him, tempting him with such thoughts. And yet, she was still here.

Kyla.

He had been wrestling with it for days, and the end result was always the same. Roland told himself he had needed to bind her to him because she was the countess, and he was the earl. Together they would be responsible for a dynasty, the creation of which was to be his nightly delight.

But fate, of course, had laughed at his confident plans. This wasn't mere lust he felt for her. Not infatuation, nor any of the other pallid emotions he had encountered before for a woman.

He loved her. He loved her as sure as he had loved anything, including his family and his home.

Oh God, he loved her, and what was to become of him

now? She would never truly accept him, all of him, not with these unspeakable ghosts that stalked him.

Kyla smelled the stale wine on the air, noted the tumbled amber of his hair, the circles beneath his eyes, through the lurid teal-and-purple light. Roland was looking down at the desk again, shaking his head slightly, saying something too soft for her to hear.

She walked over to the window and pulled on the brocade cloth. It came loose but then stuck on something; she pulled harder, ripping it where it had been caught on the iron bar at the top of the window. The heavy bundle fell in slapping waves to her feet, and the room was flooded with sunlight. Kyla kicked the material away from her and leaned over the windowsill, pushing the latch back and opening the glass until she could smell the ocean air. Then she came back to the desk.

She had his attention now, by God.

He was staring up at her, trying not to squint in the sudden brightness.

"Kyla?" he said, his voice sounding slow and scratched, as if he were waking up from sleep.

"My lord." She folded her arms across her chest.

Roland brought up a hand and rubbed his eyes, then looked around at the room, almost in surprise. "You are here."

"I am. And you are drunk."

"I'm not." He laughed, a self-mocking sound. "I wish I were. I was trying."

"I would speak with you, my lord."

He leaned back in his chair, regarded her with shuttered eyes, then shrugged.

"Pray, speak."

But words fled from her tongue. To cover her disorientation she made a show of choosing a chair to sit in, a small one opposite his, leather-backed and carved of oak, then arranged her skirts in precise, graceful folds.

He was still watching her, silent. His fingers formed a steeple beneath his chin.

"How do you fare?" she asked at last, at a loss for anything better.

"Passing well, my lady."

It was so obviously untrue she thought he must be taunting her, but his mouth was twisted in not quite a grin, more of a grimace. She decided to let the moment pass.

"I have not seen you much of late," she said instead, keeping a tranquil tone.

He said nothing. She saw his eyes flick to something over her shoulder, then back to her.

"No doubt you are busy. No doubt your duties as earl keep your days filled."

He gave a peculiar half-smile to the desk, toyed with the gold chain on it, drawing it out along the flat surface, making a twisted pattern out of its links. An S. A triangle.

"No doubt," she continued, watching his fingers work with the bright metal, "you prefer the company of darkness and wine to that of your wife."

"Is that what you think?" Roland looked up at her, right at her, for the first time. His eyes were feverishly bright. "Is it really?"

She lifted her hands in the air, a gesture of resignation. "What else?"

"You don't want to know." He stole another glance over her shoulder, looked away.

"Yes, I do."

The chain became a straight line, the locket exactly in the middle. He placed his hands on either end of the links.

She was beginning to lose her hold on the patience that had kept her in the chair. He was ignoring her again, stonestill, staring down at the locket. Kyla shifted, began to rise, when he spoke.

"She was younger than you when she died."

He said it low, almost a private thought that took them both by surprise.

"Who?" she asked.

"Eleanor. She married young. Too young, I thought. Fifteen." He leaned back again, closed his eyes, sighed. "Ah, perhaps it's not so young."

Kyla frowned, glanced down at the locket. It was a disk of gold, a design of some sort in the middle, a Celtic cross, or a lover's knot.

"But she was so happy with him. She loved him so much, she said. I had to believe her. James was a good man. And I knew he had loved her for ages, watching her grow up. It almost killed her when he died."

Kyla looked up at him again but his face was blank. He had found that spot behind her. He was watching it with detached interest.

"She was five months pregnant, and James had to go and get himself lost in a storm at sea. There was nothing we could do. He should not have been out. But he was."

She moved in her chair, uneasy with the tale, his focus gone to that place behind her.

"This is what you consider all day?" she asked, perplexed. "This keeps you in here?"

"I had to leave, you see," he said, pinning her with his look again. "I had to. Henry sent for me. I couldn't refuse him, it was a command. A campaign in the north. He needed me, and he needed my men. I had to go. It didn't matter that it was only a fortnight after the death of James."

She nodded, frozen in his look.

"I was gone, do you understand? I was gone, and so were almost all of the men. There were only the women, the children, my father, and his guard. That's all. It had always been enough before."

There once was a queen. . . .

Elysia's words came back to her, held shades of ominous new meaning.

"Kyla." He said it like a caress, aching, startling her with his pain, the turquoise eyes fully on her again. "Leave me now."

"I can't," she said. "I can't leave."

Roland laughed. "No, I suppose not. My fearless Kyla. Would you like to hear the rest of the tale?"

No, she thought.

"Yes," she said.

"Siren's Cove, that very place where you were felled, my love, netted the island two ships while I was away. Most of the crews drowned. A few survived, climbed up to shore. No more than twelve and seven men, all of them half-dead by the time they were found." He picked up the locket, rubbed his fingers over the design. "It was our way, then, to take in strangers. My father did what he had always done; rescued them, gave them food, clothing, a place to bed until they grew strong enough to leave on their own. Only these men did not leave."

The queen loved everyone. . . .

"Eleanor seemed to have befriended one in particular, a lad about her age, sixteen then. I suppose he told her wild tales of the sea, beguiled her with made-up stories. She had always been enamored of stories. And this lad—Justin was his name—convinced her to convince our father that the men needed a little more time to recover. A few weeks more, and they would be on their way."

Roland opened the jeweled box. The inside was lined with faded satin, perhaps once a royal blue, now lavender-gray and splattered with water spots.

"Three days later, at dawn, these men massacred everyone they could. They had been fit for days, after all, but spent their time learning of the castle—how many people, how many soldiers, what they could steal. They were pirates. They had been pirates all along."

Kyla felt her chest constricting, her hands clenched on the arms of the chair.

"My father fought them, I am told, but he was old then, and his guardsmen were taken by surprise. Most of them were killed immediately, before they could even leave their beds. A few of the pirates went down with them, but not enough. They kept my father alive. Perhaps they meant to use him as a hostage.

"Marla has always been one to rise before dawn. She was out in the woods that morning, gathering herbs, when she heard the commotion from the soldiers' quarters. And being

Marla, the first thing she did was slip back inside the keep through one of the tunnels, something the pirates had not managed to discover. We did not use them so much then, you see. She had Madoc and Seena gather the children and the rest of the women, had them hide in the walls of the keep. And then she went to find Eleanor."

He picked up the locket again, dangled it from his fingers, watched it swing.

"Instead of Eleanor, Marla found Justin."

Do as I say and they won't have to die. . . .

"It seems that at sixteen he had inherited the captain's position among the pirates, since the other two captains had died in the wrecks. He won this position through his cunning and his brutality. Even at sixteen the other men held him in fear, recognizing the evil in him that my sister had never seen."

Roland dropped the locket from his fingers into the box. It landed amid the satin with a thud that seemed heavy in the quiet room.

"Marla refused to tell them where the others were. She thought Eleanor had escaped and joined everyone behind the walls. But they brought her out when Marla wouldn't yield. She was in her eighth month of pregnancy then."

Kyla closed her eyes. She wanted to shut out his words, she didn't want to hear about this. She knew what happened next.

"But then, they never really cared what Marla had to say. They had what they wanted, after all, their booty and the Earl of Lorlreau. They made my father watch as they took turns raping both women, and then they killed him when he fought too much. They left Marla and Eleanor for dead. Eleanor almost was."

Roland closed the lid to the box very carefully, as if the slightest wrong move would break it. His voice had no emotion at all. "I was told that Justin took particular delight with Eleanor. That he insisted on having her despite her condition."

Her cheeks were wet. Kyla had no memory of when the

tears started, she didn't feel them except for the coldness against her face.

"Marla delivered the baby right then. She knew there was no hope for Eleanor, but she was determined to save the babe. Eleanor found the strength to hold Elysia in her arms for a moment before she died.

"Two days later I returned to Lorlreau. We had intercepted Marla's messenger before he reached London."

He smiled at her now. "Two days. It doesn't seem so very long, does it? Two days earlier, and perhaps my sister would still be alive. Perhaps my father would still be the earl."

Her voice caught in her throat—she had nothing good enough to say to him, she had nothing to take away the horror of his tale. She could only shake her head.

"Did you know that just behind you, over your shoulder," said Roland in a faraway voice, "I see a great emptiness. But in there, beyond the empty, is something like fire, and screams. Bodies. Blood. A great deal of blood. Women are screaming at me. Men are pleading. I can't quite make out what they're saying. I can't quite . . ."

His voice faded off, almost bewildered.

"You can't what?" she asked, hushed.

"I can't remember," he said, looking to her. "I can't remember what I did to them."

"To the pirates." She made it a statement but it sounded like a judgment, falling hard into the silence.

"I found them. All of them. It wasn't hard. It was almost . . . easy. I found them within a week. Some were in taverns. Some were in homes." He took a ragged breath. "And I just can't remember what I did to them."

"But they are dead?"

"Oh, yes," he said softly. "They are quite dead." He exhaled, a sharp sound. "You asked me once how I became the Hound of Hell. Now you know."

Roland's gaze slid off of hers, he seemed pained by her again. "And now, someone is stalking you. Someone means to kill my wife, against all reason, against all sanity. And I am afraid that I will join that insanity should anything happen to you."

Her head was swimming, it took her a while to sift through to the meaning of his words. Roland sat back, looked weary again.

"Now you will leave, my countess. Go back to your rooms."

"No." She stood up. "Now you will listen."

He didn't stop her, but he wouldn't meet her gaze. He scowled down at the box.

"I don't care what you did." She took a step closer. "Do you hear me? I don't care. And I don't care if you never remember."

He looked up, beyond her.

"I don't care about that at all," she said fiercely. "I won't let it ruin you. I won't allow it to ruin us."

The air trembled in her lungs, she dragged it in, willing him to believe. "Nothing about the past can be changed, and I have seen enough of death and dying to hold me over forever. We cannot go back and fix what was done. Those days are over for you, and they are over for me. I will not have them hiding behind us in the darkness, or in the light. I will not let you live in those moments, and I refuse to dwell there any longer. I refuse!"

Her voice rose, became almost a shout.

"And I will not have you lingering in the shadows, Roland Strathmore! Do you hear me? Whatever you did before right now, right this moment, doesn't matter at all! You will come out of this room and you will be my husband, and I don't want to hear any excuses. Because the past is a dead thing, too. And I am sick of death!"

She paused, pushed her hair back, searching for the right words to convince him. "I want *life*," she ended, softer now. "I want life, and I want you."

He was shaking, covering his eyes, and for a moment she truly feared for him, that she had said something he would not recover from. She went around the desk until she reached his side and then he pulled her down onto him, holding her so tight she almost couldn't breathe, and he was pressing his lips into her hair, laughing into her temple.

"Don't you dare laugh," she cried, enraged. "Don't you dare!"

"Oh my God," Roland gasped, still squeezing her. "I love you so much."

He shocked her, took the temper out of her and left in its place something numb, something that made her speechless.

He wasn't laughing now, perhaps he hadn't been before, because the wetness she felt on her face was not from her own tears, not just hers. And when he looked at her she saw the tropical spark again, but no trace of mirth, only bright sobriety, compelling warmth.

"I've never spoken of those days before," he said, wondering. "I never could."

"They have no power over you," she replied, "unless you allow them to."

He pressed his face into her neck, holding her tight again, a long, sustained moment that left his arms faintly trembling. She reached up, ran her fingers through his hair, caught the gold there and let it slide over her palm.

"My fearless wife," he said finally. "Mayhap I'm not as strong as you think."

"I am not fearless. Only a fool has no fear." She closed her eyes, leaned her head against his shoulder, comfortable, sturdy. "But I think you are stronger than you know. I imagine you might even survive a whole winter on your own in the wild Highlands, if you had to. Of course, I could give you a few tips first."

He laughed now, really laughed, and relief swept through her. She felt the warmth of his lips seeking her cheek, the curve of her jaw, and turned her face to his, letting him capture her lips.

"I love you," he said, tasting her, shifting until she was alone in the chair, and he was on his knees in front her, leaning into her, so intense. "I love you. I would never survive anywhere without you, I don't know how I managed for so long. I love you."

"I love you, too." The words came from her heart, perfect truth, perfect clarity, at last. "Roland, I love you."

He pulled her deeper into his embrace, his hands sliding down her arms, then up again, to the soft curve of her breasts. He breathed in her scent—flowers and flame and woman—let it surround him, let it saturate his soul. Her hands were light on him, she pressed her fingers into his shoulders and pulled him closer still, cradling him between her legs.

Her gown was loose, loose enough, he thought, and proved it by finding the creaminess of her skin beneath the silk, the linen, tracing the long lines of her legs until he found the center of her, and she was gasping now, shocked and excited together, a whimper caught in her throat.

He leaned into her, used his other hand to cup her buttocks, urging her forward, closer to him as he kissed her, ruthless and hard. She was panting against him, using her hands to find his arousal, to torment him with her touch until he thought he would go mad with it.

He pushed her hands out of the way and freed himself, not bothering with the rest of their clothing, his tunic, her bliaut. Her skirts became a sea of froth at her waist, and then he was pushing at her, he was inside her.

He moved in a sharp thrust and she met him there, holding onto his arms, head thrown back, baring her neck to his mouth. He was guiding her with his hands around her hips, rocking forward, slow, which was all he could bear. He thought he might die from the exquisiteness of her, God, so hot and wet and tight around him, and then she began to move and the sun exploded behind his eyes, he gave himself up to it at once, helpless to stop, and she cried out and bit her lip and collapsed around him in magnificent little shudders.

Her forehead rested on his shoulder, he felt her lips brush his skin around the collar of his tunic. On his knees still he bowed his own head to hers, breathing hard, and then he picked her up and moved them both down to the thickness of the Persian rug beneath them, rolling on his back so that she would be on top.

She lay pliant and warm across his chest; he smoothed her skirts to cover them both, then relaxed, exhausted and feeling a peace he had not known before.

"Don't ever leave me," he mumbled, half-asleep in a patch of yellow sunshine.

Her reply came fair and lucid, clear as summer skies.

"I won't."

Chapter Fifteen

ORNING CAME WITH the welcome awareness
of being cradled in her husband's arms, something Kyla had
missed more than she could say over the past few nightmarish days.

The nightmare was over, she was sure of it. The worst was
past them now, and the proof was that Roland slept beside
her, peaceful and calm, strong and close throughout the fantasy spell of last night. He had come out of the study with her
yesterday, come out with the surety back in his step, no more
silent wrath.

He seemed a changed man to everyone but her, escorting
her to dinner last night with a smile on his face once more,
laughing at some sally made by Elysia, conversing easily
throughout the meal as he used to do. Only Kyla, and perhaps
Marla, could see the pale shadow of the sadness that lingered
in him still. Kyla was not surprised at this. That he could
come this far after what he had put himself through was
miracle enough for her. She would help him one day at a
time, until even that shadow was banished.

And a part of him would always be, she supposed, the
Hound of Hell. He would never be able to relinquish the
warrior in him, nor would she want him to.

He had smiled and laughed all right, but still he scanned
the hall for their enemy, still he held a lengthy conversation with Duncan, who kept nodding gravely and glancing
around.

Kyla liked that part of him, she decided, the protective man. She understood it, since it matched her own spirit. She would become his protector, as well.

People were shocked by the change, Kyla could see, but pleasantly so. Dinner had marked a new beginning as far as she was concerned, and her smile had echoed her husband's, the man she loved.

She had heard the amazed whispers, people wondering what had gone on behind the closed door to their lord's study, with him enclosed with the countess. Roland had only chuckled, inscrutable, and proposed another toast to his lady.

She had gotten light-headed with all the wine she drank for his toasts to her.

They had made love late into the night, exploring each other with a newfound tenderness, an endless wonder and delight that lasted until she had been unable to keep her eyes open any longer. And then he had rocked her to his chest, held her safe under the covers of the bed and whispered his love to her once more as she drifted off.

It was the most amazing thing that had ever happened to her.

So that this morning, as he slept still, she looked down at him—sweetly chiseled lips, long brown lashes, straight brows, elegant nose—and Kyla felt her heart fill up again with gratitude, that she could be given such a splendid gift as Roland Strathmore. That she could love him, and he her.

He opened his eyes, caught her looking, and grinned. "I love you. I'm starving. Let's eat."

Breakfast was even merrier than last night, news of the change in the earl having spread to just about everyone by then. Kyla had thought it important that they join the rest of the people of the castle for the meal, to prove the change that had been wrought the night before was not just myth or wishful thinking.

Roland had not protested. Well, not very much. Not after he was done kissing her, at least.

When both Kyla and Roland emerged from the master chamber, Thomas and Berthold had accepted his presence with their usual impassivity, but Kyla caught the look of surprise that passed between them when they thought she was not watching. However, when Roland dismissed them outside their door, saying pleasantly that they looked as if they could use some sleep, neither man argued, only bowed and walked away.

Roland draped an arm over her shoulder and kept it there until they were seated in the great hall.

He seemed confident and at ease, in charge of his estate. He held on to her hand and periodically pressed a kiss upon it around the courses of the meal, causing her to blush for no good reason, causing him to kiss her more.

Marla was bold enough to ask about this change, and did so over a warm loaf of bread she was passing around.

Roland considered the question thoughtfully, then replied in a low voice, "I have been saved by my lady. What else?"

Marla gave a slow smile, and Elysia nodded.

"I told you she would," said the child to Harrick.

"You did," he agreed.

Kyla merely shook her head. "You have saved yourself," she said to her husband, who looked down at the table, then kissed her hand again.

***

"WHERE ARE WE GOING?"

Kyla stepped carefully around a delicate cluster of flowers growing near the center of the trail, aided by Roland's hand on her arm.

"It's a surprise." He gave her that special smile of his, the mischievous one, and it tickled her until she had to smile back, curious but trusting him.

He had disappeared after breakfast but shown up again just a few hours later, telling her he had in mind a journey for them both this afternoon.

The sun beamed down on them now, casting short shadows over the grass and flowers around them, showing off the subtle hues of all the colors of nature.

It was a beautiful day, a glorious day, Kyla thought as Roland walked beside her with his roguish smile. Yet it was odd how deserted the land seemed. Usually there were people everywhere, bustling around, working.

This afternoon the paths were empty save for her and Roland. Even Thomas and Berthold had not reappeared.

"Almost there," Roland said, and a bird warbled a short song beside them in a pine, a complement to his words.

She knew this path, she had walked it before on the day of the thunderstorm. Today there were no clouds in the sky, only a long blue horizon, and then behind the grove of giant trees was the meadow of the rabbits she remembered, full of clover and people.

People everywhere, tables set up in the grass, garlands of flowers draped from them, food, drink, even musicians. Kyla stopped where she was on the edge of the meadow, amazed, but Roland's smile had grown broader, then broader still as the people of Lorlreau spotted them together and let out a cheer.

She turned her head and looked up at Roland and he down at her. His smile vanished, became a reflection of serious turquoise.

"We never had a proper wedding," he said quietly.

Kyla couldn't speak, though her mouth opened, searching for the words. There was something wrong with her, there was a knot of something in her throat, she couldn't seem to swallow around it.

Roland took both her hands in his, brought them up to his lips and kissed them, never looking away from her. The sunlight glowed around him, golden contours, celestial warmth.

"Will you marry me?" he asked now. "Again?"

He had planned it all for her, she realized, he had gathered together his people and his dreams, and it was just for her, to please her.

A real wedding. Not rushed vows in a darkened chamber but promises offered openly, here in front of his family, his friends, her new home. Just for her.

"Yes," she said, because it was the only possible answer that came to her.

Marla approached, laughing, with Elysia beside her, both of them wearing circlets of flowers in their hair. The child carried another one for Kyla, fresh blooms of white and violet, delicate dark green leaves, and Kyla knelt so Elysia could place it on her head, where it tilted drunkenly to the side until Roland straightened it for her.

Marla and Elysia went skipping back to the crowd and Roland began to lead her forward into the thick of the others, down the center aisle they had created amid the heavy grass and clover, to Harrick, standing serenely in the center of the meadow.

It was unexpected magic, it was bewitching joy, to repeat the vows that Harrick spoke for them, uniting them again before God, before them all, with the wind singing through the boughs of the trees and the ocean echoing along, distant and deep.

Roland kissing her, holding her face with both hands, his lips warm and light against hers, an exchange of breath between them, and then they were showered with flower petals of all colors, bits of rainbow gliding down from the sky around them as everyone cheered again.

Magic, this feeling of wonder she had now, accepting the congratulations that came thick and fast from the people. Someone handed her a silver goblet of wine, matching the one Roland held. They locked arms and drank to each other, and Kyla had to fight not to smile as she drank, the sweet headiness of the wine filling her up, the sun bright in her eyes.

The crown of flowers fell off her as she tilted her head back, and Roland swooped it up and put it on her again, followed by a kiss. The crowd laughed and applauded.

The food was delicious, the wine and ale filled every cup as they were toasted again and again.

Kyla sat beside Roland on the special bench placed in the middle of the tables for the two of them, and her face hurt from all the smiling, and her laughter was giddy and still a little disbelieving. Roland held tight to her hand through it all.

Tangled up in the gold of his hair were the flower petals,

velvet pastels against his shining brilliance, and it gave him a fanciful air, a demigod amid the innocence of summer.

"I love you," said the god to her, a frame of trees and sky around him.

"I love you, too," Kyla replied, and then gave a radiant smile, because she couldn't help it, her happiness was so overwhelming.

After a long while they all drifted back into the keep but the mood was unchanged, and many stayed in the great hall with the musicians as the benches and tables were put back, the leftover food and drink brought in.

Roland kept Kyla beside him, his arm around her shoulders as he stood talking to those who still came up and wished them well. He nodded his head and a few flower petals came free, dancing down to the ground at his feet. Kyla gave a little laugh, then leaned her cheek against his shoulder.

The men he had been talking to drifted tactfully away. Roland glanced down at her, a warm, sleepy look.

"My lady, would you care to join me upstairs?"

She understood the message in his tone, the invitation, the way his hand began to stroke her arm, and felt her heartbeat quicken.

But before she could respond another man approached; Duncan, looking worried.

"My lord. A word, if you please."

Instantly Roland latched on to the undertone of urgency in Duncan's voice. Kyla caught his transformation, from lover to warrior in a fraction of a second. He let go of her shoulder with a final squeeze, then walked over to his captain.

The two men stood off to the side, conversing with their heads together, arms crossed. As she watched them Kyla felt a sudden chill flow from her spine to her fingers, an uneasy feeling that was reflected in the grim lines of Roland's mouth, the hard glint in his eyes.

Conversation in the great hall hovered and died, leaving only the occasional clink of metal on wood, shifting murmurs of guesses as to what the two men could be discussing.

Duncan had finished speaking. Roland looked over at

Kyla, his glance almost involuntary, a reflex. He turned back to Duncan.

"Gather your men. We're off."

Duncan bowed and left. Roland returned to her, his eyes distant now. He took her over to a nearby table, the one where Marla sat with Harrick and Elysia. Everyone stared at him, waiting.

Roland sat on the bench but perched on the edge, as if ready to spring up and leave in a second. Kyla fought the urge to pull him back farther, to keep him there.

"Kyla." His voice was serious, distracted. "Can you recall hearing anything about a note in regard to the death of your mother?"

"A note?" She had an unsettled feeling in her stomach. "No . . . wait. Only the one you referred to, my lord. From the message saying you had a note to clear my father's name. Is that the one you mean?"

Of course it wasn't, she knew it wasn't, and when he shook his head the uneasiness in her increased, became a cold tingling in her legs, a dryness in her mouth.

"No," he said. "Not that one. Another. You don't recall ever hearing of such a thing?"

Numbly she shook her head.

Marla asked, "What is it?"

Roland stood. "I don't know. I'm going to go find out. I have a message from the mainland, an urgent one from one of my men. He has said he must speak only to me, but he's not yet to the shore, he sent a man ahead." He looked around the room. Several of the soldiers had left already, leaving cups and plates unfinished on the tables.

Kyla grabbed his sleeve. "Don't go," she said, and then hated herself for saying it. She made her fingers release him.

He sank back down beside her. "I'm sorry, my love. This is not the way I imagined us spending the rest of the day, believe me. But you know I have to go. I won't be long. I'll send someone to summon your guard. You will be safe."

He leaned forward and kissed her, hard and fast.

"I won't be long," he said again, and then left.

She watched his back, watched the way all eyes followed him as he strode from the hall.

"Don't worry," said Marla, but there was something like a frown in her voice.

"It will all be over with soon," Elysia said, and took a bite of bread.

---

*K*YLA HAD NO APPETITE for food or drink after Roland was gone, only a gnawing anxiety that she could not explain away. Marla had patted her sympathetically on the shoulder and invited her to go herb gathering with her, but Kyla had declined, knowing what poor company she would be.

"I think I'll take a rest," she said, trying to sound unconcerned.

"An excellent notion," Harrick approved. "Roland will be back by the time you awaken."

Elysia said nothing, only hugged her tightly, using one hand to trail her fingers along the golden belt around Kyla's waist as she pulled away, tapping the handle of the dagger there with her fingers as the last thing before releasing her.

Kyla's hand came to rest on the hilt. She studied the child thoughtfully as she was led away with the other children.

"Shall I escort you to your rooms, my lady?" asked Harrick.

"No, thank you."

"Alas, I'm afraid I must." Harrick took her arm. "Your husband would never forgive me for not doing so. He is such the gentleman about these things, you see."

"Oh, really?" She had caught the amusement in the monk's voice and took his arm graciously, willing away the strangeness she felt.

"Indeed. Perhaps you've noticed that Roland puts all of our manners to shame."

She gave a little laugh.

"When he wishes," Harrick qualified.

Her chambers were empty and quiet, the covers of the bed already straightened, everything tidy and neat and undisturbed, as if the wonder of last night and the magic of this afternoon had never happened.

But it had. It had, and Kyla concentrated on that as she lay down alone in their room. She had placed the crown of flowers on the trunk by the window, and now it let off a sweet fragrance that carried across the room to her. Kyla rolled over and hugged Roland's pillow to her, preferring to inhale the lingering scent of him on it. She rested her face against the softness. She was not tired. She didn't really want to rest.

In fact, just staying here, listening to the silence gather around her, was not helping at all. What was the matter with her? She sat up abruptly, shook her head. She was behaving unreasonably. There was no cause for this knot tying her up inside, no need for the quivering alarm racking her, which made her stand and begin to pace the floor.

This was ridiculous. She was her own worst enemy, feeding this insecurity from within. What she needed was to get out, and regretted that she had dismissed Marla's invitation so quickly. Perhaps she had not gone far yet. Someone was sure to know where she usually went for herbs. Kyla would join her, after all.

When she opened the door she was somewhat surprised to see neither of her guards standing there. No doubt Roland's message had not gotten to them yet. Or mayhap they had gone with him to the shore, and another guard would be coming. No matter. She would instruct someone to tell her guard, whoever it was, where she went.

In the bailey she found her maid, Meg, and asked her if she knew where Marla might be. Meg scrunched her eyebrows together and thought about it heavily, then replied that most likely the lady was in the meadow next to the creek with the bog.

Kyla looked at her blankly.

"I'll take you there," offered the girl shyly.

Kyla glanced around the bailey, at the bustle of people newly intent on their work, at the shielded looks being thrown to her.

"Yes, thank you," she replied.

Meg led Kyla to the gate of the keep, casting her eyes down to the ground. Kyla followed her with her own eyes fixed ahead of them, scanning the horizon for what, she couldn't say. She remembered she had neglected to instruct anyone to locate Thomas and Berthold, but then gave a mental shrug. She would ask Meg to do it after they had found Marla.

They followed a stone path that faded off into the green darkness of the woods, away from the meadow where they had been this afternoon. Meg looked up finally, threw Kyla a tremulous smile.

"My lady! My lady!"

Both women turned around at the voice, coming from behind them. A man was running toward them, waving.

"My lady!" he called again as he approached. He slowed when he saw them waiting for him, then bowed low when he was close enough.

He was tall and balding, familiar enough to tease the corners of her memory but Kyla couldn't quite place him. He was not, however, the brown-haired man, and so she faced him with polite inquiry.

"Yes?"

"My lady," said the man, breathing hard. "I have a message for you from my lord."

"A message?" Her heart began to pound.

"He bids you to join him at the shore, and sent me to fetch you."

"Only you?" she asked, looking around him.

"Your men await us there," said the man. "I am Titus, my lady, a lieutenant in Duncan's guard."

Again came that teasing familiarity. She had seen this man before, but she could not capture an actual memory of him. He seemed harmless enough, with warm, dark eyes and a reserved smile. If he was Duncan's man, she might have noticed him at the meals, or in the bailey. Perhaps even at the ceremony today.

Beside her the young maid was clasping her hands together, staring up at her mistress.

Titus was waiting. Kyla was moving before she was aware that she had made up her mind, back down the path.

"This way, my lady," said the man, taking them in a new direction, down a different set of stones, opposite of the way she had expected to go.

"Isn't the pier the other way?" Kyla asked.

"We have two piers, my lady," replied Titus. "We are going to the smaller one."

Kyla looked at Meg, who frowned but nodded.

They walked briskly over a field of green grass and tiny golden flowers, the low thunder of the ocean growing stronger and stronger, the wind picking up and pressing her skirts back.

Kyla could see no pier, but now she did see a cliff ahead, and then she could make out a narrow strip of wood stretching over the water. A single boat bobbed on the waves. A man sat in the boat, waving at them. Titus waved back. There were no other people that Kyla could see.

Beside her Meg's footsteps grew slower.

"This way," said Titus, sounding impatient.

"Where is my husband?" Kyla demanded.

"On the shore, as I said, my lady."

"He is not there." Kyla came to a halt, pulling Meg back to stay with her.

"Oh, not this shore, my lady. I beg your pardon. I meant to say your husband is on the mainland shore, awaiting us."

"On the mainland shore?" Meg's words were tinged with disbelief. "This is not the pier to go to the mainland. If you try to row there from this pier, the currents . . ."

Meg's voice trailed off as both women saw the anger slash across Titus's face, a broken instant before his blandness resumed.

Kyla looked at Meg and took her hand, as if to lead her forward.

"Run," she ordered, picking up her skirts and taking off the way they had come, dragging the startled girl behind her.

For a moment it seemed to work. Her feet ate up the distance, she could see her maid from the corner of her eye, almost keeping up with her as they kept their hands tight together. The wind was an aid now, pushing them forward, also pushing forward the sound of their pursuer, his grunts and heavy steps.

Then she felt a hard tug that pulled her off-balance, their hands ripped apart. She saw Meg go tumbling down, a tangle of skirts and a shrill scream.

"Lady Kyla!" yelled the man, loud and forceful. "Come back or she dies!"

Kyla regained her balance, still moving. A look over her shoulder showed Titus on top of the girl in the field, holding her head up by her hair, a knife to her throat. Kyla slowed and stopped. She turned around and began to walk back to them through the grass and flowers.

Meg's breath was coming in gasping whimpers; Kyla understood the feeling, wanted to cry for her—for them both.

"A wise decision." Titus smiled, warm again, and Kyla saw him in her mind somewhere else, not dressed in the plain garb of a soldier. He had on a hat, some fancy thing, velvet and plumes. She scowled at the memory and then it was gone, and she saw only the knife pressed to the white skin of Meg's neck.

"Let her go," she said into the wind.

"Come closer," he replied.

She did so, close enough so that both of them knew she would not be able to run again.

"Now release her. You don't need her, only me," Kyla said.

Titus moved the knife swiftly, prompting a sob from Meg as Kyla raised her hands in protest, but he turned the hilt around and slammed it into the temple of the girl, letting her slump to the dirt.

"You're right." He seized Kyla's arm, twisted it up behind her back exactly as the black-haired man had done. "I don't need her."

He took her over to the cliff, down the carved steps that curved to the pier, to the other man, waiting in the boat. Kyla wanted to shield her eyes from the brightness of the sunlight on the water but couldn't. And anyway, she knew who was in the boat.

The brown-haired man stood up and took her by the waist as Titus lowered her down. She didn't dare fight them, not yet, since he had not released her arm but rather twisted it back farther, creating a screaming pain in her shoulder that she would not allow to show on her face.

She was shoved to the bottom of the boat, pressed down by Titus's foot.

"Row," he said to the other man, and she felt the boat begin to move across the waves.

For a long time all Kyla heard was the labored breathing of both men, Titus presumably from the chase, and the other man from his efforts at the oars. The ocean water slapped and splashed up the sides of the boat, sprinkling her with drops. A slant of sunlight blinded the eye she had facing up, leaving her to stare at the bottom of the craft, at the cold water sloshing back and forth inches from her face.

Her right arm was pinned beneath her, and next to it she could feel the hard metal of her dagger, pressed up against her hip. Titus must not have seen it, lost in the folds of her skirts. She began to slowly move her hand toward it.

"Quite a chase you have led me on, my lady," said Titus in a mellow voice.

Her hand stilled.

"Across England and up to Scotland and back again. If only you hadn't gotten yourself captured by Strathmore, we might have come to know each other so much sooner." Titus shifted above her, then pulled her upright, still sitting on the bottom of the boat. She closed her eyes against the sudden sunlight, turned her head away but Titus took her chin and pulled it back to face him. She opened her eyes.

"If only . . ." he sighed, and his touch on her chin became something different, a mockery of a caress.

She yanked her head back, freeing her chin. "You are a fool if you think these islands won't be crawling with soldiers searching for me."

Titus beamed down at her. "How lucky for me I am no fool, then. Of course I know that. But since I took the liberty of intercepting your husband's message to your guard, it's going to take them much longer to realize you're missing than we need to escape. And we may also thank Strathmore for his little surprise wedding this afternoon, as well. The suddenness of it has sadly thrown off the castle staff, I fear. They probably won't notice you're gone for quite a while."

The boat took an especially hard hit into the dip of a wave, knocking Kyla into the planking behind her, making Titus look at her with pretended concern.

"I do hope you forgive my methods of seeking an audience with you, Countess," he said. "I simply had to get you alone, away from your bothersome husband. My rendezvous point is not far at all. In fact, you almost discovered it at the cove. That day you came across my friend here"—he indicated the rowing man, who refused to meet her gaze—"signaling to our accomplice on the other isle. I really think we must blame Strathmore for separating my men, assigning one to the wrong island. But still, I am sure Victor is very sorry he hit you so hard, aren't you, Victor?"

The brown-haired man ignored them both. He seemed to be struggling somewhat with the oars.

"I chastised him, of course. He wasn't meant to drown you, merely to hit you hard enough to daze you, so that you could be searched, perhaps questioned. But then the watch came, such a mess. . . . And Ivan was so distraught over the whole thing. Ivan was your creature all along, I think."

"The black-haired man," she said.

Titus rolled his eyes. "A softhearted weakling, sorry to say. He didn't want to hurt you, he said. Couldn't stand the thought of even harming a hair on your head. And I'm not after your head at all, as it turns out."

"You killed him." The wind whipped the ends of her loosened braid up and around, tossed it into Titus's lap; he caught a strand and examined it thoughtfully.

"I had to. He was ready to go to Strathmore and beg for his mercy. I think—" Titus laughed, malevolent. "I think he fell in love with you, dear girl."

Another memory jarred Kyla. Lady Elisabeth, who had called her the same thing not so long ago. Another piece of the puzzle fell into place.

"I know who you are," she said coldly.

"Do you?" He smirked at her. "Good for you. I wondered when you would recognize me."

"Baron Caxton." She spat the name, though it had no other meaning to her. Jared Caxton. She had seen him at court more than once, it seemed like years ago. He had not moved in her parent's circles, and yet his name was connected with Lady Elisabeth. . . . Hushed rumors she had overheard, titters of conversation deemed inappropriate for young ears. . . .

She remembered now. Lady Elisabeth had been the mistress of Baron Caxton.

He laughed. "At your service, my lady. Well, not really. I rather think you are at mine."

"What do you want?" She couldn't help the question, but was proud that her voice came out steady.

"My lord," Victor interrupted. He was now quite clearly fighting the current. Kyla noticed how the little boat was moving sideways, despite the man's dragging on the water.

"God's blood, you imbecile, can't you do anything right?"

"I'm trying!"

The boat was moving swifter; a lazy spin had taken the bow. Kyla squinted and turned her head, looked past the two men who were arguing with each other and the tide. Somehow she was not surprised to see the jutting black and gold of the rocks to her left, and now her right. They were spinning closer and closer to the land. Hadn't Meg tried to warn them . . .

"Shove over!" Caxton thrust the other man to the side, took over both oars. "Watch her!"

The brown-haired man clambered past Kyla to sit behind her. She ignored him, intent on the approaching shore.

"You can't do it, you know," she said.

"Shut up," hissed Caxton, panting. The water was much rougher now, cresting past the rim of the boat.

"We are going to crash." Kyla sat up taller, put both hands beside her on the edges of the craft. "Look at all those ships out there. All of them were destroyed. Yours will be no different."

A strangled cry came from Victor. "Look!" He pointed to the rocks. "Look at them!"

Caxton turned his head, red-faced, sweat running down in rivulets, mingling with the spray. His eyes bulged.

Kyla looked and saw only rocks, tremendous black-and-gold rocks, becoming larger as they rushed toward them.

"They're so beautiful!" said the man with brown hair. "They want us! Can't you tell? They want us! They want *me!*" He came to his feet shakily, making the boat tilt dangerously in its spin.

Caxton had stopped rowing, was staring at what the other man pointed at with appalled fascination, mouth open.

Kyla held fast to the side of the wooden boat as it heeled up toward the sky, and just before it overturned completely she heard the same voices she had before here at Siren's Cove: feminine laughter, sharp and clear.

She stood up and dived off the side of the boat.

As she hit the water she heard a crash, a terrible splintering sound that might have been the boat smashing into the rocks. She heard a man scream.

And then she was submerged in the turbulent ocean, torn from the boat and the men, struggling to reach the surface against the weight of her skirts. Kyla felt the soul of the water beating against her, a ripping current that grabbed her and carried her off, she didn't know where. The water was black ice, impenetrable, and she was as helpless as the little boat had been.

She couldn't find the surface, it was useless, she was going to die here in the water, just her and the men and the mermaids. She was going to die at Siren's Cove on what had started out to be the happiest day of her life.

But then her head broke free of the frigid depths and she came up gasping, swallowing more water than air, thrashing her arms and legs in an attempt to stay afloat. Great, dark, hulking things flashed by her, her skirts caught and tore against the rocks, and she rushed past it all, still a part of the current with no free will. She could only struggle to keep her head up as she was moved into the heart of the deadly cove.

Kyla had no feeling left in her limbs; she had no idea if she was swimming or just being carried on the tide, but the sound of the surf was filling her ears, the reverberation pounding her body, a rhythm she could not escape, louder and louder until she knew she was going to be crushed by it at any second. The cold blackness sucked at her feet—it was a race to see if she would drown beneath the waves before she could be pulverized by them.

Then someone was there. Someone had her under the arms, someone was kicking with powerful strokes to the safety of the beach, taking her with him.

He pulled her out of the water and dragged her onto the sand, a young man she didn't know, who looked down at her with worried eyes and said, "Countess? Countess?"

The watch. Of course, it was the watch. Kyla reached a hand up and tried to hold his arm, tried to tell him about the danger, about the two other men, but he was laying her down softly on the beach with an intent look out at the water.

"I'll be right back," he said, sprinting away.

"No," Kyla tried to say, but it came out as a cough, choking her. When she was able to look up she saw him bringing Caxton to shore. Caxton, with his arm around the watch's shoulders, staggering up the beach.

Kyla rose to her knees, wanting to scream, able only to hear the strained cry that came from her as Caxton smiled at the young man and then stabbed him with his knife.

The watch fell, astonished, to his knees, and then onto his face in the sand. Caxton pulled the knife out of his ribs and looked over at Kyla.

She found her feet in the shifting sand and stood, swaying. Caxton began to lurch toward her.

Chapter Sixteen

KYLA FLED UP the sandbar that led to the tower. Behind her she heard Caxton, swearing, attempting to run after her.

Her skirts were hampering her, a soaking weight that slowed her down, cost her precious time as she heard him gaining on her, coming closer. She stumbled and her fists closed on handfuls of sand. She flung it behind her as she cried out in fear and anger and kept climbing.

At last she was at the top. The wind was even brisker up here, slamming her gown forward and then back, pulling her sideways as she looked around for a place to run to. There was only the tower, looming above her. Kyla ran around it until she found the door. The wind had pushed it open and kept it that way, and she plunged into the darkened interior.

A horse looked at her with mild eyes from the middle of the dirt floor, chewing slowly on a mouthful of hay. It must belong to the watch. In the second it took Kyla to consider untying it from the peg in the wall and riding out she saw the shadow of Caxton fall on the floor behind her.

The rest of the room was empty but for the stairs that circled in a spiral up the walls, hugging them without a railing. She raced for them without thought, slowing only to pull her sandy skirts up to her knees before running on again.

"Lady Kyla." Caxton started laughing, a dreadful, hitching sound. "Where do you think to go now?"

The stairs were much steeper than they looked. Her lungs

were on fire, she couldn't take a breath that was deep enough to quench the burning. And still he came behind her, a gurgling laugh chasing her higher and higher, until she was almost crawling to the top. It took all of her strength to push open the trapdoor that led to the roof of the tower.

When she did the wind caught the wood and snatched it from her hand, smashing the door back against the floor, leaving the opening gaping above her. Kyla climbed through.

The roof was an empty circle of stone, only a crenellated edging of giant gray blocks between her and the sky. Kyla struggled to lift the trapdoor again, to shut it before Caxton could come up, but the wind had not yet shifted, and she did not have the strength to make it close. From the darkened square a hand darted out, pressed against the wood as she struggled to lower it. Kyla saw his face appear, still smiling.

She let go of the door and backed up, thinking furiously, searching for any weapon at hand.

There was nothing. There was only her dagger.

She unsheathed it and held it in front of her. The wind was tearing at her hair, tossing it into her eyes and out again.

Caxton stopped.

"My dear girl," he began.

"What do you want?" Kyla yelled, holding her dagger the way she had been taught. Caxton eyed it cautiously.

"What do you think?" he called back, good-natured despite the hostile gleam in his eye. "What else could it be, my child? I want the note, of course. The note."

He took one step forward. Kyla took one back.

"There is no note," she said. "It was a ruse, made up by my husband, in order to trap me."

For the first time Caxton hesitated, looked genuinely puzzled. "Of course there is a note. Don't think a lie will fool me, my lady."

"There is no note!"

"There is," he countered, coming forward again. "I signed it myself, dear girl, much as I hated to do so at the time. And now you have it, and I want it back. I need it back."

Kyla looked around quickly. He was backing her up

against the stones. If she let him continue he would have her in no time.

"I don't know what you're talking about!" she cried over the wind. As if chastened by her voice it immediately died, leaving an echoing calm around them.

"Of course you do." Caxton sounded perfectly composed, reasonable, as he approached her, holding his own—much larger—knife. "Your prevarication now will gain you nothing, Kyla. I have searched Rosemead, I have searched this godforsaken castle, I have searched the whole of England, I think, for the note, and the only possible place left for it to be is on your own person. You know what I want. The note your mother gave you before she died. Give it to me and I will let you live, fair Kyla."

"My mother?" The air left her in shock. She stared at him. "My *mother?*"

Caxton saw his moment. He rushed her at once, coming toward her in great, lumbering steps and she backed up as fast as she could, slashing at him with her blade when he was upon her, crying out in a fury, twisting away from him at the last moment on pure instinct.

She had cut his hand, a deep gash, and he yelled and turned, reaching for her still with his own knife. But she had been closer to the edge of the roof than she thought, she must have been, because as she whirled out of his way he moved to follow her, but his momentum was too great. He slammed into the stone that had been behind her and it stopped him short at the knees, causing him to fall forward, to topple over the edge.

He screamed, truly screamed, and when Kyla turned around she saw one hand still grasping the edge of the stone, then the other.

She stood still, trembling, when she heard his voice.

"Lady Kyla!"

She walked over to him, still clutching her dagger.

Caxton was hanging with both hands from the lower ledge. She could see his legs flailing for purchase against the air.

Far, far below him were the inlet, the jagged rocks, the angry water.

"It was you, wasn't it?" She leaned out through the gap in the stones next to him, out of his range. "It was you who killed my mother."

"No!" Caxton cried, still trying to smile at her.

"Yes!" she screamed back at him. "It was you!"

"It was an accident!" One hand, the one she had cut, slipped a little. He brought it back up frantically. "I didn't mean to do it!"

She said nothing. Her grip was tight around the dagger. Caxton began to babble.

"She came for Elisabeth that day, she came to take Elisabeth away from me! Elisabeth was too weak, she had listened to Helaine for too long. She would have left me, even knowing that I would come after her, the silly bitch. So she took the note from my hiding place and gave it to Helaine, damn her—for 'protection,' she said! I finally had it in my hands, I had finally managed to steal it from Gloushire and that fool of a woman delivered it to her friend!"

"My mother," Kyla said quietly.

"I have . . . to have . . . that note," said Caxton through gritted teeth. "Give it to me, and I will let you live."

Kyla leaned over the stone, examined the man hanging on to the edge of the last solid thing between him and death.

"Tell me," she invited in a velvet-smooth voice. "This note. What did it say?"

Caxton didn't reply, turned his head to the left and right, looking for an escape. There was none.

"It was a debt note, wasn't it?" Kyla continued, remotely surprised at her own logic. "You owed money to Lord Gloushire."

Sweat was dribbling down his face. The tips of his fingers had turned from pink to yellow to purple now. The cut on his hand left slippery blood to run down his wrist. He expelled his breath at last, watching the blood. "Yes, yes. Money. I owed him everything, do you understand? Everything! More than that! More than I could ever pay!" Caxton looked up at her, desperate and chilling at once. "He was going to go to the king, he was going to tell Henry!"

"And you killed my mother for this. A piece of paper."

"You don't know! She was going to ruin everything. She had the note, she had Elisabeth's ear. She was taking Elisabeth away from me, persuading her to go away to the country while the debtors tore me to pieces, destroyed me. Without the note, Gloushire had no proof I owed him anything. But Helaine was going to ruin it all, she said she would take the note to Henry herself!"

One of his hands lost its grip; Caxton let out a huff of fear.

"How did you do it?" Kyla asked.

"God's blood, help me up, my lady!"

"Tell me how you did it, first!"

"I . . . I hit her! It was an accident, I swear! I hit her to get her away from Elisabeth, but she fell and hit her head. That's what killed her. We had to do something! Elisabeth was in hysterics, she didn't see the solution as I did. Kill Gloushire, put Helaine in his bed. Simple! Brilliant! Everything was fine! Elisabeth did as I bade her, as she was used to doing. She was mine again, she *had* to be or else she risked the king's wrath with me. Everything was . . . *fine*. . . ."

"No," Kyla said. "You made the blame fall on my father. But you still didn't have the note."

"Helaine wouldn't say where it was! She taunted me with it, she said I would never guess where she had put it, that it was in hands safe from me!"

The wind was returning slowly, an upward gust that cleared strands of red from Kyla's eyes.

"And you thought *I* had it?"

"It had to be you! I know it's you! Your father would have turned it over to the king if he had it, and you are the only other person Elisabeth said Helaine would trust!"

A belted thrust, sharper than any dagger, to remind Kyla that her mother had had such faith in her. She clenched her teeth against the pain, spoke coldly down to this man, this embodiment of selfishness and evil.

"Did you kill Elisabeth, as well?"

"No! Not her! Elisabeth took her own life, I had nothing to do with it!"

"Nothing to do with it? Nothing such as forcing her to conceal the murder of her close friend, for example, to save you? Nothing such as that?"

His fingers were slipping backward, one by one.

"My lady," he pleaded. "Help me."

From below them came a sound, unexpected, floating on the air. Unearthly laughter, forming into wisps of words.

Come to us. . . .

Caxton's eyes grew wider. "It's them," he said, hoarse. "Did you hear them?"

Kyla felt dizzy suddenly, the world tilting at her feet. She leaned against the stone in front of her, put a hand over her eyes.

"Lady Kyla, you must help me," came Caxton's cry.

She was going to do it. Against all reason she was going to aid her mother's murderer, simply because she could not, she *would* not be a murderer herself. She only had to make the world stop spinning and then she would—

You are ours. . . .

The laughter came stronger now, ghostly and heartless; there was really no mistaking it. Caxton's breathing grew strangled. Blindly Kyla leaned forward to put her hand over his, to stay his fall.

Someone behind her stopped her, pulled back her arm. In the next second Caxton let go, silent as death, plummeting down to join the laughter.

Marla had her arms around her, Marla held her tight and wouldn't let her look over the edge.

"It's fine now," she said, solid and sturdy. "You're fine."

The dizziness faded to nothing. Kyla stepped back, wide-eyed.

"I was gathering herbs nearby. I saw you come up the cliff and run to the tower," Marla said, answering her unspoken question. "I saw that man chase you. He had a knife. By the time I made it up here, he was already doomed. I heard what he said."

"It was him." Kyla felt a high-pitched buzzing in her head now, delayed nerves taking over. "He killed her."

"I know." Marla spoke softly. "And he deserved to die."

"Those voices . . ."

"What?"

"Didn't you hear them? Women's voices, laughter?"

Marla studied her, then shook her head. "No. But I don't doubt you did."

The haze in Kyla's head cleared abruptly. She moved away from Marla, turned, confused, in a circle.

"There's a watch down below," she said. "He's hurt. On the beach. We must help him."

"Your husband has already found him," Marla said. "I saw them bring him up off the beach just now."

"Roland? Roland is here?"

She heard him now, calling out her name. There was panic in his voice, despair.

Kyla raced to the trapdoor. "I'm here! Here!"

Marla came beside her as Roland emerged from the darkness at a leaping run that catapulted him onto the roof, a wild man with frantic eyes. He focused on her, only her, and with a few short steps yanked her into his arms.

"My God," he said, shaky, into her hair, "my God, you're all right."

She clung to him, pressed herself into him, let the weakness in her legs have its way now that he was here.

"You're all right," he said again, deeper now, his hands strong and sure on her back.

Marla murmured something about seeing to the wounded man below and edged past them both.

"Wait," Roland called, lifting his head. "Where is he? Where is Caxton?"

The look between Kyla and Marla was so quick Kyla thought she might have imagined it. Marla addressed Roland.

"He fell to the rocks, my lord. It was an accident."

Kyla closed her eyes. She felt Roland's heartbeat against her cheek, rapid and heavy.

"An accident?" Roland said.

"Aye." Marla went down the stairs.

Kyla opened her eyes and leaned her head back to look up at him. "How did you know to come here?"

"Luck," he said, and then managed a dry smile.

"Your lucky star," she remembered.

He kissed her hard, just once, then cradled her head beneath his chin.

"The star was your little maid, my love. She came running back to Lorlmar just as we were returning. I had met my man ashore. He told me he had discovered that Baron Caxton had bought a man in Henry's army, Reynard, who joined my hunt for you and your father. It was Reynard who ordered the attack at Glencarson. So I knew it was Caxton who was still pursuing you."

"He killed my mother," she said, and the words were still so raw that she had to stop her lower lip from trembling, bit down on the inside of her cheek.

"I know, my love. I know. Reynard was arrested in London. He confessed all that he knew." Roland gathered her close again. "I died a thousand times over when I came back and saw your maid. I knew that Caxton had disappeared from London a fortnight past, amid rumors and lies. It seemed logical that he would come here, looking for you. When your maid described the man who took you . . ."

His voice choked off; he ducked his head and cleared his throat. "We guessed where the boat would be headed. There are very few places to land on this side of the isle. And there was the cove. Somehow I knew you would end up at Siren's Cove."

She reached out a hand and brushed the hair from his brow. "I'm safe. I'm not harmed."

"I cannot live without you," he said roughly. "If you had died, I would have as well."

"I love you," she said, and it was enough to lighten the pain in his eyes.

⟶ ᏽᎷᎷᎾ ⟶

𝒯HE CANDLELIGHT WAS DIM and flickering, but it gathered in the rounded stones decorating the hilt of Helaine's dagger and threw back their colored glare with shifting accents.

Kyla looked down at the sharp blade resting on her palms, then up at Roland, and next to Elysia.

"Go on," said the child, resting her elbows on Roland's desk.

Marla stirred in the shadows of the study, Seena and Harrick behind her. Madoc elbowed past them all and placed a brazier on the desk next to Kyla.

"That's better, now," he said.

Roland was looking at her intently, a silent offer to take over and finish the task for her. She tilted her head at him and offered a slight smile, then shook her head.

The hilt was warm gold, the stones smooth. When she held the dagger up close to the lamp she discovered the tiny metal latch underneath the hilt, against the cold steel blade, almost invisible. She pressed against it with her fingernail. Too short to move it.

Roland handed her his own dagger, a deadly pointed tip.

She pressed it delicately against the metal tongue and the latch gave way with a barely audible click. And then the hilt was loose, free of the blade. She eased the two pieces apart.

How often had she puzzled over this, Kyla thought as she carefully placed the naked blade on her husband's desk. How often had she seen Helaine wear this dagger at her waist, and yet never use it. She had always wondered at her mother's carrying it, such a contrast to the calm woman that she had been.

The blade was sharp and keen, just as Elysia had predicted. But it was the hilt that interested Kyla now.

The hollow darkness inside the gold was not quite empty.

The paper jammed up inside of it had been folded up very tightly in order to fit, so tight that only the outer edges were wet from the sea water that had managed to leak inside. As Kyla drew out the document with gentle fingers and unfolded it on the desk, everyone in the room leaned closer to look.

"The note to prove my father's innocence," Kyla said into the silence. "It existed, after all. And I had it with me all the while."

"You could not have known," said Roland.

"No," she agreed, and stared down sadly at the writing.

Marla, to her left, gave a little gasp when she read the amount. "Who could borrow such a sum? Who would lend it?"

"A hardened gambler, and the cousin of the king, in that order," Roland replied. "Caxton had lost his entire estate to Gloushire. He had utterly disgraced a noble name. And then Gloushire demanded repayment, and Caxton panicked."

Kyla said, "He destroyed my entire family. For what? For money." She closed her eyes, suddenly weary. "Only that."

Roland's hands came down on her shoulders. Elysia sidled closer, reached out and found Kyla's arm, leaned her head against it.

"Not your *entire* family," said the girl.

The watch was going to recover. Marla had cleaned and dressed his wound, pronouncing him lucky to have the puncture miss his lungs. Kyla had gone with Roland to thank the man for saving her and found him surrounded by a bevy of concerned women, his wife and mother and three sisters. He had actually blushed at her gratitude, then thrown Roland a stifled look as the women began to regale the countess with other tales of his daring. Kyla had smiled at him and said she was sure none of it was exaggeration.

Victor was dead. Like a spurned offering, his body had been tossed ashore by the waves, broken and empty. Kyla could not find it in herself quite yet to feel sorry for him.

And Caxton . . .

It had taken more than that initial comfort in the tower to

lead Roland away from the blackness that was so familiar to him. When the body of their enemy had been found, smashed against the rocks, she could only patiently accept the sharp anger she had felt still coursing through him. If she waited, she knew, she could reach him more easily.

Back at Lorlmar they had retreated to their rooms and she had held him tightly, letting him feel her solid heat while she soaked up his, a flexible harmony of give and take between them.

After a while he came back to her from the verge of darkness, stroked her hair, helped her bathe and change her clothing and then changed his mind and made love to her instead, taking them both to heaven instead of hell.

It was justice, he said to her later, in the study, that Caxton had died while trying to kill her.

"Justice," Kyla had echoed, and agreed, thinking about the sirens' voices.

Now she looked up at the ring of faces surrounding her where she sat at the desk, dear, loving people who had adopted her and made her one of their own.

The questions haunting her had been answered. She was free from the doubt and anguished confusion that had been following her for months. Kyla had even found, albeit through a twisted path, the man she loved, her husband, and with him a new family and home. Surely it was a most precious gift.

Nothing would ever erase the past, she knew. But now when she thought of her brother, the pang that came with his name didn't seem quite as horrible as it had been before. Seemed almost, in fact, a resigned sorrow that was more of an ache than a mortal wound.

She thought there might always be a kernel of sadness in her heart at the loss of her old life, her adored family. But Kyla realized now she could go forward into her future with a lighter heart.

She *had* a future. And that was miracle enough to be thankful for.

The paper beneath her fingers was thin and crinkled, the writing now not so important as she had thought.

"Give it to Henry," she said to Roland. "Prove to him that I was right about my father."

Roland leaned closer—warm and fragrant and cherished—and in front of everyone he brushed his lips to her cheek, then gave her his crooked smile.

"We'll do it together," he said.

Epilogue

*S*UMMER IN SCOTLAND was a glorious sight, and even the ruined village of Glencarson was not immune to the stunning deep blue of the sky, the vivid carpet of green that covered the ground, splashed with wildflowers.

Kyla knelt at the base of the rough stone cairn that blended in with the mountain it rested against. She gently took the handful of bright purple thistles Roland gave her and placed them on top of the rocks.

"Be at peace, Alister," she said. "Be at peace."

The baby in Roland's arms cooed at the sound of his mother's voice. She looked up at her son and her husband, smiled at the sight of them both against the cloudless sky.

Roland smiled back, bouncing the baby, the turquoise of his eyes echoed in the child's.

Kyla stood up and took her brother's namesake from Roland. "Hello, beloved," she said down to him. "Hello, little Alister. What a sweetheart you are."

With Roland's hand on her elbow she walked away from the cairn, down the rolling slope of the mountain to the level field where the village used to be. The blackened remains of the huts didn't seem so out of place to Kyla in this remote Highland location, the burnt beams now scarce, most having fallen back to the ground, dissolving into the rich earth.

The manor house was not so diminished, and it was here that Roland led them, up to what used to be the main entrance, now a framed hole to an open space of walls and birds and vines.

He put the leather bag he carried down in the doorway, the gold coins within shifting with heavy clinks.

Kyla turned around, faced the breathtaking hills surrounding them.

"It is not full restitution," she called out, knowing she was heard, "but it is something."

The hills held on to their secrets. No one came running out to greet them, to claim the gold. But Kyla knew they were there, watching. The people would emerge after they left.

A slim young lady on horseback waited for them down on the old road with the rest of the horses. She raised her voice, clear and light. "This is good," Elysia said.

Kyla and Roland, looking into each other's eyes over the tawny head of their son, agreed.

About the Author

Shana Abé lives in Southern California with her husband Darren and two house rabbits. Yes, the rabbits really do live in the house. Shana can be reached at ShanaAbe@aol.com, or write to her at:

2060 D Ave. de los Arboles, #180
Thousand Oaks, CA 91362